Slave to Success

Clenching his jaw and his anus tight, Eugene said nothing. Was what he wanted out of life worth this price?

Eugene was overwhelmed by the thought and tears of self-pity came to his eyes. Then, without warning, she was there before him, her black, almond-shaped eyes like bottomless pits of lust, a small sarcastic smile on her lips while one long, painted nail scratched down his chest. He breathed in heavily of her intoxicating perfume; oriental, heady. The marbles were pressing on his prostate gland, creating a riot of strange sensations as his body fought his mind, the one trying to eject the foreign bodies, the other trying valiantly not to. Yet her scent flooded his nostrils; she was so lovely, so desirable, but he could hardly believe the strange thought that came to him. As though bewitched, he realised he would take this, and more, for the privilege of finally entering her body.

Slave to Success
Kimberley Raines

BLACK LACE

Black Lace books contain sexual fantasies.
In real life, always practise safe sex.

First published in 2002 by
Black Lace
Thames Wharf Studios
Rainville Road
London W6 9HA

Design by Smith & Gilmour, London
Printed and bound by Mackays of Chatham PLC

ISBN 0 352 33687 0

Oh! I am fortune's fool . . .
William Shakespeare

1

Olanthé leaned her elbows on the stone balcony and scanned the flecked ocean. Her shadowed eyes sought the sails of a lonely yacht, intermittently flashing in the dying rays of the sun. To her Eastern senses, the sea was a strange thing, huge and frightening – more so than the desert she was used to. She felt an almost primeval terror brush through her at the thought of a single, lonely sailor, eyes narrowed against a keen wind, going forward across that huge expanse of water into some secret destiny in the encroaching darkness.

She shivered, wrapped her arms around her body and told herself it was because the European summer was not warm enough.

A door opened behind her, and closed softly.

Sadness warred with anger as footsteps trod gently up to her, and strong hands wrapped firmly around her tiny waist. It was time for him to go. As the slave, named Enigma, pressed his body firmly, possessively, against hers, she felt the rough stubble of his chin on the top of her head, and a jolt of desire sprang up in her middle. She didn't look around. She would have known it was him; she knew the sound of his softest breath, the musky scent of his body and the nuances of his temperament better than he knew them himself.

'Did you have a good day, my sweet Lady?' he whispered.

'Fruitful,' she replied, her voice harsh and angry because he was pleased to be leaving.

'I'm glad.'

She sensed his eyes echoing hers, seeking the escaping yacht, and believed him. In spite of everything she had done to him, and in spite of his wish to go, he truly did seem to care. She shuddered faintly, yet it was not with any kind of fear. It was more an electric feeling of anticipation.

'Make love to me, Enigma.'

'Enigma is gone. I'm Michael now. You can't order me to do anything any more,' he breathed softly, his lips against her hair. Yet he pressed closer, and even through his clothes she could feel that he was already aroused and ready. She grasped firmly at the ornamental iron-work that ridged the balcony, her tense knuckles white, but she did not turn. Michael nibbled softly at her ear, his tongue lapping warmly, his breathing quickening. She made no outward show of enjoyment but, even as her eyes were following the dying trail of the lone yachts-man, her mind was turning inwardly to the pleasures of the flesh.

Michael was good. Oh, yes, Michael was very good.

'Don't go,' she whispered urgently. 'Stay with me. I'll make it worthwhile. You know I can.'

He gave a dark chuckle against her back, and his hands slid within the flimsy fabric to nestle her breasts; he knew them intimately, every swell, every curve. 'You'd be the death of me, my siren. I've been yours for a year. I've fulfilled my contract, and it's time for me to leave.'

'I'll give you anything you want. Money. Houses. Land.'

'You know what I want. Freedom. And the money you owe me.'

'Damn you. Is that all?'

'That was the only reason.'

'Bastard!'

Her voice was a harsh snarl, but she knew he was right. He was already lost to her. More than any other slave she had ever owned, he had never really been hers. 'I could force you to stay. I could have you chained like a wild animal.'

'You could. What then of honour?'

'Honour be damned.'

Although he had been hers for a while, she knew in his mind he was already running; had been for the whole of this last year. All the time she was beating him, hurting him, using him, he had never been cowed – not really. Her body was moving to his, tiny movements, no more than a prickle of excitement below the surface of control, but he sensed it. He knew her so well. Damn it, why did she always have to lose them just when she had trained them to know her needs before she even knew them herself?

His hands, large hands that could do damage if he wanted to, moved over the surface of her body with such finesse, such gentleness, such *passion*. She shuddered and leaned her head back against his chest, and closed her eyes, relishing the mounting tension.

His nuzzling lips caressed her neck. Her hair moved at the contact, prickling her scalp, and she shuddered deliciously. Michael trembled against her, and she knew he'd felt her response. He was sensitive to her moods, her passions – her anger.

'Don't get cross, Olanthé. Not this time. Promise?'

'I won't.'

She really meant it, but her temper was not so easily controlled. She gave a small sob of denial and turned suddenly in his arms, her clawed hand slashing for his eyes before she was even aware she had done it.

He reacted instantly, catching her wrist mid-air then, grasping her other one, spreading her arms, controlling her. 'Bitch,' he whispered, and her lips reached up to his. 'Beautiful, sexy bitch.'

She opened her mouth to his seeking tongue, fighting against his hands while revelling in his dominance. 'Oh, God, fuck me,' she said, thrusting against him.

Dark eyes gleamed with humour. 'Of course. When I'm good and ready.'

'Bastard!'

Her white teeth snapped, but he evaded them, holding her struggling body easily, wedging a shoulder under her chin, forcing her back until she stilled, accepting him once more. Hands outstretched, she was pressed painfully against the stone balcony while he continued his almost casual tasting of her flesh, his lips pressing in tiny pecking movements along her cheek, down her neck and across her straining breasts. How dare he? Her eyes followed his dark head while her body moved to the ancient throb of sexual desire. His tongue darted, teased, leaving dark stains on the silk, then she felt the fabric tear as one of his knees roughly forced her legs apart.

'Bastard!' she spat, hating the sound of whining in her voice. 'I won't let you leave. I'll make you stay with me. If you leave me I'll cut your balls off! I'll kill you!'

'Mm,' he whispered against her breast, as if she had been murmuring sweet nothings. Then he thrust his mouth against hers, and she was drowning in the taste of him, his tongue filling her mouth, stopping her vindictive words and her breath in the same instant. Even as she fought against his control, her body responded, and wetness seeped against his knee. Her tongue found his, wrapped around it, and she drew him in as if she'd never let him go.

She saw his dark eyes narrow with lust and felt the harshness of his jeans abrade her aching cunt. She moaned softly as he moved against her, and gradually his forcing tongue eased.

She drew a ragged breath. 'I won't hurt you,' she promised. 'Not now.'

'Fucking right you won't,' he said, and, ignoring her struggles, he tied her right wrist to the ornamental railings with a trailing end of silk. She gasped at the jolt of desire that speared her, and he held her left wrist painfully against the cold metal as he ripped her dress, seeking another restraint.

'You dare –!' she gasped, eyes flashing.

'I dare. Enjoy it while it lasts, my sweet,' he agreed with a degree of malicious pleasure. 'I know I'm going to.'

He wrapped the shredded silk tightly, and she felt her wrist grow numb against the cast-iron railing.

'I'll kill you, Michael!' she swore. 'I'll have you boiled in oil and your balls roasted on a spit!'

'I'm leaving,' he said softly.

His eyes pierced hers while she fought against the restraints, torn between the wish to tear him apart for daring to restrain her, yet not able to control the waves of desire that flooded her at his action.

Then suddenly they were still, remembering.

Michael groaned, knelt, and pressed his head against her heaving breast for a long moment but, when he looked up, Olanthé saw lust and pain come together as his hands met and parted, ripping the fabric through, exposing the golden skin to the cooling European air.

Beyond the balcony the yacht drifted over the horizon and was gone.

Olanthé leaned her head backward, closed her eyes, taking pleasure in his domination, in her powerless state. Michael began to kiss her. At first he nibbled gently, one breast, then the other, as though he were trying to please her rather than himself. Then his own urgency seemed to take over, and he was sucking painfully hard, drawing her swelling nipple into his mouth and squeezing it. His hands were caressing her dusky skin, moulding the breasts as he suckled, his fingers digging into the soft flesh with undeniable urgency.

Olanthé moaned gently as the roughness of his caresses stoked her desire for him into a burning need, yet still he teased himself upon her captive body, prodding between her legs, revelling in his infuriating ability to hold back the tides of his lust.

In spite of herself, she was impressed. She had taught him well.

Finally he lifted himself to his feet, harshly forcing her legs further apart with his own, thrusting himself up into the available space as though he could break through his jeans and impale her by the simple expediency of need.

'Christ, my sweet bitch,' he said, grinning. 'I'm going to miss you, and no mistake!'

'Stay. I'll do anything you want. Please stay.'

He smiled in the gloom, white teeth mocking, dark eyes glittering. 'What, the bitch says please? Well, well. But you're a liar, fair torturer. You promise things you haven't in you to give. You're a tease and a siren and a whore. I'm leaving, and I'm glad, but I'll miss you all the same. There'll always be a secret place inside me where I'll cherish these long moments. It wasn't all bad; not by any means. You know that's how it has to be. That was the contract. That is always the contract.'

There was a long silence as his eyes drilled into hers.

She felt anger rise. 'I can make you stay. I can call Ali and have you whipped until the blood flows.' Then she thought of Bran, and how angry he would be. Mocking eyes caught hers, as if he could read her mind. Then she gasped as he ripped the dress to the hem, and reverently slid the remnants of shimmering fabric from her golden skin. Desire rushed through her. His eyes razed across her full breasts, and down to her shaven pussy. Then he bent and suckled possessively once more as he released his zipper, pushing his jeans down over tense hips, freeing a massive erection.

'Fuck me!' she commanded. 'Now!'

'Oh, yes. Because you're a beautiful whore, and have the sweetest little pussy I ever saw. But you know what, my dark beauty? You have the foulest temper, and some nasty little tricks for hurting a person. Our contract is at an end; I won't be seeing you again. I'll fuck you all right, and with this fuck I thee divorce.'

She made an angry sound that melted into pleasure as the swollen cock slid relentlessly into her body, impaling her. Her eyes glazed, and she went inside herself.

There was nothing except the hotness of him against her; in her. He lifted her thighs, pushed himself upright, and she rose with him, joined by the thickness of his cock. Her mind dissolved into two parts; one part being herself, stretched and filled by pulsing warmth, the other being him, dominant, erect, filling her.

She heard him gasp and felt him freeze against her while their minds melded, then softly, gently, he began to ride her, using her for his pleasure. Her hands flexed and clenched involuntarily within the fine silk and hard steel of her bonds as his coarse pubic hair abraded her clit. She wanted to touch him, to claw him further into herself, were it possible. Michael controlled her, body and mind, and she delighted in it.

She knew he had to leave though. His own bondage was at an end. That was how it was. Yet although she accepted him leaving, at the same time she hated him for going. That was the excitement and the pain and the pleasure. Her body lifted, responded, and her lungs cried out with the pleasure of their bonding. For a while there was a silence of passion, of gasping breath as his hips moved, and she felt the thrust of his pierced cock-head beating at the gate of her womb as if trying to gain entry.

The pain was an aphrodisiac.

'Where are you going?' she gasped out, her words in sync with his heavy thrusting.

'The nearest American embassy, for asylum,' he replied, a faint humour in his eyes.

'Don't go.'

'It's time.'

'I need you.'

'You don't. There'll be another soon, I know.'

He thrust hard, and harder, and she rode on the heat and hardness of him until he came with a cry of release, pulsing hard, almost anguished.

For a moment they stood, locked, his hands clenched on the railings, hers almost numb from the force of her own weight on the unyielding silk. Then he pecked a kiss on her cheek and backed away, eyes bright with amusement. His depleted erection slipped out of her, leaving her empty, hollow.

'I'll never forget you, Olanthé. Never. That's a promise. My last promise.'

He backed away slowly, hands outstretched as if she were some dangerous creature that would leap and tear out his throat. Had her hands been free, she might have. She tore madly at the bindings, but they held.

Then he was gone.

The empty space left behind was wider than the ocean that crashed behind her, and Olanthé felt a cry of betrayal rise from her guts to her throat. The sound she made was scarcely human.

By the time Ali came in she was a quivering wreck; her wrists were torn and bloodied within their expensive bindings.

'Go after him!' she ordered harshly. 'Go and get him back. Don't let him leave. I command you!'

Ali could have done this easily, and without compunction, but did not. He knew his Lady well enough to know she did not really mean him to obey. 'It was time,' he said gently. 'Let me bathe you, my Lady.'

When he had freed her, she pressed the wounded wrists to her lips, taking pleasure from the pain because Michael had caused it. Ali was right, it was time. Michael was gone. Life moved on.

Ali tended her hurts as he always had.

'Bran has been in touch. He's set up a meeting for you. We have to leave tonight.'

'I don't want to do it. Not again. That was the last time.'

Ali smiled. 'If you don't go, Bran will be cross.'

She felt a flicker of interest stir her senses and was tempted to cross his will.

'Once it's all set up, you can go home, and Bran will help you to forget for a while.'

During the flight she opened the album and forced herself to look at the one photograph she had of Michael. Stroking her long finger down the hard planes of his face, she allowed herself to recall the memories for one long, lingering moment. She leaned her head back for a while, almost sleeping, but not quite. The soreness between her legs was reminder enough, but soon even that would be gone.

Eventually she opened her eyes, and deliberately turned the page.

Another picture awaited her there.

Her finger caressed the golden hair, the perfectly formed, possessive mouth, and a tiny smile creased her cheeks. He was as different from the dark and enigmatic Michael as it was possible to be.

'He-llo, my Greek Adonis,' she crooned gently to her next assignment, and to her own surprise felt a faint flicker of interest blossoming inside her breast.

2

Eugene Styros shielded his eyes against the spotlight. As they adjusted, he became aware of the woman sitting on a high stool before him, dark robes blending into the shadowed room, concealing her body and face from his squinting gaze. Though of Eastern origin, the shapeless, black garment held nothing at all of promise, and was relieved by no more than a narrow letterbox across the bridge of the nose which allowed her freedom of sight, yet hid her from his view. All that was visible between the heavy, dark folds of fabric were the tips of her pink polished fingernails and the merest glint from a pair of hooded eyes, rimmed in kohl. In the subdued lighting wrinkles and deformities alike would have been hidden from his view, and all he could gather was that she was neither stooped nor overweight.

He had been well versed in the protocol required for this audition and stood where he was required to stand, yet even as he bowed awkwardly from the hips – an unfamiliar movement – his neck craned slightly in an attempt to penetrate the veil. Seeing nothing, his imagination raced: was she blonde or dark, was she married or single, was she ugly or pretty? Hell, it didn't matter what she was like: she was rich.

'Rise. Lift your head – let me see you.'

Her lilting voice, soft, clear and melodic, neither wavered with age nor held the innocence of youth. Shadowed beyond the circle of light which blinded him, he realised she could have been fifteen or fifty. He rose hesitantly, then set his chin high, his shoulders back. Clever repartee rose to the tip of his tongue and was swallowed. Speak only when requested to do so, the crone had commanded, but it was hard not to try to sell himself.

An actor by aspiration if not success, and presently resting with ill grace, his extrovert need to be recognised rebelled against the dictates of this peculiar audition; yet more than any audition he had ever attended, this one could decide his whole future. If he could not speak words, his body language would do it for him. He had that much skill.

The lady gave an amused chuckle that belied the initial image of Eastern female subjugation before the superior male, and did he also detect a small amount of sarcasm behind her words?

'Ah, a proud spirit. I like that. Something to be tamed and shaped; and also a pretty face, indeed. It would look well on the screen. You see, I have read your résumé. What kind of star do you want to be, my hero? A porn star?'

Eugene scowled.

She laughed softly. 'What, more than that? My, you do have aspirations towards greatness. Perhaps, after all, you will rise to grace the world with your beauty, but not just yet. First there is desire, then there is adversity and determination, followed most assuredly by tenacity.'

He wondered at the grace inherent in the slight movement as she shifted position. She seemed to straighten her spine beneath the weight of fabric before continuing, 'Indeed, I wonder if you have sufficient of either?'

'I believe I have, Lady. It's why I'm here.'

'Determination, yes, but in the face of adversity?'

'Just give me the chance.'

'But what about talent ... don't you think an element of talent is required?'

His lip curled. 'I've got talent as much as anyone else out there. I just need the money to get the screen tests.'

'That simple? They only have to see you to love you?'

He flushed. 'It's all about money.'

'Life, or the film industry?'

'Both. I've got reason to know.'

There was silence as they digested the bitterness in his voice, and Eugene wondered, just for a moment, if he had gone too far. The inherently rich never wanted to know the problems of the inherently poor; but when she spoke again there was no anger, just a musing intonation.

'Are you prepared to learn that it is not, I wonder?'

He gave a dismissive shrug. 'I'll do what you want for a year, then I'll have the money to find out.'

'You know what's required of you?'

'I believe I do.'

'You are innocent, my pretty youth, and have no idea at all what you're seeking at my hands. Like those before you, you have free will and may choose to abort at any time. Do you choose to continue?' she asked.

'Yes. I do.'

He said it formally, all too aware of the connotations implied by his chosen words. If he succeeded, this would be a marriage indeed, for better or worse, and one that would shape his future; the commitment as binding and holy as the word of God, or he would fail in his own personal quest.

'Very well. Take off your shirt.'

The soft words, spoken with the merest hint of a foreign and exotic accent, startled him. She neither rose her voice nor dictated, yet there was a quality to it that was as hard as iron, daring him to disobey her.

He had no intention of doing so. Betraying not the slightest hesitation, he lifted hands that had never known hard labour, pulled the shirt free of his waistband and unbuttoned it: first the cuffs, then the front, from the open neck downward. Slowly, and with deliberate sensuality, he gradually revealed a broad chest covered in a fine mat of golden curls, before flexing muscular shoulders to allow the shirt to slip from him, unheeded, to the wooden floor at his feet.

'Turn around.'

He turned his back to her with the conscious knowledge that hours of training had carved his torso with muscle and that the sun lamp had bronzed his skin to a burnished gold. He paused for a moment to give her the chance to admire the sight, before slowly rotating full circle. How could she not be impressed?

There was a moment of silence, but no word of encouragement – no praise, no gasp of admiration – as he displayed himself, slightly unnaturally, to her inspection.

'What are your origins, Eugene Styros?'

'My father was Greek, my mother Scandinavian.'

'Ah, hence the golden skin and blond hair, a strange combination. You say "was". Do you have living relatives?'

'None.'

'So no one relies upon you for financial support?'

'None save me, Lady.'

'Nice answer. Take the rest of your clothes off.'

He removed his shoes. Then, with protracted exaggeration, he stood up straight, unzipped his flies and pushed the trousers and underwear over his hips in a single fluid movement, bent over and stepped out of them. Then, with disdainful disregard for the trappings of society, one foot nudged the small pile of clothes aside, his movements graceful, balanced. Naked, he stood, once again, to attention, feet slightly apart, hips thrust provocatively forward. He had looked in the mirror often enough to know the exact stance to best display his body.

Satisfied he had nothing he should be ashamed of, his chest expanded and his buttocks automatically clenched slightly, making them small and tight, the movement thrusting his relaxed penis into prominence. The blond hair cascading surfer-style to his shoulders was echoed by a riot of slightly darker curls between his legs, nestling around his genitals then fading into a fine golden down along the length of his shapely thighs. He was no gorilla, no macho, thick-necked stud, but a Greek god personified – and he knew it. Physically, he had inherited the best parts of paternal and maternal parent, though he had experienced little of the other parental obligations society might have expected them to show to their unexpected offspring. An indiscreet coupling, a brief explosion of joy, another unwanted brat spawned and deposited in the great pool of human debris that littered the free world.

But Eugene had an advantage. He had the face of a model: a chiselled chin, eyes like chips of green Mediterranean sea, a sensuous mouth and prominent cheekbones. He was classically beautiful and, in spite of an inauspicious beginning, ambitious. He had envisaged film-star fame a thousand times; he had dreamed it, tasted it, and had no doubt it would eventually be his. A while longer, a few more bit parts, and he would be discovered, thrust into stardom by his sheer beauty. He believed he was also a good actor, yet was cynical enough to know that you did not have to be able to act to become an icon. You just had to be seen by the right person.

And for that privilege he was prepared to sell his soul.

'Let me view you. Turn around, slowly,' she commanded.

He turned, knowing in his most secret of hearts that whatever her age, this woman could not possibly be less than impressed. As he turned his muscles flexed, rippling provocatively, displaying him to best advantage. If you've got it, flaunt it; and he had it in abundance.

He was facing away from her when she said, 'Stop! Lift your arms. Stretch upward. Now spread your feet wide. Wider. That's better.'

He stood there, stretched in a star, every muscle tight as he could make it, and was gratified by her response. 'You have a nice body. Now touch your toes.'

Legs wide to a point that was almost uncomfortable, he bent at the hips and put his hands to the floor. In his mind's eye he visualised the scene he was presenting to her: the small puckered knot of his arse, the slightly uneven weight of his testicles snuggling in their golden nest, and the tip of his cock hanging limply behind. In his heart he also knew that the heat in his cheeks was not entirely due to blood pressure, but to embarrassment at the ignominy of his position, which was no doubt her intention.

She required him to stay there for what seemed an interminable length of time. It was tempting to simply rise, and turn, saying with a knowing smirk, 'Seen enough, Lady? Does my arse excite you? I'll give you a quick one, if you're lucky.' But he knew it was his ire talking, so he bit his tongue. Do exactly as you're told, the crone had said, no more, no less, or the audition will be terminated. He had known then that the unseen woman would push him, see how far he would go. He gritted his teeth. Why should he feel embarrassed, ashamed, if she wasn't?

'Move towards me.'

He hesitated for a fraction of a second. Like this? But she hadn't said rise, turn, and walk, so he began to shuffle backward, with difficulty, using his fingertips on the floor for balance, each small movement pulling his calf and thigh muscles. It was an undignified, graceless movement, and it irritated him to have to do it.

'Now stand up. Turn to face me.'

He complied, gratefully, thankfully realising that he had correctly interpreted her previous command. The light was no longer directly in his eyes, and he gazed intently at her face, trying to assess the lines around the heavily mascara-ed eyes for age. The eyes narrowed. He was sure she was smiling.

'Now I would like to take the measure of your tool. The man I employ must be able to perform on command and should be well endowed. You may stand easy and do what you need. You have five minutes, and you may not take your eyes from me.'

Eugene swallowed.

With his charismatic looks and manner, it was easy to seduce a woman. He had done so on many an occasion, the expected erection rising gloriously to command for, in so doing, he was pleasing himself. He could also please himself in other ways, more private, with equal enjoyment. He just had to be in the mood, to think about it, and it was there in his hand, fat and eager to please. But to stand here naked, in front of an unknown woman, and bring the blood pulsing into his genitals? He closed his eyes slowly, then flashed them open again. No, this had to be done fully conscious and aware. To command. It was what she had ordered, what she wanted; and there was reason enough behind her request. Easy for a woman to fake interest, to feign orgasm – not so easy for a man.

Yet, without his eyes closed, he could not bring any of his favourite images to mind, no matter how much he strove to do so. Instead, he stared at the black pits of the woman's eyes and felt, for the first time in years, the terror of failure. It seemed that if he failed in this, he had failed in everything.

He took a deep breath and a handful of uninterested flesh. He kneaded, concentrated. He could do this. He could. His other hand went up to his chest and began to tease his nipple, rolling it between thumb and forefinger and, just when he was despairing, he began to feel the faintest response. That tiny buzz of contact flowered, stiffened, became a taut line between chest and groin, and his whole body began to grow tense, the hair follicles on his legs rising and prickling with the growing need.

Satisfaction was tempered by relief.

Never before had he felt such an intense sense of achievement at gaining an erection, but never before had he produced one so blatantly and so clinically. The dark eyes bored into his, and he found himself being drawn towards the unknown woman until all of his senses were wrapped within that core of contact between his eyes and hers. Nothing else existed. He drowned in her dark eyes and shared his enjoyment with her, for even as he pleasured himself with the exquisite tremors in his body, it was as if he were pleasuring her; touching her, rubbing her ripe breasts with his open hands, twirling her nipples in his fingers rather than his own.

He began to gasp. Now the energy was flowing. He could feel his sense of balance going, his awareness being pulled relentlessly inward towards the glowing, unseen core. He wanted to lean on something, to get on his hands and knees so that he could concentrate on the pulsing demand of his cock rather than have to maintain balance in this unnatural, upright position. His knees trembled. His legs clenched tightly, his toes curling on the wooden floor. Now his fingers were fast, but more gentle, more specific. The thumb and forefinger of his right hand closed over the head, and slid back, closed over, slid back. He could feel it building inside him like a dam waiting –

'Stop!'

His chest heaved, he breathed in small pants, yet he froze instantly, his hand still circling his cock, lubricated by his pre-come. Just for a brief moment he had forgotten where he was. Now it all flooded back. His mind worked on several levels: partly steeped in need and wishing he could just finish the job, partly jolted, surprised but ecstatic that he had been able to perform so adequately upon demand, and one small part of himself ashamed of his present situation.

'Very well. Get dressed. You may go,' she said.

Suddenly it was over? He turned to his clothes and, as he dressed, the erection partially died but, as he had expected, the internal euphoria did not. He knew he was going to have to relieve himself at the earliest opportunity or he would explode, yet he had no idea whether the performance of a lifetime had achieved anything other than his own lack of self-respect.

He stood hesitantly for a moment, poised as if to ask the question, perhaps to beg, but did not. If his perfect body and admirable performance had not impressed her, there was nothing he could say to alter that fact. He began to walk towards the door, dejected, humiliated, but filled with a new determination that he would simply not allow this present failure to colour the rest of his life. He would succeed in spite of her! He wasn't going to be beaten, no way.

He put his shoulders back defiantly and strode to the door.

'One month,' she said as his hand was on the handle. He swivelled urgently, faced her, almost disbelieving his own ears. 'If you still want to do this, sort your affairs out. You will be sent instructions and a cash advance and be expected to leave in one month. Can you do that?'

'Yes, Lady. I can.'

'Brace yourself, stud. You'll come to me with nothing and leave with a future, but it won't be easy, I promise you. And there is one last condition . . .'

He waited.

'When the time comes that your earnings exceed ten million a year, you will agree to pay me ten per cent of everything you earn from that point forward.'

Eugene was startled. 'Why would I do that?'

She chuckled. 'How badly do you want my money now? Take it or leave it.'

He thought for a second, no more. When that time came he would hardly notice the loss, besides which he could always pay some high-flying solicitor to get him out of it, pay her off, because what woman would allow it to be dragged through the courts that she had hired a paid stud?

'I agree.'

Out of her presence, even the disapproving glare of the old crone could not stop him from letting out a whoop of jubilation as he thrust his fist in the air and uttered a heartfelt 'Yes!'

3

Informed of Bran's arrival by the low thump of the helicopter motors, Olanthé took a deep breath and turned to greet him. Bran never changed: he was still that pale, suave Englishman dressed in the understated elegance of the very rich and very self-assured. She felt the familiar jolt of desire wash through her body at the sight of his sandy-lashed eyes and slender frame walking towards the front door. Moments later, Bran crossed the room in a couple of elegant strides and reached to sweep her into his arms, his normally cool sea-grey eyes alight with pleasure. Olanthé pulled back her hand and slashed him viciously and emotionlessly across the face.

'You bastard,' she said. 'Where have you been?'

He ignored his reddening cheek. He snatched her hands out of the air and held them in the small of her back while he kissed her. 'Mm, I do like it when you're angry,' he murmured.

She struggled against his grip and her own volatile temper, then her body betrayed her and sank towards his, melting into his embrace. 'I've missed you, Bran. I've missed you so much. Don't go away again.'

'I must. That's how it has to be.'

He was nuzzling her neck as he replied, and his hands were doing wonderful things to her body, turning it to jelly inside. They explored each other with the fleeting desperation of long separation, then Bran's shaking fingers carefully undid the clasps of her sarong, and the fabric slid from her in an expensive puddle.

She gave a faint laugh and scrabbled unsuccessfully with the buttons of his shirt before ripping them apart. Olanthé knew that where she was all fire and fury, he was control personified. They were fire and ice; excited by the difference. Where she lost her temper and her control easily, his occasional anger was all the more terrifying because of his rigid control.

But presently control was not the issue.

They fell on to the pile of cushions and rutted like animals, biting and sucking and scratching in the height of frustrated lust. Bran came almost instantly, leaving Olanthé stewing in the height of frustration, but she knew he would make it up to her later. This was always the way of it.

Bran stretched out, relaxed in the aftermath of sex, with his long fingers clasped behind his head. She lifted herself on to one arm and watched him, stroking an absent finger along the length of his torso. What was it about him? He was tall and slender as a willow, but not in the first flush of youth, not by a long way. He had neither the Greek-god stature of Eugene nor the debonair smile of Michael. In fact, he was very British. His serious expression, pale skin and patrician face epitomised his upper-class background; but there was something more – something indefinable that made her bend to his whim and his will.

'If you ever leave me I will kill myself,' she whispered.

Those pale eyes turned to hers and a faint smile tilted the corner of his thin, chiselled mouth. 'If you ever leave me, I will find you and kill you myself,' he replied.

The response warmed her, and she reached down to suck one of his nipples into her mouth and rasp it round and round with her tongue – not because she expected to rouse him so quickly, but to assert ownership, to wash away any lingering remains of the other women he had been with.

His eyes, half closed, didn't leave hers. She knew he was taking in every tiny detail of herself, reminding himself of her. She knelt up, reached for the oil and began to gently smooth it into his pale body. She worked quietly, softly, teasing her fingers into every crack and crevice, revelling in the hardness of the muscular body, so different from her own.

Eventually she realised he had fallen asleep, or into a state bordering on sleep. He had been travelling a long time, and working hard. She maintained the slight pressure for a while, then sat carefully back on to her heels and waited, so as not to disturb him.

There was silence around them, just the faint, comforting sound of the fountain outside, the fitful swishing of sand brushed by wind, and a faint murmur of voices as the household slaves went about their duties. The sun tipped towards evening as she waited, and the brightness of the day subtly changed to the brightness of evening – the harsher fall of shadow, the increasing coolness in the air. It was never truly dark in this place at this time.

Eventually Bran stirred and, as she looked down, she realised he must have been watching her unawares.

'How is Michael?'

'Do you miss him?'

'Terribly.'

'He's fine. He's already been taken on as a junior attaché. People have noticed him. He'll go far. What do you think of the new one?'

Her lip curled. 'He's very pretty.'

He reached up to touch her mouth, and she shuddered deliciously as the finger brushed across her lips and back again. 'He's weak, but there's potential. He just hasn't discovered it yet. I trust you will discover it for him.'

She shrugged, not very interested.

He lifted himself up on to one elbow. 'He'll be better after a month or so of your inimitable training. You'll see.'

'I don't want him. I want you.'

'I think you still want Michael. I'll have to do something about that.'

He pulled her close and rolled her on top of him, and she rippled with anticipation, tasting the faintly spicy, exotic taste of his lips. Their hands explored each other urgently, touching, sliding against satin and cotton, their bodies already stoked with the heat of wanting. Bran's long slender fingers twined roughly in her hair while he kissed her, his tongue exploring deep into her mouth. She sucked hard, stopped him from escaping for a moment, and their eyes flashed with inner fire.

Olanthé's hands pressed against his narrow chest, feeling the strong heartbeat within, and she wondered for the umpteenth time what it was about this man that made her breath shorten and her body burn with desire, more so than any other man she had ever met.

The touch of his hands against her scalp softened, moved, tingling her hair follicles, before sliding down over her shoulders and into the small of her back, pressing her even closer into his body.

'Fuck me, my precious,' he said huskily. 'Fuck me hard. Use me. It's been too long.'

She pushed herself down, sliding on to him, joining with him, then she rose to her knees. He lay acquiescent beneath her, but she felt the faint quivering of his body as desire surged and was held in check. She leaned back and began to rock gently, watching him as she did so.

His hands reached out, smoothed her skin gently, touching, pleasuring in the way only he knew how. She leaned her shoulders back, thrusting her breasts out provocatively, and his fingers moved towards the inviting nipples, and squeezed.

A tide of pleasure rose up in her. Her hips began to move at a faster pace, and she reached a finger between her legs, enjoying the feel of him inside her while she rubbed at her clit. 'Oh, God, Bran.'

He lay still, and might have been unaware of what was going on, save for the odd tremor that rocked his body and the small intakes of breath as she rode him. For a while the burning sensation between her legs was the beginning and end of her world. Her eyes shut and her mind closed in on itself, until there was nothing but the pounding sensations of her body.

'Now, Bran,' she gasped. 'Now.'

He rolled her over in one swift movement, still within her, and began to hammer himself into her. What might have been pain in another time was pure, unadulterated pleasure now. She felt a scream building up and rocked into orgasm, her nails digging deep into his back. Tuned closely to her needs, Bran stilled, let her orgasm ride through both of them, then, giving a couple of selfish thrusts, he allowed himself to come.

In the air outside, the faint whine of the helicopter motors powering up put a surprised, irritated look on Bran's face.

Olanthé was amused. 'I told him to go. You take your work far too seriously. It's just as well you have me to make sure you take the time out to unwind.'

'When is he coming back?'

'Never.'

Bran smiled, grasped her wrists and spread her arms above her head. She was trapped beneath his weight.

'Then, my love, I will have to chastise you severely for that act of selfishness. I have a business to run.'

'Your millions will no doubt carry on multiplying without you there to count them,' she said, not perturbed by his threat. 'Will you release me? I need to bathe before dinner.'

The exotic pool was roofed only by a canopy of leaves through which a speckled sunshine glittered harshly. There were many slaves working outside, cleaning the surface of the water, sweeping the never-ending trickle of dry sand from the hot stones. As the Lady Olanthé and Bran emerged, naked as the day they were born, and as innocent looking, they dropped to their knees and pressed their foreheads to the shimmering ground.

Olanthé glanced at Bran's fair skin and smiled. Even as she was a desert flower, he was a thing of ice, and not made for the heat. Already his face was lined with a thin film of sweat.

'Why you can't set up shop somewhere a little more civilised beats me,' he said.

Her brows rose and he gave a short laugh and patted her rump. 'No, you weren't made for civilisation, were you, my randy little love? You were made to tease men into submission while making them think they're using *you*.'

She gave a gurgle of laughter and trod gently down into the water; Bran followed, obviously grateful for the temporary relief. Olanthé floated on her back, looking at the ochre walls that surrounded them, beyond which was desert. This place was paradise, an oasis, in truth, surrounded for miles in either direction by a hostile landscape. What fluke of nature had put this spring here was beyond human comprehension, and what ancient prince built his kingdom here no one could recall. But one thing was certain: this was her kingdom now and, once here, no-one could leave this place without her knowledge, and survive. She floated on her back, the warmth of the sun burning between the overhanging leaves, then rolled over in the water, cooling herself.

Bran paddled beside for her a while, luxuriating in the wetness, but not as comfortable in the water as herself. For a desert flower, she was presently doing a good imitation of a water babe, whereas he, though born in a land of mist and rain, was as elegant as a landed fish. She grinned at his uncoordinated movements, and he subsided against the shallow steps.

His brow lifted. 'Dare you laugh at me, madam, your lord and master?'

She swam up to him and knelt, peering at him from beneath lowered lashes. 'My lord and master is not pleased with his woman?'

Bran stood in one easy movement and held his hand out for the towel proffered by a vigilant slave. Olanthé followed him into the shade of the leaning palms. Her black hair trailed into the small of her back and she stretched her arms up, soaking up the warmth, spreading her hair in the dry air and letting it fall. She was already steaming gently, and hardly needed drying, but Bran began to dry her all over, dwelling minutely on every little patch of skin as though she were porcelain.

At first she watched him work, the tip of his tongue protruding with the concentration he was putting into the task, then the roughness of the towel began to generate a new feeling inside her, something more primitive, more vital. She leaned her hands against the red-ochre wall, closed her eyes and spread herself wide to his ministrations. The towel moved in tiny circular motions over her belly, her back, down her arms, down her legs, towards her inner thighs.

She made a small mewling noise of pleasure, but he moved back out again, teasing, tempting, before circling his way back inward towards the place she was willing him to touch. She gasped as the towel abraded slightly and then moved away again.

For a moment she was alone, left with nothing but anticipation, then she felt the faintest touch between her legs, a featherlight touch that parted her and pulled upward in a long, slow movement before reversing, disappearing. She pressed her hands into fists and shuddered more deeply, knowing it for what it was.

The first slash of the crop caught her fully across the buttocks, and she gasped with shock. The dinner gong sounded, but she knew better than to move. 'That, madam, was for sending my helicopter away.'

Bran's voice was chilled, and she strained to hear the nuances, whether he really was angry or whether he was faking it. Without seeing his eyes, she could not tell. The crop rose and fell, rose and fell, and with each stroke she felt a burning line form on her buttocks and thighs. In her imagination she could see the lashes, criss-crossed like lines of fire over her rear end.

She did not know when the pain turned to pleasure. One moment she was taking Bran's punishment with stoic acceptance, her brain numbed by the continuing slashes, the next she was delighting in it, moaning softly with pleasure as each stroke landed like a burning brand on her libido. She knew the true strength in his arms, she had experienced his anger in the past, and this was not it.

'Kneel.'

She heard the quiver of excitement in his voice and knew, without looking, that he had re-stoked his own fires at the expense of her inflamed flesh. She knelt against the stone seat and braced herself as he knelt urgently between her parted legs. She jumped as he unexpectedly pushed his thumb into her arse, lubricating her briefly, before thrusting himself inside.

She gasped as she stretched to accommodate him, locked for a still moment, quivering with excitement, then Bran put his hands firmly on her flaming buttocks and began to ease himself in and out. She cried out at the rasping sensitivity of that union, the unique strangeness of it that always shocked her by its intensity.

Bran worked himself backward and forward behind her, using her, rubbing his hands on the ridges of lash-marks, panting with the excruciating pleasure and constriction.

'Play with yourself,' he grunted, not ceasing his long, slow strokes, and Olanthé's hand reached down between her legs without much bidding. She was so aroused it took just a touch before she jolted into orgasm. As if prompted by her tiny shudders, Bran thrust hard a few times and followed with a pained cry.

After a moment he pulled free, and walked down to the water to wash. Olanthé rose to her feet with difficulty and followed more slowly. Bran's slow smile dawned as he followed her progress. 'That's going to be sore for a while,' he said with satisfaction. 'And when it's better I'm going to pay you back for Michael.'

Olanthé scowled, and winced as she eased herself into the water. 'I only did it because you told me to.'

'That's true, my angel, but you didn't have to enjoy it so much!'

Within a week Bran had ceased to think of his pressing business concerns and was losing that slightly desperate look of a man who knows he has something really important to do and should be getting on with it. Olanthé revelled in his company, knowing their days together were being devoured all too quickly.

As usual, he would depart when her next assignment arrived.

4

The Mediterranean sun burned as Eugene kissed goodbye to Greece for a while. It was here he had returned, at the end of the long month's wait, to drink with old friends for the last time rather than heed the siren call of Hollywood, which had barely recognised his existence. There he had been a hopeful face among millions; here, one was the friend with no name – stranger was not a word in the native Greek tongue – and it was here that his roots felt strongest whenever a challenge strove to destroy his self-confidence. Here, on the white beaches, he was king.

He linked arms with the friends with no names who were his present companions and delighted in the secret knowledge that one day his face would be recognised over the globe. His name would be household, and his image would adorn the walls of adoring fans.

Oh, yes.

But before that could happen he had a task to perform, and he intended to attack it with the dedication that was the trademark of his ambition. He would succeed. This task would lend him the credence he needed in order to be seen in the right circles. This present assignment, more than any other, would shape him into the man the world would know.

Swaying to the plunking of a Greek zither, sober, but drunk on anticipation, he viewed the women who swayed with him and made his choice. Older than him, experienced and probably married, the woman's dark eyes had smiled at him more than once, and he knew he was not mistaken: she was his for the taking. He watched her for a while longer, then made his way outside to lean on the wall, and wait.

Sure enough, she came.

Without words they slipped from the taverna and made their way, single file, down a small path to the beach. The moon was almost full, lighting the surface of the sea with twinkling ripples. He thought how beautiful life was, how much he had already, and wondered why it just wasn't enough.

He turned to the unknown woman and began to undress her. There were no words between them, no kisses, no false pretence that this was anything other than simple lust on both parts. When she was naked he quickly threw off his own clothes and led her down to the sea. There, in the warm, knee-high water, he washed her, cleaned her for the taking, and she stood there, enjoying the feel of his hard hands on her softer body and the strange, warm wetness of the salt water trickling between her breasts and legs.

Then he bent his head and tasted the salt on her cheek, her chin, her throat, and on the large nipples, colourless under the moon's white light. And as he lapped and sucked, his hand slipped between her legs. Gently his finger began to glide, not into her body, that warm receptacle which he knew was aching for him, but where he knew it would best stimulate her juices. His softly working finger sensed the little nub of flesh harden and swell; he felt her breath increase pace against his cheek as she began to move gently to the rhythm of that age-old tune. Around them the sea whispered along the seashore, lulling them deeper into unity. Eugene watched her come; he felt the slight judder ripple through her body and realised that for a short while she had taken control from him, using his finger as if it had been her own, pleasuring herself to fulfilment upon it.

And with that knowledge, his erection, only partially evident, made its intention clear. It rose and swelled with the knowledge that it was now his turn, and with that simple awareness his own self became diminished. When her shudders died he would have pulled her on to him, eased her on to his throbbing cock, but once again, she took control. Pushing his reaching hands firmly aside, she knelt and began to wash him as he had washed her, reaching up to carry handfuls of effervescent water on to his shining body, to rub the surface of his skin with work-worn hands. She washed every single part of him, circling her hands over his chest and nipples, kneading his buttocks, smoothing a small finger deep into the crack of his cheeks and up into the slight resistance of his anus. He gasped and took her shoulders for support, and still she worked him until the blood pulsed urgently and every hair follicle in his body rose and clamoured for attention.

When his consciousness had turned inward, she took his hand, led him to the edge of the tide and pressed his body back into the sand. He lay and listened to the sand sucking water greedily from the sea, but in the subtle massage afforded by that lapping water, his more basic instincts had taken precedence. He spread himself wide, hands moulding fiercely at the sodden sand, the erect cock between his legs the epitome of his being, yet when she knelt between his parted legs and began to nurse gently with her mouth, he was startled. It was a selfless act he had not anticipated.

After she had teased for a short while her strokes became long and sure, her tongue and lips pressing tightly around him. One hand encircled the base of his tool, holding it available to her, forcing the blood ever stronger into the expanding length of him; her other hand gently teased at his sac and opened his arse-cheeks to the sea water, which rushed in to thrill him with its strangeness. Nothing mattered in the world save that. When he could hold himself no longer he gasped a half-phrased word of warning, but far from withdrawing, she sank herself down on to his cock to enclose as much of him as she could manage, and his spunk was teased from him by the constriction of her throat.

Then Eugene and another man's wife lay sated, side by side, like lovers on some desert island, and dreamed their own dreams. She dreamed of the fine man her husband had once been before toil and strife had made him old before his time, forgetting just for a moment that this young god who lay beside her was not hers to hold. He withdrew into his anticipation of the unknown life that lay before him, exhilarated yet strangely scared. They parted knowing the intimacy of each other's bodies, but never knowing each other's names; when they said farewell, they were the first words they had spoken, and they would be the last.

When she said farewell, she was saying farewell to an illicit, stolen moment, but when Eugene said farewell, he knew he was bidding everything familiar to him good-bye. He was the chrysalis that was going to emerge, not a gentle butterfly, but an awesome dragon. He was the phoenix who would rise from the ashes and take the new world by storm.

5

The Eastern sun was hotter and dryer than that of Greece, and the breeze held nothing of the sea's cooling influence. Instead, the inland air was permeated with the hint of exotic blooms, and an atonal instrument wailed plaintively in the distance, compounding the foreignness of the location. Drinking deeply of the spice-laden breeze, a huge sense of inevitability descended upon Eugene. This was the East, where his destiny had long been predicted in the stars, and whatever route fate had used to bring him here, to this place at this time, his arrival was preordained.

He was supposed to be here, but that did not make it any the less exciting.

As he exited the aeroplane, pausing for a fleeting moment at the top of the steps, he felt as if he were hovering on the brink of one world to another: behind lay civilisation as he knew it; before was something very different. And as he stepped forward, his heart raced, as though he had crossed some invisible boundary and would never be able to step back again.

He did not have to wait for the aeroplane to disgorge its luggage – lightly packed, as specified, he had just the one bag with some overnight things he had needed for his journey. Everything else for his needs would be provided on arrival; there would be no need for money, nor any other kind of worldly goods. It sounded monastic, religiously intent, yet he was not fooled. The course of action he had chosen would change him, but would be equally as hard as that of a zealot bound by his own religious fervour.

As he left the airport complex, navigating the official minefield with the ease of a visiting dignitary, he realised he had been touched by kismet, or hands other than his had oiled his path. Yet, whichever it had been, the feeling of entering a new and more auspicious phase of his plans was accentuated by the impressive vehicle that waited at the kerb where a bland-faced man of Eastern origin stood, in a traditional Western suit, bearing a placard stating 'Eugene Styros'.

He walked purposefully towards the car, feeling as though somehow he had bent time, sped forward in his game plan to arrive already at the height of his fame. A family of Europeans stopped and stared, wondering if, perhaps, they should recognise this beautiful man with the charismatic smile who could afford to be waited upon by a chauffeur driving a spotless limousine. They persuaded themselves they had seen a film star, a pop star, or some millionaire Western playboy. The plethora of beggars, however, were not fooled. They kept well clear of the impressive vehicle and pestered the bemused Europeans instead: a much safer target.

Eugene was greeted with a smart salute, whereupon the chauffeur took his bag and opened the rear door for him. He climbed in, glancing around the spacious interior. She had not come to meet him, then.

The door was slammed and the chauffeur climbed into the front. There was a faint whine and the window separating the front seats from the rear lowered halfway down.

'Your clothes, please, Mr Styros,' the chauffeur requested politely, swivelling in his seat to hold out his hand.

Eugene was startled. The car was stationed at the front

of a large, international airport. Now, seated inside, and with a clear view of everyone outside, he could not remember noticing if the glass was one-way. Flushing slightly, he recalled what he was here for, and realised that this was where it started. He was not wearing much as it was, but relieving himself of those few light cotton garments meant relieving himself of everything civilised and European, yet he sensed the chauffeur would not drive an inch until his reluctant passenger did as he was told. When he had handed his clothes over, down to the last small item, including his watch, the window slid back up again and, with a faint purr of a huge engine, the car eased its way through a swarm of brightly dressed Eastern women and out on to a long, dusty road.

He realised he was being reborn, coming to his new life poor and naked as a baby.

Looking around the plush, leather interior of the elongated car, Eugene knew he was committed, and that this sense of luxury was an illusion. He could discover no means of communicating with the driver, bar knocking on the dividing window, and he had the nasty suspicion that he could knock all he wanted; the driver would ignore him until they reached their destination.

He was not comfortable, in spite of the air-conditioning. His bare skin stuck to the upholstery, and with every corner negotiated, and every bump in the potholed surface, he was reminded of his vulnerability. A strange place, a strange car, an Eastern society. Even had he wanted to change his mind, to throw open the door and run, he realised in the circumstances he stood more chance of ending up in some foreign prison than making it home.

And yet, in spite of this strangeness, he found himself keenly surveying the route, following the road signs, marking his journey. At the end of this time, he would know where he had been, at any event. However, when they had travelled several miles, negotiating two towns festooned with minarets and beautiful masonry, then out on to smaller roads, the driver pulled into what seemed like an empty field. The dividing glass lowered a small way and a leather object was passed back to him.

'If Mr Styros would please to put on the hood,' the chauffeur said politely.

The window went back up again, and Eugene surveyed the hood with more trepidation than anything he had encountered to date. Without the words needing to be said, once more he knew they would wait here until he obeyed, and if he didn't the car would probably eventually just turn around and deposit him back at the airport – perhaps *sans* clothes.

He lifted the hood and pulled it over his head. It fitted snugly, the padded leather packing his eyes tightly shut, and when he managed to manoeuvre the rear zip over the back of his head and down to the neck, he realised he was also effectively gagged, for he could not move his jaw. The hood might have been made for him, it fitted so snugly. In darkness, he wondered what was going to happen next. He had expected the driver to continue, but the car remained stationery; they were waiting for someone, or something. From time to time his hands moved, itching to reach up, unzip the hood, but he restrained the impulse. Then, on the air came a thumping sound – unmistakable, even to untrained ears muffled by leather.

A helicopter! He was slightly peeved that this exciting opportunity was not his to savour, to enjoy film star-style, as he had imagined. He heard the front door of the car open, then another, and he was being pulled gently by the arm, indicating that he should slide out. His bare feet encountered a stony ground that made him wince, but he was walked along a short way until his feet encountered vegetation; grass. He stood hesitantly, hands automatically covering his exposed genitals, and felt the chauffeur's hands fiddling at the back of his head. On inspection, he realised a small padlock had secured the zip in place. So, he was not to know his destination, by accident or design.

To his consternation, he heard doors slam behind him, and the limousine departed. He swivelled in faint panic and reached ineffectually for the padlock, but his hands then fell back to his exposed parts and he turned back to face the unseen, noisy craft that continued to settle. He felt inordinately vulnerable, having no idea how big it was, or who was in it, watching him standing there, naked save for a leather helmet, like some bondage pervert.

In spite of the warmth, he shivered.

There was a rush of stinging air on his naked flesh, a 'whoomph, whoomph' of blades, then eventually someone placed a hand on his shoulder, and another on the back of his head, pushing him forward in a low crouch. He knew there was a second person present when other hands directed his feet, gripped his hands and eased him up through the opening and into a seat. Like a child who could not perform this duty for himself, a body harness was buckled around him. The door slammed, then, with a gut-dropping lurch, the helicopter rose up and sideways before settling into a steady path. Here, Eugene lost all count of time. Neither being able to see the landscape roll past beneath him, nor having any idea of direction – they could have been flying in circles for all he knew – he had no idea what mileage was covered, or whether one hour or three passed in that strange, muffled and somewhat tense darkness.

The helicopter finally drew a huge loop in the sky, dropped with unexpected speed and came to rest. Eugene felt trapped in a sense of timelessness, as if he had stepped from reality into another universe or into a dream. Now his heart was beating furiously, and nothing he could do would still it. He felt stifled by the hood, in spite of the air holes at the nostrils, and it seemed he could not bring enough air into his lungs to satisfy them. As the door opened and the rotor blades began to sweep in slower arcs overhead, Eugene realised that he was almost to the point where he was going to panic. He was eased out on to what felt like a paved surface and, with an unknown hand at either shoulder, was walked at a fairly brisk rate forward.

Within moments the air cooled and he realised they had entered a building. Hands at his neck now released the padlock, unzipped the hood and freed him. As the hood fell away, he gasped air into stricken lungs and stood for a moment, half-blinded, before beginning to take stock of his situation.

The reality was a culture shock.

Where he stood was more than simply a room – it was obviously the vast foyer to some great castle or palace of storybook beauty. Open doorways led off in various directions, and everywhere the walls were hung with bright fabrics or painted with beautiful, intricate patterns. The walls were also alien to his Western eyes, being partially formed of an open latticework beyond which other corridors and rooms were visible.

And there were people everywhere. All standing where they had obviously stopped, mid-task, to view his arrival. The women were dressed in bright, flowing trousers and tiny bikini tops encrusted with jewels, and some even had fringed masks over their faces. Similarly, the men wore trousers, but their torsos were bare, save ornamentation and jewellery, and on the feet of all were the most dainty, curl-toed slippers he had ever seen.

For a moment they stood in silence, he staring at them, they staring at him, before a harsh whisper heralded a hasty flurry of movement. The flock of bright silks parted to allow access to a woman in black, followed by an enormous, overweight man of Arab extraction, wearing nothing but a loincloth and a belt supporting a variety of strange instruments nestling underneath his flowing gut.

The garment that concealed the woman's face was a yashmak; he knew that now, he had done his homework, such as he could. And in all this place she was the only one who was covered, head to toe. But he knew it was she, for there was a kind of presence that clung to her like an aura, and which he had never sensed on any other woman.

'Welcome to your new home, slave.'

'My Lady,' he said, bowing.

'A little more humility would be appropriate for a slave,' she responded.

Eugene hesitated just a moment, then lowered himself to his knees and put his forehead to the floor, wondering if that was sufficient. It seemed to be, for she uttered no further complaint, but left him there, his buttocks in the air for a moment, before continuing.

'Slave, my name is Olanthé. This is my citadel, and you are my slave. You may address me as Lady.'

'Yes – Lady.'

'When you please me I will reward you. Thus.'

She threw a coin down; it bounced around and settled a few feet away.

'Thank you, Lady.'

'And any time you displease me I will have you punished. Ali, please give the new slave ten strokes to show him what I mean.'

Eugene looked up in alarm. 'But that wasn't –'

'Slave, the word "but" will earn you punishment, the

word "no" is forbidden. "No" uttered deliberately three times will send you home.'

He opened his mouth, took a breath, but she held up a hand guessing his intent. 'And sorry is simply a word with no value. It does not even translate into my language. Ali,' she said, redirecting her hooded eyes towards the large man.

'Lady,' Ali said, bowing slightly.

Glancing sideways, Eugene was horrified to see the man remove from his belt an object the size and shape of a cricket bat, but made of thin, whippy wood. It took all his willpower to remain there, forehead and hands flat on the floor as the man walked around behind him.

Nothing in the whole of his adult life had prepared him for the stinging slap of the paddle-shaped beater against his raised rump. He gasped with shock, his skin instinctively flinching from the blow, the aftermath of the sting travelling like fire from his buttocks up his neck and into his head. It seemed to him there was a small pause before the next blow, as if the Lady and her henchman, Ali, were exchanging a silent conversation of raised brows: will he stay the course, I wonder? It was almost to his own amazement that Eugene gritted his teeth and stayed there.

'Does my slave approve?' the Lady asked, the merest hint of sarcasm barely evident on the tip of her tongue.

'Yes, my Lady,' her slave snarled, not having envisaged any such thing, but almost as soon as the words were out of his mouth the second stroke fell noisily in the silence. Contrary to expectations, this one was not easier to bear because he knew what to expect. Instead, the blow landed in exactly the same place, on skin never before so abused, already sensitive with tingling nerve ends. He bit his lip, trying to stop himself from crying out, then released it quickly as he sensed Ali's hand raised for the next blow, realising that the last thing he needed was self-inflicted teeth marks on his perfect features.

He could just imagine the memory that would sear his mind every time someone asked the question: 'And just how did you get the scar on your mouth, Mr Styros?'

The beater came down with precision several more times. Though by the end his face was damp with tears, he had the satisfaction of not having actually uttered the mewling sounds of distress that were building up in his throat. When the last stroke landed he was too stunned to even feel relief. This was happening to him, Eugene. He was crouching on the floor, allowing another man to whup his ass.

'Very good, slave,' the Lady purred. 'Now pick up your coin and give it to Ali, who will look after your rewards until the day you leave. Stand and follow me. Keep your eyes to the floor before you.'

'Yes, Lady,' Eugene said in a flat voice.

As instructed, he followed as the small cavalcade wound its way through three corridors and into what seemed like a vast hall. Without lifting his eyes he was able to assess the amazing width and length of the room, but not the height, yet there was an echoing quality in their footsteps which told him the ceiling must be some-where far above.

This room was also more basic than some of the areas he had been through so far. In spite of its size it had a sort of functionality about it. The floor was made of flagstones and the plastered walls were bare of all but the most minimal of designs. A large fireplace to one side told him it was not always this hot, and he wondered if perhaps this room was used as some kind of a universal meeting area.

He realised there was a raised dais at the far end of the room on which there were several large, wooden chairs, padded with fabric for comfort. In the centre of the room there was a structure like a small plinth, rising from the floor in stages like steps, reminiscent of the lower half of a pyramid.

It was to this plinth he was led and, with suitable encouragement, he mounted the steps until he stood at the top in solitary splendour, facing the dais. There was no mileage now in casting down his eyes. From this position he could see everything and everybody, and was uncomfortably aware that everybody could see him – all of him, including his stinging and probably red posterior. Uncomfortably he crossed his hands in front of him, shielding some small part of his anatomy.

From above came a small creaking sound, as a wide wooden bar was lowered before him. It was supported on two fairly functional hawsers, and sported a pair of leather cuffs hanging on short chains. Realising the implications of this, he swallowed hard; but that was not all. Without a word, Ali brought two more cuffs and clipped them to the floor of the plinth at the outer edges, a suitable distance apart.

'You can cuff your own ankles,' the Lady said softly. 'Just to assure me that it is your own choice to accept that which you have contracted to accept. Don't forget, you may choose to end this at any time.'

Biting back a suitable retort, Eugene bent down and did as he was told, cuffing one ankle, then spreading his legs apart to accommodate the second. This is crazy, he muttered inside his own head, and wondered, not for the first time, if this was not all a huge mistake, and what the hell did he think he was doing?

He stood up awkwardly, feet straddled, and lifted his hands obligingly. Ali fitted the wrist cuffs snugly before going back to the wall and winding the mechanism back up. Within moments Eugene found himself standing on tiptoe in an exposed stretch. He grasped his hands around the chains above his wrists to take up some of the strain, consoling himself with the thought that, although this was an unusual position for a Western man to find himself in, it must actually be displaying his rather fine body to some advantage. His chest was tight, his waist was sucked in, and almost every muscle on his body was contracted. Yes, all things considered, he probably looked quite good.

He glanced sideways at the shapeless woman who was standing to one side, and was disconcerted to make direct contact with her eyes. He flushed and looked away quickly, hoping that this aberration had not earned him another punishment of some sort. Surprisingly, although the punishment itself had seemed inordinately severe while it was being dispensed, only a matter of fifteen minutes later all that was left was a slight soreness on the surface of his skin.

The Lady, however, just lectured in that soft voice of hers, directing her words to all present, but with emphasis towards Eugene himself.

'Slave, you'll remain here on view until such time that I allow you to begin your duties. Keep your chin up, and I don't mean metaphorically. Don't show unseemly interest in any of my brethren. You are here for them to look at, not the other way around. Don't ask questions, but answer if any asks a question of you. I'll leave you to your own reflections for a bit. I suggest, with the utmost sincerity, that you discover within yourself such humility as it is possible for a Western man to find.'

And with those words she turned and departed, leaving Eugene to his reflections. He could do little else. He was not there long, however, before people silently began to enter the room and get on with various tasks, such as setting up low trestle tables, surrounding them with brightly coloured cushions, and beginning to load them with an exotic abundance of fruit. In the same way that those people glanced at him surreptitiously as they worked, so Eugene's eyes sidled around the room assessing them while his head remained at the angle requested by his Lady.

The people who scurried about diligently were obviously servants, while here and there, it became obvious, others were overseeing the procedure. He noted it was not so much manner of dress – or lack of – that put them apart as attitude, and he wondered whether this was a fair representation of the people who lived in the place, wherever or whenever it was, for it certainly didn't seem to belong in the century he had come from.

Gradually the long tables were filled with platters of every kind of food imaginable, and it was only after scrutinising the situation closely that Eugene realised there was more variety on the tables nearer to the raised dais. There was a hierarchy. One's position at the table was determined by one's status, and the whole room would shortly be filled with everyone who could possibly exist in this place – and he was strung up like a captured beast for them all to view. For the first time, his pride in his male accoutrements was slightly less than over-whelming, and he wished they would just crawl up inside his body and hide, rather than hanging there so obviously and happily between his legs.

6

Olanthé lay on the dark, embroidered silk cover of her bed and Ali stood beside her, waiting. She wore nothing save jewellery but, even so, the dry heat of the day made her golden skin gleam with sweat. She stretched and yawned, flexing her muscles with catlike grace, before asking, 'How does he look?'

'Terrified.'

Her white teeth gleamed. 'Just terrified?'

'And belligerent, and hopeful, and embarrassed.'

'It'll do him good.'

Her smile was echoed in his eyes. 'I don't doubt it, Lady. He has a nice body, but his mind is cluttered.'

'It won't be soon.' She reached out and plucked a grape from the luscious mound of fruit on the table before her and popped it into her mouth. White teeth bit hard and the grape cracked audibly, filling her mouth with sweetness. Suddenly she stilled and tears filled her eyes as a memory surfaced.

'Oh, God, I miss him so.'

'Michael or the master?'

She shifted herself carefully. Bran's parting gift to her buttocks would take a few days to calm down. 'Don't be obtuse, Ali. Michael!'

'You missed Persu greatly, before Michael came.'

'I know I did, but that's beside the point. It's Michael I'm missing now.'

'Within a few weeks you won't miss him any more. You'll have Narcissus to see to your needs.'

'Why do you have to be so matter-of-fact? If you don't stop it, I'll have you flogged to within an inch of your miserable life.'

'As you will, Lady,' he said calmly.

She gave a watery chuckle. 'Massage me, Ali. I'm stiff and sore. It's just as well Bran doesn't come home too often; I might not survive the experience.' She rolled over on the cushions and Ali knelt beside her and began to rub oil down the long length of her back. His hands were dark against her skin, and rough with calluses, and although his touch was careful, at first it was like sandpaper along the lines of chastisement.

She gradually began to relax under the strength of his blunt fingers and, as she relaxed, so he began to work her flesh harder and more deeply, digging his thumbs into the tense muscles, teasing them apart until she groaned with pleasure. She didn't need to tell him how to please her, not any more. Ali had been her first loyal slave, and would be loyal till the day he died.

There came a time when his touch ceased to hurt; her body moved so subtly under his hands it was no more than the prickling of goosebumps on the skin, but he knew. He rose up on to his knees in order to lean over her and spread the weight of his body more equally between his two hands. From this new vantage point he began to work his way down her body, from the well-muscled shoulders to the globes of her buttocks.

She sighed with enjoyment and moved sensuously under his hands. He poised for a moment then, when no further instructions were forthcoming, began to circle her buttocks in strong even movements. Olanthé's hands began to clench and relax on the velvet cushions and she spread her legs slightly wider in invitation. Her body was physically relaxed, her flesh moving evenly under Ali's competent massage, yet there was a buzzing tension of expectation inside her head as his fingers worked closer and closer to the knot of her anus. As he brushed a finger across the puckered opening she gasped and jolted, and waited expectantly for it to happen again. She was almost holding her breath with expectation, but Ali made her wait.

'Bastard,' she muttered, then almost bit her tongue as he did it again. She imagined the secretive little smile he would have on his face had she turned over suddenly.

'Is that nice, Lady?' he whispered.

'Mm,' she agreed.

She didn't need to look to know that Ali would be enjoying this too; she had seen it often enough, his incredibly thick cock pushing against the fabric of his loincloth as he worked.

'Roll over,' he commanded.

She rolled over, eyes closed, and delighted in the feel of his hands all over her body: between her legs, down her thighs, along her breasts. When the massage became sexual it was scarcely subtle. One finger slid between her legs and pressed insistently, the grease allowing only the fleetest resistance before it slid in. She moaned as he massaged her now, his left hand teasing a roused nipple round and round with increasing strength until it was almost painful, the other working between her legs, a finger sliding in and out of her backside while his thumb teased up and down the greased hood of her clit, the sliding of his hand as sensual and erotic as anything she had ever known.

Her whole body was moving now and her knees rose and parted, hips thrusting in time with his strokes. She was inwardly consumed by her own private sexual indulgence; nothing else mattered save the feel of those electric touches on her body. She clutched at the bedcovers and let the waves of pleasure ride over her, through her.

Finally she made a small mewling sound and sucked air into her lungs until she thought they were going to burst. As the enormous jolt fired through her body like an electric current, Ali's fingers stilled, keeping the pressure on throughout the dying orgasm until she shuddered to stillness under his hands.

At last she opened her eyes and stretched luxuriously, pushing Ali away with her feet.

'I'm going to sleep now,' she told him. 'Go away and service yourself; and wake me up before the dinner gong.'

'Yes, my Lady, of course.'

He gave a small bow and left silently.

Olanthé found herself unable to sleep, though. Stretched out on top of the covers, she found her mind skipping around unconnected memories of the men who had passed through her hands. Where had it all started? It was so long ago, her traumatic childhood was like the remnants of a bad dream. Living with all this wealth, this control over her own destiny, it was hard to think of that previous existence with any degree of reality. Turning her head sideways on the rich counterpane, she glanced at herself in the dressing mirror with some justifiable satisfaction.

She rolled over on to her back and thought of her latest project – Eugene. He was physically very beautiful, firm in all the right places; he had youth on his side but, to his credit, had obviously worked at being that way. Also, for a man, he was still a few years short of his peak condition, whereas she – she grimaced wryly – she was at the age where women were considered past their prime. The thought was unsettling.

When the day came that Bran did not look at her with lust in his eye she would cover herself with sackcloth. She pondered on that for a moment, then a small grin emerged. Better still, become Madame rather than Lady, and run a whole stable of pretty girls and boys. She could still train them, after all, and when you had as much money as she and Bran had between them, well, perhaps she would have to resort to paying people to service her needs. After all, if you paid enough, people would do and say anything you wanted them to.

But it wouldn't be the same.

She rolled over on to her stomach, crossing her legs in the air behind her, and reached for the remote control. A panel in the wall slid back, incongruously exposing a television within. She flicked through the channels, watching snatches of the films she came across.

Some days she loved the old films for their black and white characters, corny scripts and all the charm and simplicity that modern films somehow missed, yet sometimes she couldn't stand them for that same reason. On other days she loved the modern films for the special effects and larger-than-life heroes, never mind that the heroes could only grunt and shoot guns, and if there was a plot you had to be clever to find it – or blind to miss the glaring errors.

So what made a film good, and what made an actor a star?

She thought of Eugene strung up in the main hall and stifled a giggle. He was certainly impressive in the chest and muscle department, never mind his more manly attributes, and he was right about money getting him through certain doors. With absent attention, she watched the screen moving. But just getting through the door wasn't enough. Forget the acting ability, or lack of it; in that field success wasn't something you could expect at the end of four hard years, like getting a diploma or a degree. With some people it was luck, plain and simple; with others it was hard work and persistence. But there were some actors who simply were stars, almost from the first moment their image was broadcast.

Bran wanted Eugene to become a film star, and why not – but how?

Eugene thought it would simply take money, but he was a fool.

Bran had obviously sensed Eugene could become an icon, but knew he needed a little more *something*; Olanthé didn't quite know what that something was, but she would find out. She usually did.

She flicked the set off and scrunched up on the bed to paint her toenails red while she thought.

7

A man entered the hall and lifted the beater of a large gong. Like the knell of doom it seemed to echo on and on in Eugene's mind. Spread as proudly, and breathing as rapidly, as an athlete at the termination of a magnificent display of physical prowess, it was as bad as he feared. His hands clenched involuntarily around the chains as from almost every quarter there was a sudden hubbub: the hall seemed to have more entrances than the Metro, and through every one of them streamed what seemed to be an unending tide of people.

Within moments, what had been an empty hall was now filled to bursting. Behind the rigid expressionless mask he presented to the throng, he was shocked to the core by his present situation, and inside his head his tongue uttered the words that would release him over and over again: no, no, no.

Yet his hopeful career would expire at the sound; he would be sent home penniless. Being good-looking wasn't enough in Hollywood. He had already discovered that you had to bribe someone to get through the door, never mind get a screen test.

The advertisement, passed snidely to him by a friend of sorts, had hinted that the enormously lucrative position was that of sex-stud toyboy. He had laughed at the joke, then later fished the advertisement out of the bin. Right the way through from the initial telephone call to the interview to the flight here he had run an argument in his mind about the pros and cons of this strange development.

And right to the time of being picked up at the airport he had expected to find himself the pampered pet of some ageing woman with a hankering for young blood. He had expected to be ridiculed a little, to do menial chores in inappropriate garb – that he could handle with the dollar signs firmly behind his eyes. But he had also expected to find himself living in a certain amount of affluence, for no ordinary woman would have been able to pay for the privilege of having a young stud, a golden Greek god awaiting her every beck and call. He had supposed also that this fictitious dame might have other house help: gardener, cook, cleaner. If so, he didn't care what they might think of him. And yes, he had expected to be required to service her body whenever she wanted, and he was prepared to do so even though she would almost certainly be undesirable to his young eyes.

All that he had taken into account, but he had assumed it would be basically a one-to-one relationship, and that perception appeared to have been vastly mistaken. He had had misgivings at the moment of handing his clothes over in the car, but not for one moment had he expected to become a slave in a whole bloody society where hundreds of people, including men, would witness his inauguration and – horror! – perhaps more. To choose to be a sex slave was one thing but, being a heterosexual man, he had assumed, of course, that his main task would be that of pleasuring a single woman on command. Suddenly he was not so sure that the financial reward was great enough for this.

The women were dressed for the most part in almost transparent silk and the men were bare to the chest, many adorned with gold ornaments, even on their nipples, which looked to be permanently pierced. One man was also wearing what appeared to be a lacework of straps around his head, holding what could only be a gag in place.

Perhaps this was a punishment of some kind, he didn't know.

Hiding his utter consternation at such an alien scene, he managed to appear to be staring straight ahead and, although he could feel heat burning in his cheeks, he presented, as far as he was able, expressionless features to the crowd who betrayed no surprise at all at the sight of a naked man strung up in their dining hall.

Perhaps this was something they were used to.

Suddenly the babble of conversation stilled, and from the door behind the dais emerged a woman. Tall and beautiful, skin the colour of natural honey, exquisitely tip-tilted eyelids curving over black-olive pupils and a riot of dark hair falling in soft curls almost to her waist; she was exquisite. She was also nearly naked, her attire so minimal it could have been classed as jewellery rather than clothes. Even from this distance, Eugene was startled at the magnetic jolt he felt run through his middle at the sight of her: she was blatantly, unashamedly sexual.

This was *her*?

He was both confused and exhilarated, having assumed her previous covering of robes to be concealing something of which she was ashamed, whether deformity or age – but he had still been prepared to serve. This new knowledge, that she was not only presentable but actually quite lovely, gave the lie to his previous conviction that any woman who desired a male slave, gigolo, or whatever, must be well past her prime, and probably quite desperate. Well, what do you know, he thought to himself in mild amusement, if the mistress wants fucking, I'll be happy to oblige!

The woman came to stand behind the table, and every person present was silent, eyes glued to hers.

'My brethren,' she began in her musical voice, 'I would like to introduce you to our new slave. He speaks Greek and English, so today we'll speak in English. This slave will be my personal challenge for the coming year.'

Challenge? Eugene thought, startled, wondering what she meant by that.

'Take a look at him. Is it not a pretty specimen? He thinks he would like to be a film star.'

All heads turned, and there was a smattering of laughter. Eugene flushed a slightly darker red at this focused attention. 'And, oh, so conceited. I have decided to call him Narcissus, after the Greek youth who fell in love with his own image. Slave, from this point forward that shall be your name. Your old life is gone, your old name is gone. You are Narcissus, and exist only to serve.' She clapped her hands. 'Let the inauguration feast begin.'

She sat down, a sensuous curling of limbs, and there was a sudden buzz of activity and noise. Hot food was brought on steaming platters, wine was poured, and within moments everyone was deeply engaged in the business of eating. Which reminded Eugene he had not eaten for a while. His stomach let out a mighty rumble that must have been heard by those near to him.

The Lady looked up instantly and, again, her eyes contacted Eugene's with a clarity that made him swallow hard. Too late, he lifted his head and stared into the distance. She made a small comment to a nearby woman, who backed away humbly, palms together, before scurrying to fetch something from a large chest. The young and extremely attractive woman then danced lightly up to the dais and, to his horror, knelt before him and began to wrap something around his testicles. Everyone stopped eating and turned to watch, food hovering untouched in their hands.

When the slave finished her fiddling and let go, he felt

the most amazing stretching feeling down below and had to grit his teeth not to bend his head and look at what he knew had happened. Christ, she had hung weights on him!

In the interested silence, the woman's voice rang out clearly. 'My Narcissus was thinking of food. He must learn that the only thing he must think of is my pleasure. In a few moments he will think of nothing else.'

There was another brief spatter of laughter, then everyone turned back to their meal.

At first Eugene found the strange pulling sensation to be vaguely pleasant, and with some mental juggling he could almost imagine the insistent tug being caused by a woman's hand or tongue as they sought to flood his tool with the necessary desire to make love. After a short while, however, it was no longer so easy to fool himself; the weight seemed to get heavier by the minute. What was initially a strange and almost erotic feeling very rapidly became a dull ache that spread throughout his body, somewhat in the manner of an orgasm but without the related charm. He was certainly thinking of his organs, but he was not thinking of them with any sense of satisfaction and, as for the Lady who was his mistress, his imagination saw him wrapping his hands around her very pretty neck the moment he was free. But it certainly focused his mind: where he had been thinking freely before, he could now think of nothing except the fiery ache in his balls for the rest of that long meal.

When the slaves were finally engaged in taking away the barely diminished piles of food, the most richly dressed of this strange community rose from their seats and gathered around, curious as children, to view Narcissus, the new sex slave, at close quarters. To his great embarrassment, however, they did not only look. Instead, they prodded his muscles, tweaked his nipples, massaged his cock to feel the size of it and pulled his foreskin back and forth, chattering like sparrows, perky and interested, inadvertently (or perhaps not) setting the weight on his balls swinging time and time again.

Giggling like schoolgirls, they touched him everywhere – both the men and the women – trying to generate involuntary movement, a gasp or a sigh from him, but it was only when a softly probing finger pushed up into his arse that he gave an audible grunt and yanked his hips forward as though he could escape that indignity. But the involuntary twitch was enough to set them giggling some more, and to repeat the invasion again and again.

It took a moment for him to realise, being virgin in this particular area, that he was being oiled, obviously in preparation for the insertion of something, and what that might be he could only stab a horrified guess at. But no, he was not to suffer that particular indignity. Eventually something hard and inanimate was pushed up against his anus, stretching it wider and wider until he gasped at the tightness, thinking if it stretched any more he would split open.

Then, just as a faint whimper almost passed his lips, his body seemed to take a deep breath and suck inward. The object passed inside him with a faintly disturbing spasm of muscle, and it was gone. He panted with a kind of claustrophobic fear. What was it they had put inside him? What would it do? Would it block his bowels? But he was given little time to ponder, for there was another pressure at his anus and the insertion was repeated again and then again. The only consolation was that the muscle gradually relaxed, in spite of his tension, to make the ingress smoother, less frightening each time, and he gathered, from the feel and size of them, that he was being filled by balls, metal or glass, the size of large marbles. He managed not to cry out, but never in his life had he experienced such an extraordinary feeling as that of his bowels being filled from an external source.

After a while the weight inside began to be noticeable, and with it came the urge to eject the foreign bodies. Even as his body shuddered at the thought, a fairly well-built man in rich, red trousers beamed at him with a wide smile, enunciating in very bad English, 'Narcissus will keep the balls inside, yes? Until he is given permission to pass.'

Clenching his jaw and his anus tight, Eugene said nothing. Was what he wanted out of life worth this price?

The man grasped a handful of his already tender balls and warned, 'You will say, "Yes please"?'

'Yes please,' Eugene blurted, a sob in his voice.

'Good. You please my Lady. After, if she agree, I make love with you, Narcissus. You are beautiful man.' And the man tapped him playfully on the buttocks as he departed.

Eugene was overwhelmed by the thought and felt tears of self-pity come to his eyes. That would not happen, no way. After all this, he would be forced to abort. Then, without warning, she was there, before him, her black, almond-shaped eyes like bottomless pits of lust, a small sarcastic smile on her lips.

'My Narcissus wants to quit already?' she asked softly, while one long, painted nail scratched down his chest almost absently. He breathed in heavily of her intoxicating perfume, oriental, heady. The marbles were pressing on his prostate gland, creating a riot of strange sensations as his body fought his mind, the one trying to eject the foreign bodies, the other trying valiantly not to. Yet her scent flooded his nostrils; she was so lovely, so desirable, but he could hardly believe the strange thought that came to him. As though bewitched, he realised he would take this, and more, for the privilege of finally entering her body.

'No, Lady,' he gasped.

There was a sudden silence, and she waited expressionlessly for a moment, before commenting, 'A forbidden word, my slave, for which I will punish you later.'

'Then what am I supposed to say?' he whispered.

'You must discover other ways of saying things, my slave. Learn to use words to your advantage. You want to be an actor, don't you? Then act. You must assure me often that you're having a wonderful time, then beg me to allow my people to continue to pleasure your fine body. It pleases me to see them do so, and perhaps you will grow to enjoy it.'

The most peculiar sensation of warmth stole over him at the compliment. She thought he had a fine body, and from somewhere the words discovered a way out. 'I'm glad it pleases you, Lady. I'll learn. I promise.'

She flicked the weight and he gasped, but the small nod of satisfaction his words generated didn't go unnoticed. 'You don't have to be afraid, my pretty Narcissus. It's only a little weight. We've got far greater ones for your pleasure, later. Only you'll have to earn the privilege. And never forget the one truth I give you now.'

She gave a cheeky smile at his puzzled expression.

'That, along with your financial reward, I pledged to send you home a new man one year from now, not a broken one. With everything that happens to you, remind yourself of that one thing. You may have to remind yourself very hard sometimes.'

'Yes, Lady. Thank you, Lady.'

'Very good,' she purred.

Eugene watched her bottom rotating deliciously on the ends of those rather incredibly long legs as she moved. He realised something important had happened, but could not quite work out why or how. A moment ago he had been ready to leave, yet at a couple of words from her, he had moved into another level of acceptance. However, he hoped she did not intend to leave him here very long. Though he had not eaten since leaving the plane, neither had he been given the opportunity to relieve himself, and it did not look like this was going to happen in a hurry, except by accident. To his consternation no one seemed in any hurry to leave the hall, and it became obvious that something else was going to happen when the slaves scurried to fold the large tables and pack them away at one end of the room, then fill the floor space before him with huge cushions.

Gradually order was restored as the cushions filled the floor and the gentry, exhausted by their labours, sank on to them, laughing and gasping with enjoyment.

To Eugene's astonishment they then proceeded to fall fast asleep.

8

As the brethren slept, scattered like butterflies on some gaudy, scented bush, the slaves kept watch, starting forward if someone muttered or moved, then slipping back quietly to watch some more when it proved to be a false alarm. The Lady herself slept among them, and it was now that Eugene took good stock of her, her long, honey-coloured legs stretched in abandon, her eyes heavy-lidded, sated, her ripe mouth slightly adrift, her hair cascading in a dark waterfall over the coloured cushion. Now and then she would move slightly, as if dreaming some private dream, and her limbs would shudder, her hips flex.

Standing in a stretched cross, unable to relieve the aches in his shoulders or calves, it was the ache in his lower body that utterly consumed him. Clenching his bowels ever tighter to stop the marbles from exploding furiously from him, he imagined the sheer noise they would generate, bouncing around the hard floor, startling the assembled sleepers into wakefulness. With this effort his balls seemed to get tighter and tighter, and insistent waves of desire were generated by the strangely packed sensation of his lower body.

Eugene found himself beginning to fantasise. Without realising how or when it had happened, he discovered that the severe discomfort had transmuted inexplicably at some stage into pleasure. The total and consuming tension, at first an overwhelming need to evacuate his bowels, gradually became a flooding erotic desire, the like of which he had never before experienced. Waves of sexual need pulsed through his balls and cock, until eventually an erection of fairly impressive proportions was pointing proudly towards the assembled sleepers before him.

It was Eugene's experience that when an erection appeared, it demanded attention. The need to relieve his extended bowels was nothing to the consuming desire he felt now to simply take his erection into his own hand, to touch it, tease it, play with it until he spurted his spunk everywhere.

He moved his thoughts to that inner desire, closed his eyes, leaned his head back and breathed softly a litany of wishes: to gently touch, feather-light, the glowing tip, feel the immediate, electrical pulse of contact. Rub his hands, oh so gently, over every part of that wonderful, thick organ until every nerve was aflame. Cup his balls in his hand, press a finger against the small knot of his arsehole. Then, finally, when his whole conscious self had flooded inward, had compacted into knowledge of only that one rigid part of his body, to take his cock in his hand and glide gently, up and down, up and down, until the internal fires burst like stars behind his eyes.

But he could only imagine, and that thought became as total and consuming as any sex he had ever experienced. He thought about touching, gliding, sucking and thrusting, while his legs stayed stretched wide and his hands curled desperately in their leather cuffs. His hips were now moving just faintly, because that was all he could manage, and any kind of movement at all threatened the precarious hold he had on the anal stuffing. In frustration, he stared down at the erection that throbbed like a purple flower.

His mouth opened and he panted in tiny breaths.

Never, in all his years of adolescence, of dawning youth, had the meaning of frustration been made this clear. Always he had been able to contain himself with a few discreet touches, in the knowledge that he could shortly secrete himself away somewhere to service his needs. Never before had he been in the position of having such a glorious erection in the full knowledge that he could not touch it, no matter how much he wanted to. And before him, the Lady slept on unaware that he was there, ready and willing to service her, to prove his manhood in the best way he knew how.

He closed his eyes and groaned softly under his breath with frustration. Yet when he opened his eyes again, a fraction later, he realised she must have heard, for she was awake, staring at him. Her body was still, and he had not heard the slightest movement, the tiniest betrayal of her wakefulness, yet she was awake.

Now she stretched luxuriously, yawned and, as if this were a signal, around her the others also began to stir, and one by one all turned their eyes to the new slave, as though magnetised. There was almost a look of wonder on their faces and he was not sure if it was the size of his erection that made their eyes widen, or the fact that he had one at all. But it was there, as tight and shiny an erection as he had ever achieved. His balls had contracted, risen, in spite of the constriction and the weight, the glowing head of his cock had burst free of its sheath and his bowels were aching with the effort of holding in the pile of marbles, which clamoured and sought exit.

Even with every eye on him, Eugene could not stop the minuscule movements of his hips, his need was too great; they moved without thought, without volition, and he could no more have stilled his body than fly. He wanted to beg her – or anyone – to come and take his tool in their hands. That was all it would have taken, a single touch, and he would have released this glorious and tightly clenched pleasure in a single fountain.

But they did not. Instead, to his horror, they freed their own sexual organs from the confinement of their clothes and were pleasuring themselves, using the sight of him as a tool to aid their exertions.

As though he were a pin-up from a porn mag!

The Lady, too, was moving subtly, her right hand nestled between her legs, stroking, teasing; until her lips fell apart with lust, her eyes half closed and her breath came in tiny pants. He knew the moment she achieved orgasm, for her whole body was racked with uncontrollable tightness and a current of ripples seemed to travel from the core of her body out to every extremity, giving the appearance of a seizure.

He had never seen a woman respond so physically to her own sexuality.

In fact, it occurred to him that he had never seen a woman masturbate, never mind see a whole group of people masturbating together as if it was the most normal thing in the world.

It occurred to him that he was shocked.

She lay back, her hungry gaze drinking in his aroused state while around her the small groans and gasps of orgasm slowly declined and stopped. Now the slaves came in bearing bowls of steaming water and, with great care, they began to wash and dry the sexual organs of their Lords and Ladies.

Eugene looked at the bowl with aching intensity; if someone would only come and wash him . . .

As if reading his thoughts, his needs, the Lady stretched, catlike, and yawned with sensuous pleasure.

'I think my slave is ready for further punishment,' she observed.

No, Eugene thought. No, no, no! He closed his eyes briefly and prayed to whatever god was listening out there. He could not, he would not! It would just take a word, that single word repeated out loud, as he had uttered it in his head, and he would be released, sent home. Penniless. He swallowed, cleared his throat, and clamped his jaws shut in case the words popped out in spite of him, and he thought of the money; the incredible amount of money.

She uncoiled her slender form from the cushions and Ali, bowing from the waist, handed her a small switch as she walked forward. For a brief moment Eugene was pleased that it was not the wide baton, but then the lady bent the switch deliberately between her hands, showing him the flexibility and strength of the small stick. He stared at it with apprehension, for though it looked like bamboo, it was something far more sophisticated: an innocent length of twig which had been lovingly cut green from the tree, honed, oiled and crafted into something that was surely not to be treated with contempt.

'Does my Narcissus approve?'

'Yes, Lady,' he said tightly.

She purred at his response and came forward. She even walked like a cat, he thought, one foot directly in front of the other, treading softly and silently on the balls of her feet. He bit his lip and could not take his eyes from her body, undulating and desirable, as fresh and wholesome as new brown bread. He was apprehensive but, even so, mesmerised by the sight. What was it about her that made him want to abase himself like a true slave and beg her to use his body in any way she wanted, when she was about to do just that?

She walked around the plinth and, when he could no longer follow with his eyes, he turned his face to the front and listened. He heard the soft swish of skin against skin as she stepped upward towards him and, though not seeing her, he would have known her from the sweet musky scent of her body. He felt himself melt with desire on the one hand, and laugh at himself for his stupidity on the other: she was about to do things to his body that were going to be decidedly unpleasant, and he was fantasising about fucking her?

He sensed movement behind him a fraction of a second before hearing the swish of whippy wood slice the thick air. A line of fire burned instantly on his inner thigh, and he took a shuddering breath to stop himself from crying out. Why had he supposed she would stick to the buttocks? And if not, where else would that line of pure pain fall? He winced in his bonds, willing his balls to shrivel up inside him. But they did not. As his cock lost the wonderful glowing rigidity it had known a few moments previously, they sank floorward slightly, pulled inexorably downward by what he had been assured was only a small weight.

Standing now to one side, she lifted his failing erection with the tip of the stick. 'Be careful, my Narcissus,' she warned in a sultry voice. 'My people want to see you enjoying yourself. And don't forget to thank me.'

For beating him? He took a deep breath but, as if she knew he was about to utter something he would regret, the little stick whipped back and laid a thin line of liquid fire across the front of his thigh. His words bit off into a grunt and a gasp, and tears flooded his eyes. When he had controlled himself, he took a couple of shuddering breaths and said, 'Thank you, Lady.'

'Now concentrate. Where would you like to be beaten, my slave?'

'On my buttocks, Lady?'

'Oh, come on, be more adventurous. It's such a little switch, and so very accurate.'

Oh, shit. He closed his eyes for a fraction of a second. 'My calf?' he suggested half-heartedly. Her sloe eyes narrowed, the switch whipped, catching him across the tight calf, and he jolted so hard he squeaked, and his feet left the floor. He clenched his buttocks hard, nearly having evacuated all the marbles on to the floor.

'Now you understand the manner of the game, you thank me and suggest another target as quickly as you can. Do try to be inventive, and don't keep me waiting.'

'Thank you, Lady. My left buttock?'

The switch instantly cut the air and shocked his nervous system once more. Suddenly Eugene did not care that a hundred people sat watching his performance – or lack of it. All he knew was that he was about to disgrace himself. He gasped in a single breath, 'Thank you, Lady, I can't hold the marbles any more.'

She snapped her fingers. 'Ali! Yasmin!' The slave called Yasmin leapt up the plinth with alacrity and presented Olanthé with a gag. Eugene nearly cried. 'You can say no,' she assured him. He shook his head, not knowing how to answer.

'Then open, and bite down.'

He opened his mouth, and she thrust a bit between his teeth, bringing the various straps up over the top of his head and under his ears, buckling it firmly in place. His mouth was pulled into the parody of a smile.

Ali then stepped up with another object, a bung on a pole. Eugene whimpered, horrified, his tongue lapping at the rubber bar, but Ali stood, brows raised, waiting for permission. Think of the money, think of the money, he said to himself. She had said she wouldn't hurt him. No, she had said she wouldn't *damage* him. He was just beginning to realise the difference. How in hell had he got himself into this mess anyway?

He thought of the money and nodded; a brief, quick nod, to get it over with.

The lady signalled Ali with a flick of a finger, and the object was pushed up into Eugene's back passage. He lifted as far as he could, almost screaming at the extra load that was wedged inside his body, extending his bowels even further. Then the end of the pole was settled into a small depression in the plinth, obviously there for that very purpose.

Gradually Eugene stilled and settled and, when he was once more in control, the Lady nodded. 'Now you will not embarrass yourself, slave. Are you comfortable?'

He nodded again, and she began to target various areas of his body with the innocent little stick. She struck his inner thighs, his buttocks, his nipples, the lifted soles of his bare feet, until he felt as though he were standing on his own funeral pyre, that his body was going to simply burst into flames and consume itself.

As she was working, and to his shock, the slave Yasmin came up, knelt between his legs and took his cock in her mouth. At first he was so focused on the awful stretching in his bowels and the lightning strikes of the cane, which bit with venomous snakelike accuracy, that even the soft, sucking pressure of her lips could do nothing for him. Then gradually, so very, very gradually, his attention shifted inward, beyond the burning surface of his nerves and into the body within. Once again the tightness of his lower abdomen began to send signals to his genitals, and to his surprise there came a time when the biting of the little cane became a pleasure that he awaited eagerly – each sting sending a shiver of masochistic pleasure into some hidden core of his brain. He recalled reading somewhere that masochism was closely tied to eroticism, but he had laughed in disbelief.

He now knew it was no joke.

And that was when he realised Yasmin had her red lips around a full and throbbing erection, and that her fingers were holding the shaft at the roots, nestled in his golden mound of hair. He was vaguely aware that the Lady was still standing there, switch in hand, but all that mattered now was the warm glowing feeling that was spreading from his cock to the rest of his body. The cries that came from his throat were mewls of pleasure, growls of lust, demands that she work faster, faster. Because he was transfixed to the floor by a pole that went up inside him, he could not move his hips in the slightest to assist; he could only lean his head back, tighten his chest with anticipation, and let her get on with it.

He could feel it building up inside him, a glorious volcano, bigger and hotter than anything he had ever known – then the Lady, with the flick of a finger, sent Yasmin back on to her haunches.

With horror, Eugene stared down at her. No, oh no, not now.

He glanced over, almost in irritation, and the lady gave a faint curl of the lip. 'Narcissus, my slave. You will learn to get an erection at will. You will learn to hold that erection in place for as long as I tell you to hold it, and you will learn not to release unless I give you permission. That is your target, your goal in this life.'

He gave a wordless grunt of denial – it was not possible! She scraped a painted nail along his lips, into his mouth around the rubber bar, toying with his tongue. 'You Western men are all the same. You think it can't be done. It can, and we'll teach you how.'

He could have cried as she walked away, taking the

rest of her court with her, and leaving him impaled. As he suspected, Yasmin was a bitch of the first order. She sat and watched his erect tool as if there was nothing else in life to live for, which in other circumstances would have been admirable.

In other circumstances he would even have appreciated her opening her pert little mouth to little Johnny every time he wilted a little, to give him a good suck and a fondle. She certainly knew how to do that, now running her tongue around the foreskin, cleaning, nibbling, now lapping at the sensitive, glowing tip, now thrusting herself down on him, now squeezing with her teeth at the base.

Oh, God, it was beautiful.

And terrifying. Christ, who were these people?

It occurred to him that no-one, including him, knew where the fuck he was, and he might never get free.

But did he want to when this was happening?

Straddled on his pole he couldn't move a muscle to help. He couldn't move with her, against her, or even away from her. He was forced to simply watch and accept while this pretty woman did things he had only dreamed of a woman doing to his most wonderful male attribute. But if she knew how to get him going, the little bitch also knew exactly when to stop. Each time he could feel the pressure building up, the excitement level of his heart increase, his blood pressure on the boil, ready to lift the lid, she would stop, sit back on her haunches and stare at it again. At those times her actions would cause to be emitted from his throat a strange noise akin to that of an animal in distress.

He had no idea how long he stood there, in that great hall, on the plinth, being orally excited by the most gorgeous little naked slave he could ever have fantasised about. He assumed they would probably arrive at a time when his tool, as sore and tired as the rest of him, would simply refuse to play; when it would just fall over limply, crawl into a hole and die. But to his own shock and surprise, the opposite happened, as though something had been triggered in his brain, some chemical, some hormone, that said, oh, for goodness' sake give in, stay up and give yourself a break. For after a while she did not work any more, she sat back and stared at him, and the single eye of his trouser snake stared back, undaunted. After a while she stood, turned and disappeared, and when she returned a short while later, preceded by the Lady, it was still there, proudly, hotly on display.

He was irritated that she gave him what he could only think of as a cheeky grin. 'Well, Narcissus? Are you beginning to feel more like a sex slave now?'

He nodded dutifully, tiredly, his proud erection not so much an object of desire as a huge, bloated wart, a foreign body attached to him like a pustulous leech, something that should be squeezed until the juices flowed out. No, it didn't feel good at all. It didn't feel bloody natural.

Now she nodded and said to Yasmin, 'Get Ali to see to him. Bathe him, clean him down, make him ready for the evening. Tonight he becomes Narcissus.'

Eugene didn't know what she meant by this, and he was torn by the relief of his imminent freedom and the horror of embarrassment, knowing the moment he moved he was going to spit marbles all over the hall; there was no way he would be able to stop them – and everything else – gushing like a geyser from his body. But it was not to be. His arms were released, but his ankles were tied tightly to the pole, holding it firmly in place, and he was carried out of the hall, face down on a stretcher, pole and all, his erection uncomfortably squashed beneath him. This was more embarrassing than anything he had ever dreamed of.

His face flamed red and stayed that way for a long time.

As he was carried along, from this undignified position he looked around as well as he was able, curiosity mixed with disbelief. What was this fucking place? Whatever it was, it was huge, with tall archways, stone-slabbed floors and, incongruously, electricity points. He was taken to a modern, tiled shower room and here, shamefully and noisily, he was uncorked and allowed to relieve himself of the objects that cluttered his insides. Then the gag was removed, he was stretched upon a marble slab, comforting in its coldness against his abused back and buttocks, and a pillow was put under his head, providing the illusion of comfort.

Slaves came and began to wash him and, to his irritation, remove all traces of hair from his body. With a fine blade and soft soap, the hair from under his arms, down his arms and legs and around his genitals was gently and efficiently removed, as were those little whorls of gold that had curled around his nipples for as long as he could recall. His nails were cleaned, manicured and polished, his nose and ears were syringed out and, when they were done, he looked down at himself to see not the Eugene he knew, but a stranger whose body was not his own.

When he was as smooth as a newborn baby on the front, the big man in a turban came up and sat beside him on the slab and undid a small roll of fabric. From this he removed a selection of bars and rings. Two bars he lay across Eugene's nipples, two rings he placed either side of his head, and one ring he carefully placed near the genitals, just in front of Eugene's still quite impressive erection.

'You say yes?' the man asked politely.

Eugene stared, astonished. He opened and shut his mouth several times, emitting negative noises, then clamping them in, because the only words he could think of were, 'Not bloody likely!' and he wasn't sure if this would be construed as no three times. He thought it very probably would.

'This not hurt,' he was told. 'Timi show!'

To his surprise Timi dropped his flowing trousers and displayed a big brown cock adorned with a silver ring, which was threaded through the thin section of tissue below where the end of his knob split, and popped right out of the hole in the crown. Christ, Eugene thought, a Prince Albert! He'd never seen one except in magazines. The big man was circumcised, so the ring sat there in full view, nestling in the crack of his exposed knob. He flicked it a few times, pulled it about a bit to prove that it did not hurt. Then he proceeded to do the same with the ones through his nipples, indicating by rolling his eyes and gasping that they also felt very good to touch.

Eugene bit his lip and felt tears come to his eyes. He shuddered and tried to suck his bits up inside his body with the power of thought. This he could not do, no way. All he had to say was no – and that would be the end of it all. For what if he said yes, and it all went wrong? He could end up having his knob turn black and it having to be amputated. He'd heard the stories.

And what about pain? He knew, without a doubt, he could not do it.

Perhaps sensing this last thought, the big man said, with a huge smile, 'Me, doctor.' He then produced a small syringe. 'You go to sleep a little. You not feel hurt. Yes?'

Eugene gritted his teeth and gave a fractional shake of his head, so small that it was almost unseen, but they all knew what he had done. He'd blown it. The doctor pursed his lips a bit, then pointed to an earring, quietly giving the new slave another chance.

'This ten thousand dollar bonus.'

Eugene blinked. The man pointed to the other earring. 'This ten thousand dollar bonus.' He pointed to the nipples. 'These ten thousand dollar bonus.'

'Each?' Eugene asked, stunned.

He nodded, and his finger caressed down his chest to the waiting Prince Albert ring. 'And this ten thousand dollar bonus. But only if you say yes to all. Lady says you keep bonus even if you not stay for year.' He gave a fleeting grin. 'You will enjoy. It make good sex.'

'Christ,' Eugene said, looking at the innocent little bars of metal with new eyes. 'And I wouldn't feel a thing?'

'You feel nothing. I good. I do many times. No problem.'

'You make sure I feel nothing,' Eugene threatened.

The needle slipped in, and after a few moments the doctor began to get out a pair of pliers and various other instruments. Eugene felt a little panicked by this and tried to say, 'But I'm still awake,' only to find that he could say absolutely nothing. His tongue was thick in his mouth and his muscles felt like jelly. In fact, even though he could see his body lying there on the slab, elongated out of perspective before him, he couldn't move a muscle; and so, perforce, he watched the whole thing, which wasn't quite what he'd had in mind. The various sites were cleaned with disinfectant. A pair of clippers punched earrings straight into his ears, and the bars were inserted into his nipples with the use of little plastic sheaths, which were then removed. By the time the doctor came to his cock, the erection had died, but it was a little disconcerting to watch the man stuff a piece of plastic tube into it and begin to work a thick needle through the flesh and out of the plastic tube. Although he could feel nothing, he shuddered internally, a jolt of panic in his middle. When he opened his eyes again, the ring was in place.

He was then rolled over on to his stomach and the other side of him was cleaned as efficiently as the first, while he discovered there were little holes in the table for his nipples and his cock, and a padded hole for his face.

He stared at the floor for a while, almost distanced from reality, then, as the feeling gradually came back, he felt hands working all over his body, scraping, cleaning, putting balm on the faint marks left by the switch. When they had finished, soft hands teased at the sore flesh of his back, working his muscles and rubbing sensation back. It was then he discovered the doctor had lied.

Every puncture hurt like bloody buggery.

Only it wasn't so much hurt as an insistent throbbing, which was probably only bearable – certainly in the cock department – because Yasmin didn't come back to stimulate him into rampant erection once more. Not that that was any consolation, for the piercing notwithstanding, the desire to come was still with him, as demanding and unrelenting as ever, differing only in that the end of his knob felt sore and strange and uncomfortable – and he was sure the anaesthetic hadn't quite worn off yet, that there was worse to come.

Eventually he was escorted to a small bedroom.

It was there, chained loosely to the four corners of the bed, he was left to stew in his own miserable juices for the night, and the only consolation he could think of was that they hadn't offered him another ten grand to do his nose or his tongue.

In the darkness of his own mind he accepted the true depth of his own greed, and a small internal devil told him the discomfort he was suffering was well and truly his own fault. The padlocked restraints did not hold him uncomfortably tightly, but they were enough to stop him examining his wounded flesh, which, he supposed, was the whole point. He groaned fractionally as he tried to make himself comfortable, knowing he would never be the same again. Why had he done it? He was a bloody pansy with earrings, nipple rings and a bloody Prince Albert in his knob. He lifted his head and looked down at himself, able to do little else. Who would want to hire an actor adorned like a woman? Why had he done it? The answer echoed around in his own head, and he tried to deny it, while knowing it was true: it was greed, plain and simple. But greed for what? It wasn't just the money, he told himself. That was simply the means to an end. Or was it? Was the thought of all those millions the sole reason he wanted to be an actor?

He shuffled about on the bed, but sleep evaded him as the enormity of what was happening to him gradually sank in. He knew he had been awake for most of the long night by the time he heard sounds of stirring beyond the door to his room.

Eventually two matronly women came in and wiped him, top to toe, with flannels and scented water, chattering to each other all the time in some foreign tongue, ignoring him for the most part as if he were simply another chore in their daily routine – which, he supposed wryly, he probably was. When he was cleaned and patted dry to their satisfaction, to his extreme embarrassment, his various piercings were closely inspected and discussed. Next, they lifted his head and allowed him to drink via a straw, and then they disappeared.

For the next few days he existed in the little room, at night chained to the bed and during the day his arms chained loosely to the small of his back, for the sole reason, he supposed, of stopping him from examining or touching his own piercings. He was allowed the freedom to pace up and down, but nothing else was provided for his entertainment. He was soon bored to absolute and utter distraction.

He saw nothing of Olanthé at this time, but the man called Timi examined his piercings twice a day, the women washed him once a day and Ali was a constant visitor, sometimes bringing small amounts of food, but certainly not enough to satisfy his griping hunger, and sometimes taking him for constitutional walks out into a sandy courtyard bound by tall walls. The sky above was wall-to-wall blue and he could only suppose that wherever this place was, it was far from the sea. He was bored out of his mind, frustrated, and angry with himself, but he noticed after a few days that the violent bruised swellings of his piercings had died down and were healing with astonishing speed. He realised he had lost track of the days and was beginning to see this routine as the beginning of a long year of grinding boredom, when the routine suddenly changed.

The women who washed him were replaced not by Timi, but by Yasmin, who quickly climbed over his recumbent body. He stared at her as she began to tease at his cock, and she grinned cheekily back at his dismayed understanding. Maybe the healing wound had something to do with it or maybe, he thought with irritating rationality, there had been something in the drink but, whatever the reason, it took her merely a moment of teasing with finger and tongue to produce the desired effect.

'Bitch,' he whispered softly as the familiar pleasant buzzing started in his loins and spread outward in consuming need. Once he was well and truly rampant she left him alone once more, writhing with unconsummated need.

He decided that when someone came in and freed him

he would smack them on the nose and say to hell with it. But when Ali came in and began to buckle some kind of harness around his shoulders, he grimaced and accepted without complaint. Then he sat up and allowed Ali to strap his wrists to this contraption behind his back.

It was only a year, he said to himself grimly. Think of the money.

He sighed deeply and closed his eyes, knowing it was not going to be that easy.

Ali then strapped his ankles to each end of a short pole and hoisted him to his feet. The pole kept his legs apart and made it extremely difficult, not to mention embarrassing, when he was requested to walk. Yasmin had done her job well and, as he shuffled along, legs wide apart, arms behind his back, his cock stuck out like a flagpole before him.

It was, he thought, a nightmare from which he was sure to wake up soon.

That, or it was going to be a bloody long year.

9

Olanthé leaned back against the cushions and watched Narcissus shuffle awkwardly into the room on the end of a collar and chain, led by Ali. He was further humiliated, she could see, by the fact that Ali tethered the chain to a pillar before departing. A shiver of desire darted through her as she cast her eyes over his nakedness. He really was very, very lovely.

She stretched luxuriously, her imagination already in full swing.

The slave Narcissus could not hide his curiosity any more than his nakedness, and she saw him take in the rich décor and her near-naked state in the same avaricious glance. With a certain amount of malicious amusement she moved sensuously on the bed, opening her legs to give him a clear view of everything, knowing that in spite of her orders he was unable to tear his eyes from the juicy morsels within. She would hazard a guess that no woman had ever displayed herself to him like that before. She saw his cock jolt slightly and was impressed in spite of herself. He was certainly attractive and sexual enough for the most discerning of women. It was exciting to have a man, an angry one at that, rampantly aroused by your body, yet chained to a pillar, unable to perform.

'So, how do you like your ornaments, my slave?'

His lips compressed, but he said nothing.

'You have permission to speak freely to me,' she commented, leaning back on one elbow on the rich cushions, crossing her ankles and plucking a grape from the table beside her with almost absent-minded precision.

'I didn't expect –'

Her dark eyes gleamed with humour as his eyes finished the sentence. 'So I gather, but I made it worth your while; you could have refused, but you didn't.'

'I didn't think I was allowed to refuse.'

'No?' she said innocently. 'I wonder what gave you that idea? But if you want to go, just say so. My word is my bond. You can still go with fifty thousand dollars and my good will.'

Eugene took a deep breath and snapped, 'I didn't say I wanted to leave.'

'You didn't have to say it,' she replied with a degree of indifference. 'It's written all over your face.'

'I didn't expect –'

'To be treated like a slave?' Her voice was scathing, and he winced. 'Why not? Did you expect to live an easy life for a year, perform a few sexual acts and walk away with a few million pounds in your pocket?'

His flush told her that was exactly what he had expected. Michael had not been so naive, she reflected; but better not to dwell on Michael. He was special; one of the few who happened to cross her path just now and then. 'Very foolish, wouldn't you say? Didn't it occur to you that I could have bought those services for considerably less than I'm paying you?'

'Perhaps it was, but you knew I thought that. And you don't have to keep me chained up like a dog,' he said petulantly.

Her voice was harsh. 'You're chained up like a slave, and you're not the first to experience it by a long way; but don't fool yourself. Some slaves have no choice – you do. You're here because you choose to be. Because of greed. If you don't want to be here, say the words and I'll send you home.'

She waited for a pregnant moment.

He bit his lip, swallowing his ire rather than retort, and her voice softened fractionally. 'You're chained because it pleases me to see you so, but also it's for your own good. The piercings will heal much quicker if you can't touch them. Most of the horror stories you hear are either because the piercing has been performed by amateurs, or because secondary infections have set in from scratching, or not being clean enough. Yours will heal quickly on all counts. Two weeks more and you will hardly know they had never been there. Trust me.'

He glanced down at himself. The brightly inflamed nipples and throbbing cock had already healed astonishingly well, and almost seemed like part of him. Already the panicked feeling of having alien artefacts pushed through his skin had diminished to a weird kind of acceptance. 'Did you do this to humiliate me?'

'No.'

'Then why?'

She gave a secretive smile. 'You'll find out.'

He scowled and pulled uncomfortably at the bindings around his wrists. Olanthé lay back and feasted her eyes on him. Belligerent, as Ali had said, and embarrassed, and not a little afraid. It was a good combination that stirred a warm feeling in her breast. There was nothing quite as exciting as having a slave force himself to do your bidding unwillingly, and to take undeserved punishment without complaint. These actions never ceased to send a shiver of pleasure through her middle; and to be able to culminate this humiliation by forcing them to perform acts of sexual gratification on the perpetrator of their discomfort was an aphrodisiac second to none. She stretched and uttered a small mewl of satisfaction. The fact that they probably enjoyed it too rubbed salt in their egos.

She fleetingly felt sorry for the millions of women around the world who would benefit from her teachings, if only they were allowed to be freed from the sexual restraints of society. Women who were taught to believe that sex was an immoral act, and that enjoyment of the act would bring eternal damnation; or that their bodies were solely for the use and pleasure of a single male. Not unintelligent, she realised that most of these teachings were derived from male domination, but she would remain forever baffled by the fact that those men could not understand that the sex would be so much better for all concerned if those same women were allowed to enjoy it – wallow in it – as she did. After all, something as wonderful as sex was the stuff life itself was made of, and could not be sinful.

However, though she was no stranger to the many societies the world had to offer, the constraints of society would remain forever an enigma to her – which was one of the attractions of her desert hideaway, and the reason so many people who came here to work for a short while ended up staying.

She stretched back and watched Narcissus eyeing her with something akin to dislike. He did not realise yet that it was himself he did not like very much, not her. It was funny how different men were, and she had known a few. This Narcissus was a strong man lurking inside a weak one, whereas Michael had been strong from the first moment she saw him, and his capacity to take pain or embarrassment in grim, stony silence was incredible. She had sensed in him a self-destructive capacity and knew he had accepted her offer not because he coveted the money, like the others, in spite of what he said about being a politician, but because he had needed space from a reality he couldn't cope with.

Bran had been dubious when she told him that. He was rarely wrong, and it seemed he had proved her wrong this time, but a small niggle of doubt remained. Michael would be a good politician, and he was far, far more interested in being a good politician than a rich one.

With Michael it had not been so much that she had given him the space as that he had grasped it himself with both hands. Then, healed by time, he had gone back to life with a vengeance. That he would be successful, and eventually rich, she did not doubt. Bran had a good nose for a potential target. She smiled softly at the memories of her last meeting with Michael. He had done everything she ordered – and not always willingly – until the day his contract was finished. At that point, his obligation honoured, he had taken back control in no uncertain manner.

Which she had enjoyed, on reflection.

She knew she would treasure that moment in time. A soft, introspective smile curved her lips. She thought he might even miss her a little. A shiver of enjoyment went through her at the recollection of Michael's parting gift; and in the same moment, regret. She would have liked to keep that one, but they all had to go in the end, nothing could change that.

And there was Eugene, her Narcissus, glaring at her as though his predicament were all her fault. She smiled inwardly. Perhaps it was, but she had learnt a long time ago that when a weak man gets sufficient incentive he sometimes discovers strengths he didn't know he had; and Narcissus was incredibly vain, expecting his looks to earn him a future and suffering his present humiliation only with that final aim in mind. Maybe he would succeed yet. She studied him, thinking there must be some reason Bran chose him over the others. He was, after all, a hollow excuse for a potential star, but perhaps he could be forgiven for being this way; his incredible physical beauty was without question, and he certainly had some inner drive to succeed, even if he thought he could do it the easy way.

One thing Olanthé knew from experience: there was no easy way.

He was watching her now, distrust in his eyes, and she let him wait – the tension was good for him. Besides, she liked that look on a man's face. She had seen it before: the wary one, where he was stunned by his predicament, wondering what she was going to do and whether he had the strength to go the whole term. They didn't all make it. Most, but not all.

She still wasn't sure of Narcissus but had been surprised at the way he handled his rough inauguration. He had shown a little more stamina than she might have expected, but then again, he was incredibly greedy for success.

She stood up and walked towards him, knowing the effect she had on him. It was the effect she had on all men, whether they liked it or not. It was both a curse and a talent. He stiffened, and she saw his muscles tighten involuntarily as she approached. She unclipped the lead that chained him to the pillar and led him towards the bed.

'Kneel,' she said.

With some difficulty he obeyed, falling forward on to the bed, trying to protect his sore places, before dropping to his knees. Ignoring his quick intake of breath as his newly acquired piercings were pulled, she clambered on to the bed before him and sat on the edge, knees spread, giving him the full benefit of everything she had to offer. She was pleased to hear his breath shorten, and see his eyes contract almost instantly with lust.

Her lips curved slightly and she leaned back, lifting her heels from the floor. 'Lick me,' she said.

She saw his face go rigid with shock. What was it about men, that they thought it was fine to persuade women to do certain things to their bodies but it wasn't proper for women to demand the same? It was a bit like saying men could sow their wild oats but the women who went with them were whores. That she could never understand.

'Lick me!' she repeated harshly.

Almost timidly, Narcissus obeyed, and she was sure he was not enjoying the experience. He was doing nothing for her pleasure either. After a moment, she pushed him away with her foot. 'You'll have to learn to do better than that if you want to earn your money,' she snapped.

She stood, walked to the open window and leaned her hands on the sill, but from the corner of her eye she saw dejection slump his shoulders, and she knew her caustic, calculated words were having the right effect. He was wondering if he could take this humiliation for a whole year; whether he could actually please her sexually; whether he would be kicked out because he could not; and whether the whole slave thing had been an awful mistake in the first place. In short, his self-confidence had taken a bit of a knock.

'Tell me about *Casablanca*,' she said suddenly.

'What?'

She turned, hands on hips. 'The film. *Casablanca*. Tell me about it.'

'But I – I've never watched it.'

Incredulity marched across her features. 'You've never watched it?'

85

He shrugged. 'I don't like old films, and black and white ones are the pits.'

She sat on the sill and rocked one foot to and fro, then gave a short laugh. 'You haven't got a clue, have you? You think you want to be a film star, but you don't think you need to be an actor. You want to make films, but you haven't done any research. That is the classic romantic thriller of all time, and you, my budding film star, have never seen it?'

He flushed red again at her scathing tone.

She gave a brittle laugh. 'Well, perhaps you're in the right place after all. Perhaps you've found your niche in life. It doesn't take a particularly large amount of intelligence to be a sex slave. Just a good body, and you have that. Lean forward on to the bed.'

'Why?'

'Because I want to hit you. You make me want to hit you.'

He bit his lip and stared at her for a moment, then leaned forward on to the bed, carefully trying to avoid snagging his nipples. Olanthé glided sensuously over to a chest, anticipation already warming her, and peered into it intently for a moment, before making a decision. She pulled out a thin switch, watching him take note as she did so.

From his wince she knew he wasn't fooled by its minimal size; he knew she was going to hurt him. His hands clenched behind his back and he made an involuntary movement to squeeze his knees together, but he was thwarted by the stretcher between his ankles.

She started slowly, a single lash, not even too hard, and waited for his harsh indrawn breath to be slowly released before laying the second alongside the first.

'*Casablanca*,' she said, laying a slow stroke with every third or fourth syllable, 'was made in 1942 with Ingrid

Bergman and Humphrey Bogart. It's a work of art, the definitive classic movie. It's also been called the most romantic film of all time. Who starred in it?'

The tiny crop landed squarely on his left cheek at the final syllable. He squealed, leapt from the bed and then managed to draw himself back up, panting.

'I said, who starred in it?'

'Humphrey Bogart,' he whispered hoarsely.

'And?'

'And – uh –'

Whack. 'Ingrid Bergman! What year?'

'1945.'

Whack. '1942. You'll learn,' she said grimly, 'even if we do have to do it the hard way.'

She talked softly about the emotions the film gener-ated in the breasts of those who watched it, the meeting of past lovers, betrayal, regret, unrequited love and noble sacrifice. As she spoke, the dark, smoke-filled atmosphere filled her mind, as did the sound of the piano, backed by the almost monotone grating slide of Bogart's sensuous voice.

Oh yes, it was a film that moved a person.

After a while her monologue started to dry up, and she came back to the present with a small start of surprise. Narcissus's backside was a single swollen mass of red, and though he wasn't making a sound, his cheeks were wet with tears. She also discovered she was well and truly aroused by the sight.

After throwing the small switch aside, she took a pot of liniment and poured some into her hand. Narcissus tensed visibly as she knelt behind him, and he made a strangled cry as her hand began to smooth the liniment into his throbbing flesh. He might have thought this was further punishment, but Olanthé knew more than he could possibly guess about dealing with the aftermath of a good beating. She smiled as she gently rubbed his protruding rear end, knowing the movements would eventually arouse him.

She kept working until he ceased to wince at every stroke of her long fingers, and she saw the first signs of tightening in his scrotum. Then her massage became one hundred per cent sexual. She greased him and rubbed herself hard against his sore backside until he was moving gently in time with her own compulsive movements.

'On the bed,' she whispered.

He clambered awkwardly on to the bed and rolled over on to his bound arms as indicated. His face was tense and his cock stood like a swollen flagpole. He stared at her wordlessly as she turned, straddled his face and began to masturbate right above his eyes. As she began to writhe in time with her sliding finger, he gave a strangled sigh and tried to move, to respond.

'Sh! Lie still.'

He froze, and she continued, leaning forward to gently lap at his sore nipples. She didn't know whether he was gasping and quivering from pain or excitement by the time she came.

Flushed with exertion, she rolled away and lay on her back for a moment before turning her face towards him. He was staring at her in frustration or consternation. She gave a slow smile and reached out to smooth his mouth with her wet finger.

'You're going to have to wait a couple more weeks before having sex,' she informed him wickedly. 'But as you see, my slave, I can find ways of using your body while I'm waiting. The one thing you must never forget is that you're here for my pleasure, not your own.'

She rang a bell and a female slave, who must obviously have been waiting outside the door, entered instantly. 'My Narcissus needs a bath, and get Timi to put clean dressings on his piercings when he's done. I want him presented back to me in two hours, ready and willing.'

10

'Come on, sweetie, let's get you bathed and salved,' the slave said with a cheeky grin as she walked him down a wide corridor.

Eugene was slightly shocked. 'You're American!'

'Wow, you guessed!'

'Yes, but I –'

She put her head on one side. 'You're surprised that an American would want to be here? Buster, there's people from Oz, Europe, the Middle East, all over. Why should it surprise you? It's a way of getting out of the rat race. Lots of the people here have come from split marriages, unhappy backgrounds, whatever. Besides, it's a good living, a bit of fun, sex whenever you want it, and you get well paid for your trouble.'

'You get paid?'

She gave a real belly laugh. 'You think we were all kidnapped and sold or something?'

'No, but –'

'You did! That's rich.' She stopped in the middle of the corridor and faced him, hands on hips. 'Well, disabuse yourself, buster. I'll let you into a little secret. The slaves get paid and the Lords and Ladies do the paying. Depends on how much money you've got as to what side you end up on. And it's all one and the same in the end.'

'You mean – you're not really slaves at all?'

'Of course not.'

'And you can leave whenever you want?'

'Within reason. We get a contract, and if we don't fulfil

it, whatever the terms, we get penalised. Same as you. We've all got our reasons. Some people just stay for a year, some have been here forever; once they get here they don't want to leave.'

'But what about *her*?'

'Olanthé?' The slave gave him a sidelong glance. 'Buster, she's for real. She owns this joint, and I, for one, wouldn't get on the wrong side of her. I suggest you don't either. There are two ways you can earn your money – the hard way, or the very hard way. Here we are.'

The bathroom was a huge, tiled area, utterly modern and lined with mirrors. The slave filled the bath, whistling as she did so, then relieved him of the collar and cuffs.

Eugene inched himself down into the lukewarm water. The slave waited patiently, but once he had settled and was able to take the weight off his arms, she indicated the shackles at the end of the bath, either side of his head. He gave a wry grimace as she fitted them snugly around his wrists.

'Does she think I'm going to run away or something?'

'Fat chance of that, here. There's a hundred miles of desert in every direction. If you run out that way, you're dead, pal. No, it's to stop you doing yourself a mischief until you're all healed,' she said, and reached down to caress him briefly, and unemotionally, between the legs, which he found distinctly unnerving. 'And to stop you from playing with yourself. It's not allowed.'

'I'm not allowed to play with myself?'

'You're not allowed to wank. Not unless Olanthé says you can. Your body is hers, and believe me, there'll be times you wish it wasn't.'

'I already wish that,' he muttered as she left.

He settled himself in the bath and closed his eyes, and as he relaxed, he felt tears pricking behind his eyelids.

Nothing, but nothing in the world was worth all this humiliation, surely? And what did it matter if Casabloody-blanca was made in 1942? Who the hell cared?

He shifted faintly and winced, but the bath was doing the trick, and gradually all his aches melted away into the warm water, as did the feeling that he wanted to cry and go home. Yet what was home? He did not have one, not really.

What was it she – Olanthé – had called the people? Her brethren? She made it sound like some sort of cult. Thinking about it, maybe it was at that. A sex cult. Or a cult for masochists. He opened his eyes, peered down at his cock and winced. He would never get used to seeing something sticking through it, and that was for sure. First thing he was going to do when he left this godforsaken place was to remove the damned thing and let it grow over. At least – did the holes grow over? He vaguely recalled hearing they did.

He pushed himself back slightly to touch one ear with his finger. It was hardly painful to the touch now. Sighing heavily, he sank back even further into the water. If it was saline, it wouldn't do his ears any harm to get doused either. Why did she want him sporting jewellery though? What was it about piercings? Was it some kind of owner-ship thing, having to wear her house colours like a brand perhaps? Or was it simply a test, to see how far he would go? Instinctively he realised that was the truth. As the water cooled around him, Eugene began to think about the fact Olanthé wanted him back in two hours. How long away was that? Not long enough.

He felt like he had already been in this place for months, not just weeks. What had initially seemed like a good money-making scam now seemed more like a prison sentence, a huge chunk of his life wasted, locked into something bizarre and frightening. Worse than prison even, because prisons let you have televisions and didn't torture you. Well, not the kind he envisaged anyway. He'd seen them on television; the inmates had better accommodation than his last flea-ridden bedsit.

The door opened and Timi came in. Eugene looked at him more carefully this time and saw beyond the turban and loincloth. 'Where are you from?' he asked.

'Me? Russia,' the man said with a belly laugh. 'When the economy collapse, I work for two years with no pay. My family starve. Then, when I think I no good for my family, I offered this job. I send good money home to my wife, to my children.'

'Don't you miss them?'

The big man stilled, turned away and busied himself with a speck of dust on his loincloth for a moment. 'Yes, I miss. But it not so good to be with them and watch them starving, no?'

'No, I guess not. Couldn't they come here?'

'I not want my wife and children here,' he said shortly.

'I can't think why.'

Timi ignored his sarcasm and inspected Eugene's nipples and cock with close attention to detail. 'Heal good. Much quickly here, too, because it's dry and hot. When I get enough money I go home to wife and children. Now I here.'

He shrugged philosophically and was removing the cuffs as he spoke. Eugene climbed out on to the warm stone floor. He reached for the towel, but the doctor snatched it from him, telling him, 'You stand, so. I dry.'

'Oh, for goodness' sake!' Eugene muttered, spreading himself into the required star. As the doctor dried him, he peered back over his own shoulder to see that his swollen posterior had calmed down to a fine meshwork of little lines, which, he guessed, would probably be gone in a day or so. Except that he had a nasty feeling they would probably be replaced by others. He winced visibly as the doctor dried him, but the soak in water had already helped calm the swollen flesh, and it didn't hurt as much as he was anticipating.

'Now you come to Lady Olanthé,' the doctor said, walking towards the door and indicating for him to follow.

Eugene was nervous about walking along a corridor stark naked – it went against everything society had instilled into him – but the people he passed on the way knew no such qualms. They gazed at him curiously, assessing his potential, admiring his physique, some of them even visibly stirred, sexually, but there was not the slightest hint of amusement in their eyes. That, he thought, was the strangest thing of all, that they were so used to seeing naked men with rods and rings in their knobs and nipples that they took it for granted.

His interest in his surroundings, though, was tempered by a very real apprehension about what was going to happen next. He guessed that the previous boredom, nearly two weeks by his rough calculations, had not been indicative of the rest of his stay. He realised he had merely been given time to heal from the rather unpleasant and unexpected piercings, and now he was going to discover what Olanthé expected of him. He had not, in his wildest dreams, thought of this kind of scenario, and had he known, he was sure he would have baulked before committing himself. In fact, in all likelihood he would not be here. There was something about actually being here, though, that made him grit his teeth and bear it, almost a perverse, masochistic determination.

But, as Olanthé had so cuttingly observed, it was not what he had expected at all. She had known full well he had been expecting to live the easy life as a rich bitch's gigolo for a lazy year, damn her. Whereas, far from whispering sweet nothings in some old bag's ear and rutting with her once or twice a day, the tables had been turned on him. Instead of being the expected toyboy, he was simply a toy. Maybe an object of desire, also, but an object all the same, whose sole function in life was to provide sexual stimulation to an exotic and beautiful woman whose boundaries of eroticism exceeded his previously naive comprehension.

All in all, this made him feel rather inadequate.

He recognised the doorway to her private quarters and tried to recall everything she had been saying about *Casablanca*. He wouldn't put it past her to put him to the test, damn her eyes. She was not there, however, and the doctor pointed beneath the large curve of an internal archway to a small plinth upon which one might have expected to see a statue.

'You wait here.'

Eugene clambered up with a reluctant sigh, spreading his arms out along the waiting steel bar without waiting to be instructed, so that the doctor could secure them in that position before buckling the available harness firmly around his shoulders. His ankles were then buckled to chains on either side of the plinth, stretching him tautly, but comfortably, in an open gesture of welcome to whoever might enter the room; and there he was left alone, a living statue. Part of the damned décor, for goodness' sake.

He waited as instructed, as there was little else he could do, but after a while he realised he was strangely at peace with himself. He tried to tell himself he was bored, angry at the lack of freedom, but behind the inactivity of his body, his mind was in overdrive. While his body was shackled and unavailable to him, his mind was freed of pressure for the first time in many years. It was a strangely disconcerting freedom. He had no obligations to anyone or anything simply because the ability to react had been taken away from him.

His eyes roved. Behind him lay the bedroom, but this side of the apartment was obviously living quarters and boasted a strange mixture of cultures, from the balustraded, carved Eastern window looking out over a sculptured sea of sand to the computer set-up on the desk in the corner. From the exotic spiced scents that wafted from a tiny brazier, overpowering the senses, to the cooling hum of an electric fan. From the butterfly-bright silken drapes that fluttered enticingly to the ornamental, captive white man draped between them.

Eugene's eyes closed, and he relaxed into his bonds, drinking in the strangeness, every so often tugging briefly, almost spasmodically, as though testing their efficacy, before sinking even deeper into acceptance of self. There was something self-absorbing about being held captive in this way, something deliciously evocative of a greater freedom.

His eyes flashed open as his involuntary sigh was echoed before him.

Olanthé did not cease to amaze him.

She stood there, slender as a willow in a pair of tight jeans and a strappy T-shirt, her hair half-scrunched up into a modern sprung comb. Her feet were bare, and forgotten in her hands hung a rush sunhat, a pair of dark glasses and a paperback novel. Although probably older than him, she looked like a typical teenager; and yet the expression on her face was not of naivety, but of calculation. The reality of his situation imploded and drove the serenity from his face. He shuffled awkwardly, impotently, as one perfect brow was raised in question.

'*Casablanca?*'

'Humphrey Bogart, Ingrid Bergmann, 1942,' he muttered.

'And?'

There was a small pause. 'You want me to repeat back some of what you were saying?'

'Like a parrot? Why not? People would assume you'd seen the film. They would wrongly assume you had knowledge and opinions, and you wouldn't even have had to watch the silly film. Wouldn't that be good?'

He heard the spitefulness of sarcasm in her voice and he tensed with anticipation; suddenly, being bound was no freedom at all. His words came out in a rush of desperation. 'If I were to make comments of that kind about a film to someone in the business who'd really seen it, I'd be shot down in flames. If you want me to make a meaningful reply, I would need to see it for myself.'

'Who said I wanted a meaningful reply?'

'I thought . . .'

'Slaves aren't supposed to think.'

'One minute you want me to think, the next you don't. I don't know what you want of me.'

'It depends on whether I'm talking to the slave, Narcissus, or to the man who wants to be an actor.'

'They're one and the same.'

'Not at all. Sometimes I want one, sometimes I will allow you to be the other.'

'How do I know which?'

'You have to learn to judge my mood, Narcissus.'

A brightly coloured fingernail slid down his skin from collarbone to groin, leaving a faint indentation, before flicking at his semi-erection. 'What's that? I made it quite clear what I wanted. You're a poor excuse for a sex slave, Narcissus.'

'A man can't just get it up whenever you want. Especially if he can't use his hands.'

She gave a smile that chilled him. 'Like any animal, a

man can be trained to do almost anything with the right incentive.'

She threw her things down on the bed, turned a chair around and straddled it before him, leaning her chin on her hands, looking wickedly childlike and innocent.

'You see, it's all a matter of perception. In Western civilisation people have too much, too easily. The senses are overpowered, the mind is clouded with non-essential trivia. The mind is a huge sponge, but it soaks up the dross from the sewers of civilisation, as well as the fresh spring water. Have you ever realised how noisy everything is? How fast, how bright, how big? There are skyscrapers, and salesmen, and adverts, and fast cars ... How long is it, my Narcissus, since you looked up and saw the beauty of a bird wheeling in the sky, or bent your neck to scent a newly opened rose?'

Eugene could not answer; he was not sure if he was supposed to answer.

'That's what I thought. So what we are going to do, my slave, is to numb the senses, which is how they would train the sex slaves in the old days. Take away all the clutter. Do you know how they would do this in the harems of old? No?'

She cocked her head, and he knew he was going to be told.

'They would cut out the tongue, put out the eyes, puncture the eardrums. When this happens, the only thing left is touch. No sight, no sound, no ability to communicate. It traps the mind inside the living body and, if all that body knows is touch, and touch is withheld until the master needs servicing, the slave is very willing and keen by then to do whatever he did not do satisfactorily before. By then the slave's very nerve-ends were fired with sensation at the privilege of touch, and he was able to put a suitable amount of ingenuity into making the event last.'

'He?'

'Or she. The Eastern Lords were nothing if not broad in their sexual tastes. Of course, the male slaves would have been castrated too, to stop them from gaining pleasure out of their own bodies. They did not just take what they wanted; they made sure the slave wanted to give it to the best of their ability.'

'By mutilation?'

'Why not? If you're Lord, no one is going to tell you no – they would be too afraid of ending up the same way.' She grinned and eyed him slyly. 'It's called sensory deprivation these days. Sounds like the ultimate aphrodisiac, no?'

Eugene discovered that every single muscle on his body had tensed; almost of its own volition his body was pulling against the restraints, testing, verging on a state of panic. She had said she would not damage him. She had promised. But how good was that promise when he was tethered fast to her whim, in the middle of a desert where no one would hear him scream?

Fear tingled up his spine.

She was waiting, almost as if sensing the internal conflict he was fighting, then softly she carried on. 'The tongue, however, played an important part in Eastern sexual activities, as you can imagine. The men enjoyed being serviced orally. It was probably the same with Europeans too, but obviously one did not admit it. So, what to do? Any ideas, Narcissus?'

He shook his head, shortly.

'As you can imagine, these Lords put a lot of thought into the problem of how to diminish the excess of senses in the slave's mouth, yet not impair the sex for the master. Piercing the tongue turned out to be the answer. It could impede speech, and stop the slave from eating, depending on what kind of jewellery was attached to the piercing – there was a very ingenious little gag I saw once, like a wide buckle, where the tongue of the buckle went through the tongue of the slave. But by the same token, with a different kind of jewellery, this piercing could increase the sexual enjoyment of the slave's owner substantially. Are you following me?'

Eugene nodded, and her hand snapped out and clenched around his balls.

Water flooded his eyes and he gasped, 'Yes, Lady, I'm following.'

'Good,' she purred.

She uncoiled from the chair and walked behind him, and he struggled to follow with his eyes as she threw open the ornamental chest. 'Deprivation of the senses,' she murmured to herself, rummaging among the hidden treasures. 'Ah-ha!'

Eugene grimly watched her approach, and he was more than a little relieved to see her swinging a black mask in her hand. He realised almost in the same instant that had she not delivered her little speech, the mask would have been viewed with greater trepidation, yet now it was by far preferable to the alternative.

'Would you like to try the efficacy of sensual deprivation, my slave?'

She stood there, brows raised, and with great reluctance, Eugene made himself say the words, 'Yes, please, my Lady.'

She had to stand on a stool behind him in order to pull the soft rubber mask into place over the top of his head. Even as the mask came down over his face, blocking out the bright sunlight, he felt a kind of peace rush into the vacuum where sight had been. She pushed something into his ears, muffling sound, then continued to tighten and strap him further into his inner self.

He jolted in panic as the internal gag pumped up to a level that displaced his tongue to the back of his mouth, and he sucked breath hard through the constricted air passage of his nose, knowing that he would die from lack of oxygen. Yet even as his hands fought in the bonds, his mind was issuing calming noises. She wouldn't let him die. She wanted him for a year. She had promised she would not damage him.

After a while his breathing calmed and, although breathing was now an effort rather than something to be taken for granted, he was bringing in enough oxygen to prevent panic. He made his hands unclench and deliberately eased the tension in his body. His head cocked, listening keenly for the faintest of sounds, but he could hear nothing at all save the sound of his own breathing. Even the faint sounds he had been subconsciously hearing previously – someone talking outside, the motor of the fan – had all diminished into silence. He knew he must look like a giant black-headed insect, with the two breathing tubes protruding from his nostrils.

Where was she? What was she doing?

It was stupid, he knew, but he kept moving his head around, as if by movement he would be able to see past the hood, hear some tell-tale sound, discern what was going on in the room. His eyes strained. He sucked against the gag, swallowed. Was that light he could see, or was it just the memory of light flashing behind the subconscious, like an amputee still feeling pain in the amputated limb? He strained some more.

Utter darkness. Utter silence.

Olanthé draped herself on her bed and watched her latest project come to terms with the totality of her control. His buttocks clenched, unclenched, his shoulders strained, his hands tightened spasmodically into fists, then eased. She saw the effort he had to put into the simple act of not fighting against the restraints, against the gag and the blindfold. Every so often he jerked as control left him, then he would pull himself together again and gradually, gradually, his whole body seemed to slither into a state of relaxation. All movement ceased. He might have been asleep, he was so still, but she was not fooled.

At first you fought, because domination of the body was contrary to everything you knew to be true about yourself. Then you resented the bonds, but accepted. Then finally a relaxed state bordering on delirium crept upon you unawares. She knew what it was like, for she had been green, naive and oh, so confused when Bran had first subjugated her to his whim by the flick of a finger, by a cold word, by the sheer strength of his personality. She had been angry and excited, chilled and thrilled, but never had she refused what he had asked – no, demanded – of her, and never had she regretted their chance meeting. Never.

She lay back and was warmed by the sight of Narcissus's broad shoulders, the tapering back narrowing down to the tight globes of his buttocks. He was a feast for the eyes, a lovely specimen. He hung there, captive to her whim, spread for her pleasure, to love or to whip as she pleased. She knew he was wondering which it was to be, and she left him wondering. The tension and fear and euphoria of his captive state would rise and fall like the tides of the ocean. His mind would be consumed by it, overpowered.

A trickle of excitement shuddered through her. Her hands slid softly across her breasts, and a jolt of pleasure fired through her body. She gave herself up to the moment, spreading her legs wide on the bed, drinking in the tension and fear and strange calmness of the slave who awaited her. Her hands became more urgent – they were not her own any more; they were hands belonging to another who knew how to smooth the soft skin into a state of expectancy, to warm the hair follicles until they rose in anticipation.

She writhed softly with need, holding on to the moment, denying herself, then gradually her hands moved down to the shaved lips between her legs and parted them softly. They were flushed and throbbing with need, as was the small bud of her pleasure. She reached for it gently with one finger and jolted, already roused to a heightened state. While one hand manipulated a nipple in hard, almost painful twists, the other finger began to move fast, gliding, sliding, first one side, then the other. The tension mounted, and the explosion began like a small knot in her belly to fire outward to the tips of every extremity, razing exposed nerve endings on the way. Her buttocks left the bed and her mouth parted as she panted in the silent screaming ecstasy of the moment. Then the waves lessened, died.

She lay for a moment, recovering, then gathered herself together.

Narcissus hung, unaware as she padded past him and turned on the computer. She worked for a while, searching the Internet for information and knowledge, also for enjoyment; but her consciousness was with her new slave all the time, sharing with him the new joys and traumas of absolute domination and subjugation. The mind played strange tricks on a person when normality was removed. Sometimes you believed you were dreaming and would wake up; but there were times you knew you were more awake than you had ever been before – when things you had long forgotten came to haunt you, to be resurrected, analysed and put back to sleep. And somehow there was healing there, because you were hanging out of time, out of place, and there was nothing more urgent to do than exist.

Narcissus was still now. He had been through panic, he had been through the tense awareness that there was something out there in the room with him, which might touch him at any time. From there she had watched him sink into the truly introverted state of self, where there was nothing outside the darkness of your own mind. The body that housed the mind was an illusion that did not exist; neither cold nor hot, it was a figment of the imagination, and the only things that existed were darkness and the contemplation of self.

It was only because she knew what it was like to be there that she could truly enjoy being the aggressor of the act. This subjugation was not a callous, cold act of aggression, but another form of loving, another form of giving, because you lived it, breathed every dark moment along with your slave.

Eventually Olanthé closed her computer down and sat before the slave, watching him closely. He was dreaming. She delighted in his dream; she dreamed it with him. She could tell by the tiny movements of his limbs that he was thinking of sex. He was moving, just faintly, to the tune. His penis was plumped and full and his hips shifted a fraction, all he was able, as he rammed into some dreamgirl. She wondered who he was loving, what moment in time had prompted that memory of pleasure.

She eventually knelt before him and reached out.

Her finger touched no more than the tip of the hair on one leg, but he jolted as though touched by an electric shock. She shifted her hand and stroked his leg, at least a centimetre from his body, but his hair follicles felt the movement of her hand and stood on end, following it. Now he was tense, as tense as he had never been before.

His awareness was trapped by the pleasure accorded by that minuscule touch.

Her own mouth parted, her body fired with echoing tension.

She reached out again, stroked the inside of his thigh, and gradually her movements became harder, more assured. Now she touched his balls, and they were tight with need. His cock was hard and strong before him, a small glistening drop of come hanging from it like dew on a freshly opened flower. She leaned forward and touched the very tip of it with her tongue, and he jolted in his bonds. His senses were so fired he knew the touch for what it was. She sensed his whole awareness descend into the tip of his cock. He was nothing; his penis was the extent of self.

She reached out. Her hands started at the backs of his thighs and spread softly upward until they reached the firm globes of his buttocks. His muscles quivered expectantly beneath her fingers. Her tongue reached forward, touched the base of his cock and slid upward.

Now he was tense, tight with expectation.

Her hands explored the muscles of his buttocks, savoured the hardness they found, and gradually kneaded and explored until one finger slid into the crack between them and touched the tight knot of his anus. He quivered, hung, and she heard the harsh breath sucked in and out of the tubes of his mask.

She slid her finger into him, and his whole body tensed, quivered outward like a bowstring. His cock thrust towards her waiting lips, and she tasted, lapped at the dew and nibbled gently at the foreskin. She felt him begin to come in the base of his shaft. There was a sudden tightening, as though everything were being sucked into that one point of his being. She lifted her head, wrapped her hand gently around his impaled crown and felt the explosion rise between her fingers. There was a rapid machine-gun fire of spasms, then he seemed to empty of tension instantly, deflated as a punctured tyre. There was a groan of relief, or pain, from behind his mask and he hung, exhausted, tense, and still in his bonds.

Olanthé smiled gently, then slid backward on to her buttocks and began to feel herself once more. This time it was different. She was feeding on the euphoria of power. He had been into the ether, lost in self, and she had brought him back from some other plane, sucked back into his eagerly appeased body. Now he stood quivering, his seed shot, a blind, frightened man wondering what was going to be done to his helpless body. He was once again aware of where he was, and who he was, but had no idea whether he had been there ten minutes or ten hours. He was keyed up with anticipation, wondering what was going to happen next.

She wallowed in her female power as she touched herself, slid a finger inside her body, damped it with her own fluids. Just watching him hanging there, desperate for sound, for sight, for something, brought her to a raging heat of orgasm almost immediately. She exploded silently, unseen, in the glory of her own mind, then sank back, gasping.

God, she loved this life.

11

Eugene knew he was quivering but he could not make his limbs behave. He had no idea whether it was because of the tension of standing in this crucified position or because he was once more intensely aware of his vulnerability. After the strangely dislocated sensation of being in limbo, he was back with a vengeance, and filled with a kind of terror he had not recalled since having nightmares as a child. It was not so much the darkness itself as the inability to see what was crowding around, watching, laughing, reaching out to his vulnerable sexual areas with malicious intent ...

He knew these thoughts were illogical – I mean, Christ, she had just wrapped her lovely mouth around him, pleasured him with her tongue. How he had known it was her tongue from that first buttock-clenching shock of contact, he could not be sure, but it had been. He knew it without a doubt. Sensual deprivation had done just what she had said it would: it had sent him hurtling into his own private hell like an express train, only to get lost on the tracks somewhere and end up in a state of stasis, mind and body separated and chugging along tracks to nowhere – and it just did not matter. He tried to recall the wonderful, heady sensation of floating he had known for that brief while. Or was it a long while? He was not sure.

Yet it had all gone, and he was now simply trapped and bound and irritated. His calf muscles were rebelling, he could feel the first twinges of muscle which were the signal that if he didn't do something cramp would follow, and the thought of the ensuing pain was grating on his mind. Didn't she know that standing in this position for lengths of time was used as a punishment in the army? That it could actually cause the blood vessels to rupture from stress? He forgot to remind himself that he was supported from above, and that the grim reality of army punishment was somewhat different.

He felt a muscle twinge and groaned in anticipation.

But he felt hands on his ankles, releasing him instantly. He knew a moment's relief. If he caught it now, and exercised properly, the cramps would simply not happen. He waited for her to relieve him of the tight heat of the hood, inside which he was sweating freely. He sucked moisture into his stretched mouth, moving his tongue around the bloated gag, anticipating the pleasure of release. Bringing his ankles together gave him a small freedom of movement, and he used it gratefully, pushing himself up on to the balls of his feet to allow a small stretching and relaxing of the whole of his body. He flexed his hips, his biceps, his shoulders, and clenched and unclenched his fists, bringing circulation back to the deadened nerve endings.

The biting agony of the cane on his thigh caught him unawares. As his legs were free, his knees buckled upward and he hung for a brief moment, shocked, in an almost absurdly foetal position, before dropping his legs with the wary knowledge that he was not to be instantly freed, that the procedure would be repeated. He mentally castigated himself for the stupid assumption that he would be.

He waited.

His feet shuffled with the agony of indecision. Was it better to keep his legs firmly closed, protecting the more tender inner thighs, or should he part them slightly, allowing his privates to slide a little deeper into the available space? But he knew he was fooling himself if he thought any of that mattered. Had she hit him from the front or back? Suddenly he couldn't be sure. All he recalled was the sudden, biting pain that slammed into his mind like a douse of cold water. Besides, where she had been just a moment ago was no indication at all of where she was now. If he knew where she was, he would lash out, damn it. Break her neck maybe. He strained against gag and blindfold, trying to hear, see, anything that would give him a clue where the next –

Aaah!

The cane caught him on the right buttock, and once again he jumped away from the pain instead of towards it. There was no controlling instinctive movements when anticipation could not be employed. His feet scrabbled at the edge of the plinth, discovered purchase, and slithered back to the centre, taking his weight once more.

Then again, and again and again until his body was alive with the stinging aftermath of the fleeting wasp stings of pain. His buttocks, his thighs and his calves were burning, and with each biting lash he jolted, unable to contain his involuntary movements, unable to antici- pate, unable to avoid.

Then nothing. He gasped, sucked air hard through the breathing tubes, his muscles a tight riot of anticipation. He would kill the bitch, just let him –

Her hands fluttered on to his thighs, and the damp soft touch of her lips pressed on his right buttock, nib- bling, kissing along one throbbing line of pain. A jolt of sexual urgency drove from the base of his skull right through his spine and into his balls. Her leg gently pressed between his in invitation, and he parted for her. He felt her kneel, slither forward, and lean back on the hands that were now grasped firmly on the front of his thighs. In his mind's eye he saw her there, arching backward between his legs, and anticipation held him rigid. The soft wet touch of her tongue on his balls contracted them instantly into small, tight marbles. His cock rose, the end throbbing with sudden pain as the piercing rebelled at the activity. She nibbled softly between his legs, her tongue and lips teasing the shaved, virgin flesh, then her kisses became harder, sucking his tight, sensitised skin into her mouth. Every organ, including his brain, seemed to be intertwined, joined with steel wire and, as she sucked, he felt explosions of exquisite pleasure-pain reach to every extremity. His fingers stretched wide and beneath the hood he felt his eyes turn inward once more. He reached up on to the balls of his feet, not to escape the pain of her touch, but because his muscles contracted so much he was arching involuntarily.

She slid through his legs and turned. He held his breath now, rampant and ready to explode at the instant of touch on his sensitive crown. Would she take him into her mouth? But no, her hands glided, touched, stroked, slid between his buttocks and up into his anus. He pushed himself towards her, but she did not oblige, and the gliding of her finger in and out of his tight hole was exquisite torture to his senses. He could have clenched his legs together, trapping her hand, stilling the movement, but he stretched, wider and wider, swearing and cursing in the silence of his mind, loving the tension and hating her for withholding the ultimate pleasure.

Then she was gone.

Although he had anticipated it, he almost cried with frustration.

He did not know how long he stood there, begging for release, but gradually the tightness in his scrotum, lacking stimulation, began to relax. He did not know if she had been sitting there waiting for it, but the moment tension left his body, he felt hands around his sexual organs. Something was wrapped tightly around them, over the top of his shaft and under the sac, binding his balls together, constricting them. The touch was instant fire to his unreleased tension; his cock once more plumped to fullness and the binding seemed in some way to be an enhancement of both pleasure and frustration at the same time.

He moved his feet involuntarily, unable to still his body, unable to take his mind from the wonderful, demanding sensation that was flooding him outward in waves from the point of origin to almost every nerve in his body. It was now that she reached up and began to unbuckle the mask from his face. He winced at the sudden onset of light and clenched his eyes tightly together for a moment, blinded by dancing red lights.

He felt her towelling the sweat from his brow as his pupils gradually contracted behind the closed lids and the blinding lights diminished. Then she wrapped her arms around his middle, stood up on the plinth on tiptoe, her body pressed between his parted legs. He felt her naked dry flesh press against his own moist skin, sending shivers of anticipation through every hair follicle on his body. Then her lips came down on his and her tongue teased into his gasping, dry mouth, moistening it with her own saliva.

Gradually he opened his eyes and began to kiss her back; he had no choice. She was whore and siren, and he could no more withstand the onslaught to his senses than he could fly. Her dark eyes were on his as sight returned, and he drowned in the spiralling depths of lust for her body. His constricted cock and balls pressed up against her belly, the sensation strangely unfulfilling. He wanted to drop his hips, to have her wrap her arms about his neck and climb up. He envisaged her sinking down on to his swollen cock, burying it in the wet darkness of her body. He imagined her gliding up and down on it, pleasuring herself, and realised he was wondering what the sensation of the piercing would be like as it abraded against the inside of her body. For the first time he was able to view it as something less than a violation of his person.

But she did not slip herself on to him.

Instead, she gave him a peck on the nose, a cheeky smile, and climbed down off the pedestal. He looked down to see his swollen, pulsing balls protruding like purple flowers from within a scarf of deep green silk that was wrapped several times around them and tied in a delicate bow. He glanced up and frustration hit him anew as he gazed upon the object of his lust, knowing he could neither have her nor, because of the restraints, satisfy himself without her.

Olanthé stood before him, her naked body glorious and golden in the shafts of sunlight. Her hair cascaded down over her shoulders in a dark waterfall and her breasts peaked through the hair like golden cones tipped with aureoles of brown. There was no hair in the crack between her legs and the lips were slightly parted to allow the small bud of her clit to protrude just a fraction.

Oh, God, he wanted her.

With inherent grace, she sank on to a couch and watched him watching her, then she spread her legs and began to masturbate softly and slowly. He saw the flush of desire reach into her cheeks and watched her eyes narrow slightly as her awareness was drawn inward. Oh, God, it was not fair. He moved in time with her, his hips thrusting as her hand slid up and down. His own mouth parted with desire and the sensations from his bound balls became ever more demanding: touch me, touch me, please touch me.

He writhed, his hips danced, and the green silk floated out of syncopation with his movements. His legs parted, then came together; one leg rose, then went down again, then he gyrated some more. Her hand moved faster now; he was sure he could see the lips of her sex swelling with need. Her eyes were nearly closed and the tip of her tongue parted her red lips, wetting them before sliding back in. His own mouth echoed hers, his tongue reaching, retracting. He saw her tension rise, it was a visible phenomenon; her heels rose from the floor, her body arched. There was a sudden stillness and he could see no movement, save for the tiny shudders that ran through her legs, but the room crackled with the tension of her orgasm.

She gradually sank into a relaxed state, and when she opened her almond-shaped eyes, almost instantly her face held that amazingly childlike, Mona Lisa glance of pure mischief. She knew exactly how tense he was, how frustrated, how angry, and how much he had enjoyed the whole thing. He also knew, from the look on her face, that she was going to leave him unsatisfied. A small groan slipped past his lips.

Her head cocked to one side. 'Say please nicely,' she instructed.

By now he knew better than to ask what for. 'Please nicely, my Lady.'

'Good slave,' she purred, and unwound herself from her recumbent state and gracefully reached forward to release him from the green silk. He gasped as feeling flooded back in, and gasped even more as she took the very tip of him into her mouth and sucked hard. His orgasm was as instant and violent and uncontrolled as that of a virgin. His legs bounced from the floor and his body turned from a mass of contracted muscle into pure jelly. His seed pumped from him painfully, with the force of a jet engine; had he not been bound, he knew he would have collapsed. He panted hard, as if he had just run a two-minute mile, then yelped as Olanthé's bright teeth playfully nipped his foreskin.

She stood and slapped his thigh. 'Right. Now you've had your fun, my Narcissus, it's time for a little more learning.'

Olanthé left her Narcissus irritatedly studying a classic scene out of Hamlet, knowing that he classed Shake-speare as something even lower down on the palatable scale than black and white films. She smiled in antici-pation. Even as he would never underestimate the importance of *Casablanca* again, so he would also come, very painfully, to have a full appreciation of Shake-speare's worth before she was finished with him.

In the courtyard she descended into the pool, dropping her robe as she went. The sun was a sandy-coloured orb and the red stone buildings seemed to shimmer in and out of existence under its intense heat. She floated in the warm water, enjoying the weightless, timeless sense of freedom the action gave her; she felt like a nymph or fairy, neither of this world nor the otherworld.

She knew she was an enigma, that she dwelt in an artificial existence funded by the corporate world beyond the boundaries of her desert kingdom. If the money stopped rolling in, she would be cast adrift on the fringes of society, whence Bran had plucked her so many years ago. She rolled luxuriously, comforted by the knowledge that such an event could never be, unless Western society collapsed. There had been too many projects, too many young people who had survived the desert and made it back out into the Western world; entrepreneurs, models, businessmen, politicians, actors – she had to dredge through her mind to recall faces, names, so many were simply lost in the mists of time: Mark, Franco, Sarah, Abayou, David, Angelo, Alison, Persu, Michael . . .

As she floated beneath the desert sun, tears welled in her eyes, falling and mingling with the water that cocooned her. She had loved them all once, but as time went by they became names, shadows, until the image melted and was gone. Only Michael was still an open sore, a wound in her side that only time would heal.

The incoming wealth from these previous successes was an electronic tide, of which the already accumulated interest alone would last her for the rest of her life, and Bran's life, and when those lives were done, well, perhaps there was someone out there waiting to inherit. She rolled again and duck-dived to the bottom of the pool, drowning the sorrows deep. When she rose, blowing water into the dry air, sorrow was laid to rest.

Life was good. Life was there to be lived, but she knew that if it hadn't been for Bran there would be no life for her; she would have died a beggar on the streets of the exotic city that had spawned her. She rose up from the pool and walked out into the air, lifting her arms and turning around and around, her feet knowing the dance from years past. The desert wind dried her skin in seconds. The soft fingers of wind touched her skin, warmed the ardour in her blood as she turned. Bran, where are you? Why can you live in that Western world and I can't? Come home to me.

She danced to the desert song a moment more, then opened her eyes. Ali sat before her under the shade of a palm.

'Bran called,' he said.

'I know. I felt it.'

'He said to remind you he was thinking of you.'

'Did he tell you how he was thinking of me?'

He smiled softly. 'I'll show you. My Lady?'

She reached out her hand and he took not her hand but her wrist in his great fist, locking it fast. She felt the integral strength of the man and smiled. 'Bran's a fool if he thinks I could forget.'

'Bran's insecure, as we all are sometimes.'

'I know.'

'I must do as he says.'

'I know.'

He stopped, turned to face her and lifted her chin with one finger. 'My Lady, I need more than that.'

'For Bran I would walk barefoot across the coals of the earth. Ali, at this moment you are Bran's mouthpiece, and my Lord. What is your will?'

He breathed in deeply, then sighed, as if scenting something sweet on the air. 'My Lady –'

She bowed her head. 'Your slave, my Lord.'

'My slave. Yes.'

He pulled a blindfold from behind him, and she stood, acquiescent, as he fitted it over her face, shutting out the sunlight. Bran, oh, Bran, I want you.

Olanthé felt a sense of peace and anticipation fill her breast as Ali pulled her across the courtyard. Her feet knew every stone, every crack, and yet she stumbled, as if the blindfold had taken away her memory. Already her senses were on fire as if it were Bran himself who was standing before her, dominating, dictating as he had from the moment their eyes met across the crowded square; he an English aristocrat, she an Arabian beggar child, neither one owning a penny more than the other.

As Ali lifted her slender wrists to the cuffs on the wall, she revelled in his mastery. Bran was harsh, powerful, and she loved him beyond reason. Her love consumed her. She did his will, she trained the young men and, God knew, she enjoyed what she was doing, but how she wished he could come to the desert, live with her, be her Lord and Master for ever.

Yet it was not to be. She was a desert orchid, exotic, scented and unparalleled in eroticism. He was an English rose, chilled to frozen perfection in the onset of an English winter. She was easily sickened by the damp climates of the Western world, and he was charred by the harsh climates of the Eastern provinces. And yet they were made for each other. Beauty and the beast. The English rose and the desert orchid.

Neither could survive in the other's climate, yet neither could survive at all if parted.

Ali wrenched her hands upward and secured them, one to the left, one to the right. She made a small mewl of discomfort, and his hands stilled for a brief moment, reminding her he was not Bran. Bran would have ignored her discomfort, he would have enjoyed it, as she did the pain of the ones she trained.

Yet this was Bran's will. She allowed herself to sink into the role he had allocated.

She stood, her bosom pressed to the warm brickwork, waiting on Bran's pleasure. He would have sent an email to Ali, precise instructions to be followed to the letter, and Ali would obey – as they all obeyed.

She was his Lady of the desert citadel, but Bran was ever his Lady's Lord.

Her ankle was grasped, pulled to one side and tethered. Then the other. In less than a moment she was pressed to the wall, out of control. She tensed, waiting. Now Ali would beat her, as Bran had demanded. He would remind her with every stroke whose woman she was, and to whom she owed allegiance and life.

She was not scared of a beating – she had been beaten

before, many times. By Bran, but before Bran too. Yet the men who had beaten her before Bran had done it because they could, because it made them feel big, manly. Bran had beaten her because he had known it was what she needed, and by doing so he owned her, body and soul. Because she wanted to be owned; being owned took away the pressures of life and living and made her complete.

Ali pressed his finger against her lips, and she opened her mouth for him. He thrust something within. Something long and thick which made her gag. She fought for control, and felt wetness seep between her legs. Her weight hung on her arms for a moment, as the delicious sensation of being dominated threatened to overcome her.

'This is Bran,' Ali whispered. 'He had it cast especially for you, to remember him by. Taste it, suck it, remember him well. Good night, my Lady.'

Euphoria fled.

Olanthé was stunned. That was it? Suck on this and remember me? Who did Bran think he was kidding? She made a mewl of anger and turned her head, waiting for Ali to react, to do whatever else Bran had ordered, but all she heard was the harsh cry of a vulture, and she scented the onset of night in the desert-dry air.

She growled deep in her throat with irritation and pulled at the restraints around her wrists, knowing that they were secure, that she would stay here at Ali's – Bran's – whim until freed. Time passed and she felt the cooler winds of evening brush around her. It could be surprisingly cold once the sun went down; even dangerously cold. There was no place on earth where the killing heat of day dropped more drastically to the freezing chill of night than this. She shivered, thankful it was not winter.

Suddenly she caught a scent on the breeze. Her body

stiffened. Her head turned as far as it would go, her nostrils flared with primitive awareness, the better to catch that faint hint of – what? Her skin tingled with anticipation. It could not be. She had heard no helicopter, there had been no warning that he would be arriving. The tension diminished fractionally. This was Bran the trickster, not Bran the lover.

This was surely Ali, doing his master's bidding.

And yet – there it was again, a particular musky hint of aftershave and male body odour, pleasingly erotic to her charged senses, and yet also confusing. She breathed deeply, drawing in the desert scents: the night jasmine, the cactus flower, the dry wind on dry sand. She was a primitive being, surviving on animal instincts from the unknown time of her birth.

It was Bran.

Ali had his own scents and she knew them; even disguised with Bran's aftershave, Ali would not smell like Bran. She gave the merest hint of a sigh, and her heels rose from the floor in anticipation. It was him. Her body fired instantly with love and gratitude and need. How it could be, she had no clue, but it did not matter; why he came in secret in the night was not hers to query. Bran was her saviour, her Lord. She waited on his pleasure, feeling the chill against her skin warring with the damp warmth that rose between her legs. She writhed softly in expectation.

What was he waiting for?

Then she heard the flare of a lighter, smelt the first whiff of tobacco. She pictured him behind her, drawing hard, his blue eyes narrowed as he surveyed her parted legs, her firm thighs, her tight buttocks. She breathed in, sharing his smoke, vicariously experiencing his antici-pation. She imagined him half-closing his eyes, breathing deeply, enjoying the cool night air as his fertile mind dwelt on the pleasures of his white body while contemplating her darker one. She knew lust would be coursing through his veins even as it now coursed through hers.

She shivered with excitement, her limbs flexing and stretching within their bonds, not seeking release but delighting in the control they exerted over her body, freeing her mind. She was a sexual object, and her sexuality was never more her own than when her body was not.

Her eyes closed, her tongue caressed the silicon cock, obedient to his domination rather than his order, flooded by desire and the knowledge that if Bran was in the mood to be lenient he would invade her body with the real one.

He made her wait.

She heard the rustling and sliding of his clothes being dropped aside, then heard the faint splashing sounds as he lowered himself into the warm water, washing the heat and sweat and sand from his body, not out of consideration for her but for his own comfort.

Silence.

She knew he was floating, drifting on the euphoria of nicotine and anticipation and domination. His pale body, almost hairless save for the tufts at groin and underarm, would be reflecting the moonlight. She knew the shaft of his cock would already be fattening with need, even as her own cunt was flooding, demanding, but he would not touch himself. He would withhold his own pleasure even as he withheld hers, not from masochism but because anticipation, deprivation, heightened the senses to screaming point.

Her imagination flared.

He would make her wait while he teased her nipples. He would gently touch with his finger between her legs, touch her back with his tongue, and yet he would leave her body unsated. He would beat her, release her, have her crawl after him on her knees before he deigned to allow her the one thing she craved almost more than life itself at that moment – his body.

Silence.

She strained her ears. Was he still in the pool or had he gone? She tensed. Was he standing behind her? Would her first knowledge of his whereabouts come in the form of a biting pain along buttocks or thighs? She tried to swallow the sound, yet heard herself release a whimper of distress. Anyone coming upon her now, she knew, would see a woman being cruelly chastised, awash with terror at the knowledge of forthcoming abuse – but they would be wrong. She was flooded with desire, the kind of desire that detaches mind from body, releases the inhibitions, drenches the soul with urgency.

Bran touched her back.

She jumped, involuntarily releasing a muffled cry. It was a soft touch; a caress with the nail which scratched slowly, tantalisingly from neck to the crease of her buttocks, sending her skin rippling in cascading, outwardly flowing waves as the skin follicles danced and fled before it. She rose on to the balls of her feet, felt her breasts pressing into the still-warm brickwork.

Bran pressed himself between her legs, pushed upward, slowly easing the fluttering muscle aside to accommodate himself within the dark warmth of her body. The long ecstasy of the moment held her in its grasp; she couldn't breathe. Her mind turned in on itself; nothing existed save the exquisite stretching and sliding and filling, and the knowledge that Bran was claiming his own.

She hung there, pinned to the wall at wrist and ankle, impaled from behind by her Lord's fat cock. Her head fell back, her senses reeling. His hands reached around, encompassed her breasts and massaged the nipples gently, firmly twisting the flesh into hard knots. His mouth fell to her shoulder, the white teeth nipped the unblemished flesh possessively, and she felt the heat of him quiver within her, yet he held himself rigid, not allowing himself the pleasure of moving.

She groaned, straining to move on him, but there was no tolerance for movement. Bran must have felt the tension in her body rise. His hands now ran over her wracked body, down her sides, between her thighs, the electric touch briefly sparking the red-hot core of her sex in passing. She shuddered dramatically, and felt his thighs respond.

There was a tense moment of stillness, as if he did not trust himself to move, then he slid slowly, surely down. She waited for the turn, for the upward thrust, anticipating, needing release, but he continued down and out of her body, leaving behind a sense of desolation as the cool night air blew against the wetness between her legs.

As he withdrew from her, abrading her dry flesh, Olanthé knew that Bran was teasing himself, not her. At this moment she was no more than the object needed to flame his own lust; but he also knew that her own lust would be sated by the consummation of his. She hung there and burned in the dark silence of her mind while her hips made tiny movements, side to side, hardly indicative of the hugeness of her frustration and desire. Had her mouth been free she would have begged him to impale her again, to use her, hurt her, fulfil her, yet he must have known this, for the sounds which emitted from the depths of her throat were animal noises, more deeply betraying the depths of her primitive instincts than words could ever accomplish.

How long she hung there, waiting, she did not know, but it seemed hours, not minutes. The wind began to chill her body discernibly, but she no longer cared about that. She simply waited, knowing that it would happen. It, Bran, the culmination of sexual desires. When he was ready, not when she was.

He lit another cigarette behind her, and she pictured him sitting there naked behind her, urgently drawing the nicotine into his lungs, his sexual needs clawing to new heights as he fed on her frustration, her absolute dependence upon him. The desire in her gut curled into a tight ball, waiting, teeth bared, claws barely sheathed.

As though she had stepped out of her body and was watching from a great height, she knew when he was ready. There was no sound, no warning save the instant his hands grasped her middle, and she was impaled upon him once more, only now the time for teasing was long past. He thrust slowly at first; the length and burning heat of his erection gliding almost painfully inside her until she stretched to accommodate the tight base of the shaft. Then he retracted equally slowly and fully, until she felt the rippling sensation of her own muscles contracting and closing as the head of his cock left her.

She felt his gasp of pleasure as the sensitive organ was taken almost to its peak at each withdrawal – then he withdrew no more. He thrust in firmly, deeply, embedding himself up to the hilt again and again. Now she rode heady waves of lust, her body at one with the organ they shared between them. She felt herself drawing it in, clenching around it, and it felt as though it reached up to her heart, filling her, consuming her. Long before she felt the culmination of Bran's lust pulse against her soft tissues as he came, she was lost in the waves of pleasure that emanated from some place deep inside her own psyche, exploding to the tips of her toes and fingers, leaving them numb, battered.

For a moment the two bodies stayed joined as one.

Olanthé could feel Bran's heart beating against her back, while his arms wrapped lovingly, gently around her torso, his panting breath on her shoulder. It was then she knew he loved her, though he would never admit this.

He reached up and released the blindfold from her eyes. She could see nothing but darkness for a moment, then shapes emerged from the gloom as her eyes adjusted. He slipped from her, released her ankles, then her wrists. She reached up a hand to remove the gag, but he slapped her hand down.

'No. Leave it. I want to know I'm still inside you.' She heard amusement in his voice. 'Well, part of me anyway. Come and wash, then I have instructions for you regarding your Greek Narcissus.'

The water was warm and Olanthé took pleasure in it for a moment, but the feel of Bran's loving was branded in her mind, and on the vague soreness of her body. She allowed the water to trickle into her stretched mouth, relieving the dryness, then Bran moved beside her, running his white hands down the length of her flat belly, over the mounds of her breasts and between her thighs. He held her there in the water, suspended, and she stretched her arms and legs out wide, floating trustingly in a star, supported by a single spread hand in the small of her back.

'You have a beautiful body, my sweet siren,' he whispered. 'I couldn't let you go even if I wanted to. I sleep with many women, the world's most beautiful women. I tell them sweet loving lies when they come to me, yet when I close my eyes it's you I see. Only you. If you're ever unfaithful to me, Olanthé, I will kill you with my own bare hands; this I promise.'

He reached out and removed the gag from her mouth, his words snaking across her belly like a chill wind. Not because she was ever unfaithful. Never. Faith was not in the men you had sex with, oh no. Bran knew that. It was deeper than that. What she felt for him was embedded deep in the soul, something that mere sex could not come near; he understood that in the same way she did. No, why she shuddered was the thought that one day she would become old and wrinkled, and he might turn from her body. When that day came he would not need to kill her; she would kill herself.

She rolled over in the water and kissed him, sharing the magic water of the desert.

Eventually Bran settled himself on the steps of the pool and nestled her body in the crook of his, her head against his chest. She waited, feeling him shudder briefly in the chill air as night clouds scudded across the sky. Desert clouds bloomed like cactus flowers, for one night only, to be instantly diminished, burnt out of existence by the new day.

Then Bran began to speak.

Softly he shared with her his life outside the citadel. He told her of the places he'd visited, the women he'd met. He told her of the possible projects he had found, and he informed her of the progress of their previous ventures.

'Do you recall how it all started, my love?'

She thought back. How had it started? Accidentally, as all the best things in life start.

Bran had stopped a young man from committing suicide, not because he cared about the man but because something in this man's sheer desperation had touched him; he had been there himself. He had brought him to Olanthé, to the dismal place in which she then lived, and between her and the desert they had healed him. That man had become a household name in the entertainment world. In gratitude he sent them part of his earnings, as without them he would not even have discovered the will to live.

Eventually Bran ground out his cigarette and stopped talking. When they made love this time it was as lovers, with all the heat and urgency of a first coupling.

12

Olanthé had discovered a variety of ways to display Narcissus to advantage, her eyes never tiring of the beauty of his sculptured muscles, even if it was often necessary to still his harping tongue. He was presently not gagged, as she wanted him to respond, which he did. His eyes blazed and his voice rose from bass to almost falsetto with each stunned word. 'You want me to make a porno film?'

Each slave took on a different persona after the inauguration rites had worn off, she mused, and not always the persona she had been expecting. Once the real world became suitably distanced, the tenets of society diminished in importance, so something of their inner psyche blossomed. Some ended up as playthings for the amusement of her brethren; some responded better to promises of seduction and some to periods of incarceration in the dark holes beneath the citadel.

Michael alone had been an enigma. No matter what punishments and pleasures she heaped upon him, she had never managed to reach that dark place in his mind that would make him hers. Of all of them he had been the most obedient, the least likely to complain when punished, and yet he had always somehow made it known it was because he chose to obey each and every individual command that his spirit had never been enslaved. So, had she failed? Bran would say not because Michael would one day add substantially to their income, and though, like all the others, he had chosen to set aside the world for financial benefit, she knew he had some hidden agenda. She learnt early on it was not just the money. He would not have hesitated to lose the fee by leaving early should he have felt the need. A class of his own. She had not changed him one iota, she knew; he was far too strong. In spite of his intense sexuality, he would have succeeded through his own inner strength had he chosen even to become a monk.

Narcissus was far less complicated; well-named after the mythical youth who fell in love with his own reflection. He was a dreamer who wanted to be hero-worshipped; ideally suited to be an icon in the film industry. His forté was simply in providing food for the imaginations of others, and so for her he had become a living statue. And Narcissus, having been given the chance to become the statue, the icon for the delectation of another, was discovering for himself that it was not enough. He had no idea that was her intention, but with every passing day Narcissus was becoming less like Narcissus, and more like Eugene, she mused. And it was Eugene, not Narcissus who would take the film world by storm. In the end, a pretty face was just a pretty face; it was the character within which animated it into something more, something which fascinated, drew the attention of the vast audience. The one was simply beauty, the other was *presence*.

He had been with her several months now, and if anything he was more lovely than he had ever been. His dark skin had paled to a faintly golden sheen, and his sun-bleached hair was growing darker from the roots, creating a look some men would pay thousands to achieve. His shoulders had thickened, his waist had slimmed and tightened; but more than that, there was a new confidence in the way he accepted his slave status, almost as though he were the master and she the slave.

However, though she had seen him stunned, humiliated, in pain, or in the throes of sexual ecstasy, she had never seen him as furious as he was now. It was quite impressive, she thought appreciatively, lending more of the macho appearance required of a modern film star. The very thing he had been lacking to date.

She must make him angry more often.

She was lounging on her bed, leaning on one elbow and perusing him, with one brow raised reprovingly at his explosive response to her suggestion. 'I didn't say porno,' she reproved gently. 'Stop looking so shocked. I said erotic, not pornographic. There's a world of difference between the two.'

'No there isn't; not in the real world,' he said grimly.

'I'll grant you there are many who don't know the difference, but trust me: I do.'

'Why would you want me to do that?'

Sarcasm slipped into her words. 'Experience? A chance to learn to act? All you can do presently is strut.'

He said nothing, but his jaw clenched; she could see anger working in the tight muscles at the side of his face. Samson-like, he pulled at the restraints that chained his wrists to the pillars in her bedroom; his chest swelled impressively, as did his biceps, and she watched with interest, wondering if he would exhale before he exploded, thinking it was just as well the chains were stronger than he was. He looked as though he would like to throttle her. She smiled inside, but showed him none of this; the confidence and machismo that had been merely an outward show before he came here were now manifesting themselves in reality. Narcissus was growing up, becoming his own man.

He just did not realise it yet.

Her mouth pursed and her eyes narrowed. 'You're very obtuse, my slave. I'm not asking you to become a screen stud. For your enlightenment, pornography consists of the close-up shots of humping: hairy balls, wet pussies and shaving foam. Eroticism, on the other hand, is an art form.'

'Culminating in hairy balls humping wet pussies,' he muttered sulkily.

She grinned openly in spite of herself. 'Possibly; but first and foremost there is anticipation, and if I've taught you nothing else in these months, surely I've taught you about the importance of anticipation?'

'Yes, but –'

'There are no buts. There are facts. Fact number one is you do anything I ask of you for one year, and you get a lot of money. Easy money.'

'With a proviso,' he sneered.

Her voice chilled again and she leaned forward, irritated. 'Nothing is for nothing, slave. The proviso that I get a percentage of everything you earn subsequent to your yearly income exceeding ten million is a clause you agreed to with aplomb. After all, did you ever in your wildest dreams think it might actually happen?'

'I wouldn't be here otherwise.'

There was a pause, then she settled back; carefully, because Bran's departing present to her buttocks and back was still tender and throbbing. 'True. That's the crux of the matter. Without dreams, life is meaningless, yet so many people wallow in the unfairness of life instead of building their dreams. One of the reasons I chose you was because you were a dreamer, in spite of your upbringing. Don't spoil it all for me by doing an about-face, or I might just end it now.'

'You can't end it. I have to. It's in the contract.'

Her lip curled at this arrogance, and she saw him wince fractionally as he realised that argument had possibly been expected, but the tone of voice could possibly have been a mistake.

'Believe me, it would take someone of a more stoic nature than you to choose to stay if I wanted you to go. Do I have to prove it to you?'

'No,' he muttered; but she knew he lowered his gaze to hide his glowering anger rather than in submission. He really was quite adorable. She felt the urge to beat him stirring in her loins. Or love him. It amounted to the same thing. She stretched luxuriously.

'You accepted a year in slavery because you want to be a film star. I'm offering you the opportunity.'

'I'm beginning to realise what an idiot I've been,' he said grimly.

'That's a stepping stone, my slave.'

His eyes snapped up. 'OK, so I'm an idiot. I've done everything you've asked. I've made a jerk of myself in front of everyone. I've let you whip me, humiliate me, pierce me, and thrust marbles in my arse for everyone's entertainment. I've watched a hundred stupid films and learnt a load of crap Shakespeare. But –' He bit his lip. 'Please don't make me be a porno star.'

'Tell me, when did you last make a film?'

'You know I didn't,' he muttered reluctantly after a pause.

'When were you last even on a film set?'

'Never!'

'So, you've never made a film. You've never been on a film set. Until you came here you knew nothing of film history. You knew nothing of acting. In fact, you knew nothing at all about the entertainment field in which you have chosen to be a star. Is that a fairly accurate summation?'

He grimaced. 'I'm an idiot, I guess.'

'But a pretty one, admittedly.'

'Christ, rub it in.'

'You've done it for yourself, I don't need to.'

He visibly slumped, defeat in every line of his body.

'Very well. I'll give you the alternatives.' She ticked them off on her hand. 'One, you make this film and, incidentally, learn everything first-hand about making films, and when you leave here you will end up with more help than you yet realise. Two, you don't do this, but I allow you to finish your term.'

He said nothing, but he stared at her, his lips tight. Her lip curled into a smile, but it did not reach her eyes. 'Oh, yes. There's always a catch, my hero. If you do the former, you might later have to live up to an erotic film finding its way on to the market, but trust me. I'm not without contacts, and people better than you have survived things that have been potentially more disastrous than that. If you do the latter, and if you're lucky, you might make it into the film industry and make out as a two-bit actor doing walk-on parts for the rest of your life.'

'But –'

'Hear me out! Yes, your looks and your cash will be your passport to Hollywood, but they may not be a passport to fame. You'll get a good apartment in Hollywood, talk to a lot of directors, fuck a lot of directors' women and maybe a starlet or two. I estimate you'll last about six months. It takes a lot of money to throw parties that directors and actors will go to. Then, when the money runs out, with a face like yours some producer or director will help you out, but at a price: you'll end up as his gigolo, his toyboy.' She threw him a calculated glance. 'If you like I can get some of our men here to instruct you in the art of gay sex so you're not too ignorant in that area for when it comes to pass.'

His face darkened with anger, and his fists clenched. 'You –'

She lifted a warning finger, but her tongue lapped her lips appreciatively – there was something so utterly warming about a recalcitrant slave, and this one truly blossomed in anger. 'Careful, my Narcissus. I'm telling you how it is without the rosy glow. You've got a pretty face and maybe now you even have the drive, but you still lack the necessary education.'

'And making this porno – this erotic film will give me that?'

'Trust me,' she purred.

Olanthé fell silent, watching the emotions ride his face. He was stronger than he had been when he first came here, if only in the fact that he no longer thought the world was his personal oyster. In just a few months the cockiness of youth had been thrashed out of him, half a year had given him the beginnings of an education in his chosen field; but nine months down the road poor Narcissus still had a lot of learning to do.

And the important part of that learning was that he accepted he needed to learn.

She raised her brows and leaned forward. 'Tell me, when you first thought of being a film star, was it because you love films more than life, or because you looked at your pretty face in a mirror one day and thought, I'm a lucky bugger, my face is my fortune? Surprise yourself, be honest.'

He visibly wilted in the ensuing silence, and she rolled over on to her stomach, crossing her ankles behind her, watching him over clasped hands as her words sank home.

'You don't think I can do it, do you?'

The wry tone betrayed more intelligence than he credited himself with.

'You were pretty ignorant when you first came here, but you're now learning all the stuff you didn't know about acting, never mind that you're doing it the wrong way round. Rules are there to be broken, after all. So do you carry on learning, or not?'

He shrugged. 'You're not really giving me a choice, but if I make a film like this it will ruin any chances of a career. I've seen it happen to others. I'm damned if I do, damned if I don't.'

Her voice was suddenly hard. 'I'm not going to force you. Commit yourself, my Greek hero. Or not. Your choice. You either come out and meet the film's scout, or you stay here, and I meet him alone.'

He shuffled uncomfortably, and she knew that he felt more vulnerable in that moment than he normally did, merely because Western society was intruding, and a civilised man in this century did not normally end up naked, chained between two stone pillars for some woman's delectation. Finally, he lifted his eyes and met hers squarely. 'Very well. I'll do it in the hope that it forwards my aim to become a film star, and if I've made a mistake, it's my fault. Is my word good enough for you?'

'It's on film for posterity.'

'Christ.' His eyes scanned the room in a second of disbelief. 'What else do you have on film?'

She rolled over on to her back, her head tipping off the bed, smiling at him upside-down. 'All of it, my slave. All of it.'

Narcissus hung there for a moment, stunned into silence. 'Oh, Christ,' he said again, then began to chuckle. 'I haven't got anything left to lose, have I?'

'Only your future, my slave,' she agreed.

* * *

Eugene did not know why he agreed. He stared at the lithe body that was draped on the bed before him, and more than anything he wanted to kneel between her legs and sink up into the siren warmth of her body.

How had she persuaded him that he would not succeed in his aims without her assistance? He did not know how or why, but he truly believed just that. She manipulated him, wound him around her little finger, and even at the height of anger, when his fingers were itching to wrap themselves around her neck, he still believed her.

He stood there, chained in her room, watching the heat shimmer through the latticed opening. Damn her, she was right about his ignorance. He had been absolutely supreme in his ignorance. Why had he supposed he could just turn up in Hollywood and the hallowed ranks would simply open to admit him because he was so beautiful? He winced at his own naivety. Why had he not seen for himself that there was a pile of learning to be done? He didn't understand that at all. Yet she had seen it, and somehow she had stimulated in him the desire to learn; and he had even begun to enjoy making sense out of Shakespeare, not that he intended to admit that out loud. The more he read it, the more something seemed to settle in place in his mind. Something to do with the emotions, the people, the twisting and turning of the characters' thoughts, not just the witches and the fights and the antics of long-dead kings in some tiny island. He had not realised before that Shakespeare could be so clever, funny, or interesting – and had never in his wildest nightmare thought he might appreciate that fact.

Damn it, he was even beginning to appreciate the early black and white films.

He flexed his muscles and shifted his weight from one leg to the other, but what he wanted to do was lower his arms, relax. A grunt of discomfort escaped his lips. His eyes flashed to where she lay on the bed, but there was no movement. Perhaps she had not heard. She sprawled in the abandonment of sleep, half-naked, beautiful, entrancing as a siren. He could not drag his eyes from her. The shimmering garment had worked its way up to expose the long length of one leg and nearly, but not quite, the area that lay between.

He stared hard, as if by staring alone he could shift the garment an extra few centimetres. The inevitable stirring of desire pricked his loins, making him wonder what it was about her that had him sniffing like a dog in heat. No matter how she treated him, he wanted her; no matter how much he had her, he wanted her some more. And yet he knew it was lust, pure and simple, that no other emotion was involved, that he would be both sorry and pleased when he never saw her again.

Common sense told him that half of his almost inexplicable desire was simply in the strangeness of his situation. What man had ever been in this situation before – slave in the hands of a raging nymphomaniac? And what normal, red-blooded man who knew of his bondage and the gloriously uncivilised sex would not have envied him for it? Yet the fact that he could not have her at a time of his own choosing was frustration beyond anything he could have imagined. She stirred, and the dress slipped slightly higher. He stiffened a little more and a breath sighed from between his lips – then he noticed the faint glint of her eyes spark from between her thick lashes.

Drowsily, her head turned towards him fully. Gradually awakening, she stared at him, drank in the chained strength of him. He saw her gaze drift down to the pulsing thickness of his cock. Her lips parted fractionally at the sight, and her hand slid between her legs. He groaned, wanting her badly, realising that just the sight of him alone was enough for her at that moment, that he was not going to be touched. His mind reached out, as if by sharing his needs, his desires, he could make her rise from the bed, glide over to him and slip her mouth over his pierced cock. Just thinking about it plumped him just a little more full, if that was possible, and he felt the slight pressure of the embedded rod move against his flesh.

His heartbeat increased, his hips gyrated and thrust against nothing, and, although he knew it was futile, he could not stop them. He imagined taking his cock in his hand and rubbing the end, oh so gently, just moving that ring about ... He had been dismayed at its insertion, but he had never dreamed that the sensations that came from it would be so fulfilling, so engrossing and exciting. The warmth of sexual desire filled his mind, increasing his frustrated need to experience again the alien strangeness of the steel bar moving about, sending shivers of something exquisite right through to the base of his spine.

She was rubbing faster now, staring at him, using his erection, his frustration as a mental stimulus to her own desires. He willed her to help him, to touch him, knowing that she would not. His fists clenched around the chains, the need to free his hands so great that he almost pulled his feet from the floor; then he sank down, knees bending, as if the weight of his own body would pull the staples from the stone pillars, but nothing he did in any way eased his ache, or the driving urge to echo her in masturbation.

Eventually he realised Olanthé was lying back watching him, lips parted, and he knew that although she must have satisfied herself, his own frustration continued to feed some other desire. He clenched his teeth against the wish to ask her, no, to beg her to give him the same satisfaction that she had just achieved. He forced himself to stand still, then closed his eyes, willing his erection to subside. But even if it did, he knew the urge would not diminish. Sex was like any other drug, for once the need had been planted in the brain, the body craved it beyond anything else. No matter that his breathing eventually calmed, the need for release lurked just beneath the surface, and would continue that way until he was able to come, and she knew it, damn her.

She slid from the bed in a single, easy movement – everything she did, every movement she made was grace-ful – and, as her head cocked to one side, he heard what her acute hearing had picked up: the sound of a helicop-ter. Damn, he thought. It was that cold fish of an English-man again, and that boded ill for any satisfaction he might get from Olanthé, or anyone else for that matter. What she saw in him, Eugene could not gather, and quite what their relationship might be, he could not guess. All he knew was that whenever the pale-skinned aristocrat turned up, Narcissus the slave ended up as truly trussed and stuffed as a Christmas turkey, and sent to learn his lines in solitary confinement, unable to satisfy himself or anyone else.

However, he soon realised this time was to be different.

'We have a few moments before I need to present our guests to the brethren. I'd like you to be with me, in your full capacity as sex slave.' She tweaked his nipples with hard fingers, then brushed his cock with her hand, and the control he had been exerting disappeared; the erec-tion rose instantly. She caressed it just a little, long enough for him to inwardly writhe and for the erection to attain rock-solid dimension, then she began to buckle the inevitable leather harness around his shoulders.

He had promised himself that when she freed his wrists he would grab her and land her one but, although the image burned brightly, he found himself obediently putting one wrist, then the other, behind his back to be firmly secured to the leather. She was not going to give him the chance to satisfy himself, oh no; but it got worse.

'Kneel down by the bed, my slave.'

He did as he was bid, and she knelt behind him and began to caress him more, stroking the tiny, sensitive ridge of flesh between anus and balls. He groaned, partially at the present pleasure of her touch and also with the sure knowledge that he was going to suffer before she released him. His hands clenched involuntarily behind his back as her own snaked around, touched the bars in his nipples, and fleetingly teased his erection, her tiny teeth nibbling at the flesh of his back.

He felt a pressure on his anus and gasped as the chilled ball of glass stretched him wide before slithering inside. His cock flicked hopefully in response to the stimulation, but she simply fed him another marble. And another, and another.

He began to feel the pressure building on the inside and, although he had felt this sensation before, memory did not lessen the impact of hard objects pressing on an already stimulated gland. She filled him until his bowels began to try to eject the mass, but he knew better than to allow this, and he breathed the shallow breaths of a pregnant woman to still the muscular spasms.

'Good slave,' she murmured encouragingly, as she began to bind him in a fine meshwork of leather straps from torso to calf. By the time she had finished and bade him stand, he could scarcely do so unaided, and when he tried to walk he discovered that each step pulled the whole network of straps so that all his sexual areas, connected by fine leather, responded to that stimulus. He bent his knees slightly to try to ease the erotic stress points, but she tapped his thigh hard.

'Stand up, stop cowering. Be a man. That's right.'

He straightened, biting back a gasp from somewhere between pain and pleasure, and glanced at himself in the mirror. The fine meshwork of straps left nothing to the imagination, not his separated and strangled balls, nor his bound, rock-hard penis with its obvious piercing providing anchor for tiny slithers of leather attached to his nipple-bars. The hard pressure of the marbles in his bowels, however, was his knowledge alone, and it was unlikely that he would disgrace himself as another strap discretely held a bung in place. He was strangely moved by the figure he cut, though, the golden mane of hair even longer in his continued confinement, wide shoulders tapering to a flat middle, strong thighs and muscular legs. His impressive stature made a captured warrior of him, a lion bound in chains, rather than a slave. He was, in short, magnificent.

Olanthé made a growling noise deep in her throat. 'Mmm,' she said, her eyes glittering with echoing approval. 'Come, it's time our film crew saw their future star.'

'Oh my God. A whole film crew?' he said, stopping short. 'They've come here? They'll see me like this?'

Her head cocked to one side, and he was dismayed by the wicked amusement in her eyes. 'Trust me, slave, they will be stunned.'

'I'm dead,' he said resignedly. 'Finished before I started.'

'Good. Then you'll say nothing. You'll not make a sound no matter what happens, and you will most certainly not answer any question put to you except by me, do you understand?'

Eugene closed his eyes briefly. This nightmare had a habit of getting worse. 'Yes, Lady.'

'Now, walk!'

She tapped his thigh smartly with a small crop, making him wince into action, and he shuffled as quickly as the confining hobble allowed him out into the corridor beyond, every step an erotic sensation designed to keep his erection proudly preceding him.

The nightmare was fulfilled when he reluctantly entered the hall, Olanthé encouraging him from behind with small, biting flicks of the crop on his buttocks. As he painfully clambered the three steps on to the central dais, a gong sounded, and as he turned to face the assembled throng every eye turned towards him. There were eight to ten men and women, dressed in expensive Western garb, sitting around the dais and surrounded by an exotic flurry of slaves, and if they had seemed slightly bemused before, now their jaws dropped instantly, one and all.

Eugene felt blood drain from his face.

He had grown so used to nakedness and sex over the last few months that it ceased to concern him, but now that he saw the shock and dawning amusement on the faces of those who viewed him, he suddenly saw it from a Western perspective. There was, he had to admit, a certain kind of humour to the situation.

'Welcome, my guests,' Olanthé said. 'I would like you to meet Narcissus the slave. Narcissus, you may bow.'

Biting back a groan of pain, Eugene bowed low, from the waist, wondering what would happen first: whether the marbles would explode from him, or whether his balls would drop, sliced through by the tight bands. But neither happened, and he stood again at Olanthé's faint tap, feeling light-headed, unreal.

This was it. He was finished.

Yet the strangers were staring at him in a way that transcended mere humour. Yes, they were shocked and amused, but they were also analysing, assessing. Olanthé glided towards the table and introduced her guests one at a time, but Eugene took in no more than the first name. Christopher Merrill, Director. Oh, God, he thought. Not some two-bit director of porn films then, but a true-blooded big-name director of major films. He shrank inwardly. The man looked over, met his eyes. He drew himself up straighter, narrowed his eyes slightly, and gave back stare for stare, then gradually the tightness of his mouth eased into a small, secret smile. If he could have shrugged, he would have done.

He most certainly had nothing left to lose.

Against all the odds he saw the man's face relax slightly from shocked bemusement into something more calculating; then the sense of communication was severed as the director turned his smile to Olanthé, one brow raised in salute along with his glass of wine. 'My dear, you have convinced me. Our harem scenes will be shot here without a doubt, and any of your people who wish to do so can be extras. Perhaps it was a happy accident that led Lord Brandon to me, after all.'

'A happy accident indeed,' Olanthé murmured, but Eugene caught the wicked glint she flashed in his direction. He knew at this moment that he was not to make a porno film at all, but perhaps be a small-part player in some major film. Christ, and he'd nearly blown it by begging to be excused. He released his held breath slowly, trying not to look as shell-shocked as he felt, but her speculative gaze was now on the director, who was still speaking.

'Your actor is to be commended. He certainly is a fine specimen for a slave; it's refreshing to see he has no hesitation in getting himself into the heart of the character. I wonder why my location team did not discover this place? Perhaps I should sack them.'

'Oh, I shouldn't blame them,' Olanthé disagreed. 'We tend to keep rather to ourselves here, you know. I am doing this only as a favour to my Lord.'

'Your Lord? Ah ha! Lord Brandon. Yes, I see. But are you going to release the fellow now, what's his name – Narcissus?'

'Oh, no. He'll remain in character the whole time you are here. He is dedicated, you see, and he knows the part of the story relevant to him.' Her voice dropped to the lilting cadence of a spell, and the film crew, as one, stilled to catch her words. 'He was captured from the invading European armies and sent to the war god's harem, where he was to be emasculated to serve the immortal beings. There they tied his testicles tightly with leather bonds prior to slicing them away, but the goddess Ariaz had seen him and coveted him.

'She made herself invisible, cut his bonds and stole him away to her magic castle in the middle of a vast desert. There she gave him the breath of everlasting life and kept him as her love slave. For many years he was happy to remain there, blinded by her beauty and grateful for her intervention, but eventually he became tired of the desert and begged to be released. In anger she laid another spell upon him, saying he could go from that place if he wished, but bade him that if ever he should speak again, he would instantly revert to his normal age, and die. And so he wanders silently from place to place, giving people the only thing he knows how to give – his passion for life. It is said the only thing which can break that spell is a kiss from the lips of a virgin bride, so the spell, of course, will never be broken.'

The was a faint silence, then Christopher gave a shout of laughter. 'By God, Olanthé, it's you who should be the actress. You nearly had me going there.' His eyes narrowed and he leaned forward. 'Will you play Ariaz for me?'

She leaned back and smiled softly. 'Ah, no, not for me the big screen. But tonight you have the freedom of my house. Anything here that's freely given, you may take with my blessing.'

'Anything?'

She cast him a sly smile. 'You may be refused, but you may ask.'

She clapped her hands, and the slaves began to pile dishes of luscious food before them. From his heightened state of awareness on the dais, Eugene saw the famous director discreetly put a napkin over his lap and cast Olanthé a look of shocked speculation, probably wondering whether he had caught the nuance in her words correctly.

Eugene was in no such doubt.

He did not know whether to be pleased or dismayed by the knowledge that tonight the slave Narcissus was not going to be honoured by Olanthé's attentions. He also guessed that Christopher, who had attained something of a reputation for getting into the knickers of hopeful Hollywood starlets, was about to be given an education he would never forget.

Clenching his buttocks against an involuntary spasm of movement, he concentrated hard on standing still, but the unbidden picture that had risen to his mind once again plumped his cock into glorious erection, and he was unable to lose it, much to the further amusement of the film crew before him.

Bran had done her proud, Olanthé realised.

The Curse of Ariaz was an epic set in the distant Eastern past, dealing with the fortunes and betrayals of gods and men, and the part where Ariaz stole the golden slave for her bedchamber was to have been no more than a tale, told as she had told it. But Bran's subtle tongue, coupled with Christopher's curiosity, had done its work. In the length of the whole film this part would still be no more than minutes long, but it would give Eugene the chance to show his body and his face to millions. Olanthé did not doubt, any more than Eugene did, that he would captivate every female heart that saw him there, tethered in the goddess's bedroom for her delectation.

It would not be pornographic; but it would most certainly be erotic.

When the meal was finished, Christopher leaned back with a sigh, before indicating Narcissus, who was still standing on the dais where Olanthé had left him. 'How long is he going to stay there? He doesn't look too good. Is he in pain or something?'

'Not yet,' Olanthé commented slyly. 'Would you like me to have him whipped?'

He cast her a surprised glance. 'He'd let you do that?'

Her lip curled. 'Oh, yes. But would you?'

'Let you whip me?' His eyes narrowed. 'Why should I?'

Olanthé did not answer, but felt a small stirring in her gut as her eyes narrowed in speculation. This man was neither young nor good-looking, yet there was something about him. An aura of power maybe. Yes, she could see that his smooth tongue and cool gaze might promise something to the hopeful starlets, yet while she did not doubt the tales she had heard, she knew in her heart that he gave nothing in return for the pleasures he took.

'When will you wish to film the slave scene?'

He was silent for a moment, and still, and she could see the top-flight director in the way his eyes suddenly committed everything – the room, the lighting, the goddess scene, Narcissus – into the playhouse of his mind.

'A month,' he said decisively. 'I'll have a good look

around, take some shots now for the lighting and send you detail of the areas we want to use, and we'll come in, take the shoot and be gone within a week.'

'A month? Time enough for broken flesh to heal.'

'Pardon?'

'I'll lay you a wager.' Her eyes locked coolly with his wary ones, then dropped to the riding crop she was bending between her long, dark fingers. 'That Narcissus will stay in character if I whip him. That he will not cry out, or beg.'

'He'll cry out,' he said confidently.

'If he does, I'll give you back the fee Bran negotiated for the use of this location, and double it.'

'And if he doesn't?'

She saw the dollar signs light interest behind his eyes, and threw the challenge. 'If you lose, you become my slave for one day and one night in his stead.'

She had shocked him, she knew. But she noticed he could not contain the flush of excitement at the prospect. Men were all the same really. Such predictable creatures. Titillated, yet scared, by anything of a sexual nature that was outside their norm. 'Well?'

'You'd whip me?'

'If I so choose; and bind you. I might also choose to do other things. As my slave, you would obey.' He shuffled on his chair, and she knew that his blood was hot for her. She allowed the flimsy material of her dress to slip aside casually, as if by accident revealing the hint of one dark areola. Her voice lowered to a husky drawl. 'Are you afraid, Christopher?'

'Christ, yes!'

'But excited by the prospect, I can see. Well?'

He gave a quick, wet grin. 'Whip the slave. Now.'

* * *

Eugene watched Olanthé shrug her garment back over her exposed bosom, uncoil from her seated position and undulate towards him. He felt something lurch inside him. He wanted relief from the packing in his lower regions, not further chastisement, and did not see why he should accept it just because the bitch was teasing the director into her knickers. He knew he was to be the fall guy and wanted to swear out loud; yet there was the contract for his small part in the film, and Olanthé was of the one part and the director was of the other.

He was just the object of their negotiations.

Yet at that moment he wanted that single small part in the film almost more than he wanted life. He bit his lip and swallowed. Olanthé gave him a single nod of satisfaction, as if, like the Egyptian goddess she had been likened to, she could read his mind. Ali walked forward at the merest hint of a nod and lowered the wrist shackles from the ceiling. Within moments Eugene was stretched into the familiar star and was having to hold his breath to stop himself from crying out. How could he ever remain quiet if she whipped him on top of that already grinding ache in his gut?

He saw the members of the film crew glance at each other guiltily, each wanting to watch but torn by the tenets of society that said they should stop it from happening, or at least walk away. They all froze, fascinated, then slipped further into shocked silence as Olanthé knelt before him, wrapping her hands around his tight buttocks. With one fleeting smile that fairly stole what was left of Eugene's breath, she took his cock in her mouth. As she teased it into submission, his agonised gaze fell to the dark head that laboured before him, then lifted towards the director, for whose benefit she was really working, and he knew he would remain silent.

Christopher was frozen in place, eyes wide, one hand in his lap.

Eugene was transported to some place he had not known existed. The exquisite pain in his bowels and the tightness of the lashings around his scrotum became amplified a hundred times as his cock rose to bursting fullness under her mobile tongue. He was moving to the tune of his blood-pulse, but knew better than to think she would finish him off. He was scarcely surprised when she lifted her head from his swollen cock and ran her dark hands up the fine golden hair of his thighs as she stood.

There were no words. She simply put one finger to her lips in warning, winked one secret, dark eye, then gathered her crop and disappeared behind him. The first slash was like fire across his thighs, but he was stretched so tightly that, even though his skin seemed to crawl from his bones trying to escape, the involuntary contraction of his muscles moved his body not once inch. Though water sprang to his eyes, he did not let out even the tiniest whimper.

'Good slave,' she whispered.

Her words were the merest whisper of a caress, and were for him alone. Wrapped in the aura of her domination, he knew he would not cry out if she burned him with hot irons. Her voice rose to a gentle sing-song, and with every other word the crop fell, landing with a resounding crack that left no one in the room in any doubt that her heart was in her work. 'And the goddess Ariaz was so angry with her slave that she chained him tightly in her chamber and had him whipped until the blood ran, taunting, teasing, persuading him to let fly the torrent of words that were building up in his chest. Yet the young Greek did not speak. He did not utter a single complaint though his skin burned like fire, and his limbs were crushed by the weight of his own pain. He stared at her with love and hatred and desire tangled in his breast, but he did not want to die, so he uttered not one word.'

Gradually consciousness fell from him.

When he came to he was lying in a warm bath of oiled water, and incense smouldered to one side, a rich, pungent scent that caught in the throat. A female slave, dark concern in her eyes, lifted a glass of water to his lips, then smiled gently and touched his cheek as he sipped. 'Not a sound,' she murmured admiringly. 'Not a single sound.'

'How bad is it?' he whispered.

'Not as bad as you think. There's no damage. You'll be all right in a few days, though it might take a little longer to realise it! But don't worry, she has other game tonight.'

Surprisingly, Eugene found he was jealous.

Just thinking about her made his hand slip to his cock, but Timi was suddenly there, restraining his wrists beside his head.

'You relax,' he commented wisely. 'She not be with the film fellow many day. Take rest while you can.'

So Eugene, perforce, took rest.

13

Olanthé stood at her bedroom window and watched night fall over the desert. The scouting crew had left an hour ago, save Christopher, who waited for her in his room. Her brethren had informed her he had bathed and dressed as instructed, in the robes of soft Egyptian cotton. She could almost feel his tension, his fear, his anticipation rise by the second. She let him wait a while longer. She looked out over the dark sand and felt the first chill of night creep across her skin, lifting the hairs on her arm.

Except the single time he was paraded into various rooms to have his pictures taken in various poses for planning purposes, Narcissus had been noticeably absent. He had been confined to his quarters for three days now, reading the film script over and over while waiting for the smarting marks of the lash to fade and heal.

He had already changed, matured, since his arrival in this place. He had learnt patience, tolerance, and many other things. He no longer paced, irritated by the task set, but dedicated himself to achieving it; not simply because she would test him on it later, but because he wanted to, which end had been the whole point of the exercise. In the silence and internal musings of his physical confinement in the citadel he had been freed of the shackles of his upbringing and had learnt how to think anew. He was ready to go, to move on to new pastures. In her own way, she knew she would miss him. Strange how you got used to having a person around, she thought.

A trickle of excitement filled her belly, and she recognised it as anticipation. When Narcissus went, another would arrive. That Bran would have someone in mind she did not doubt, but whom?

But she was not looking forward to the film crew's return. She shuddered. They would come back en masse, not a simple crew next time, but in force, invading her privacy with their lights and cameras. She resented the thought, but it was what Bran had ordered, and it was what Narcissus needed to set him on his course.

She would accept because it was for a finite time. They would come, but they would go again, and the desert would reclaim its silence, as it always did. And there were places here that would ever remain sacred to her brethren; they would make certain of that. This citadel was home to many, and not all of them wanted to be paraded like monkeys before the soulless eye of the camera, herself included.

The only pictures of her ever taken were owned by Bran, but that was as it should be, for he owned her soul. Her phobia of cameras was a legacy of childhood, so far back she could not recall who had even said the words; but it was ingrained in her psyche.

Christopher had tried to persuade her to play Ariaz, really tried.

She wondered how the famous actress who already had the part would have reacted had she agreed, and she gave a tiny smile. Narcissus would have been jealous at the ease with which she could have stepped through that metaphorical door which was so precious to him . . .

Yet she would not allow the camera to steal a slice of her soul to parade before the avaricious men of the world. Even in those distant days of poverty when her outstretched, begging hands appeared like ragged claws, there had been something about her face that made men interested. They would try to use her, rape her, film her.

She probably would have succumbed eventually, either through force or desperation, had Bran not discovered her and made her his by a single act of kindness. She thought she might have been about twelve years of age, but it was hard to tell.

She had supposed, then, that he was rich, and had been shocked to discover that there were two strata of poor people in the world. Those, like her, born to tread the hungry streets with bare feet, and those, like Bran, whose lineage allowed them to live amidst a luxury purchased by creditors. They were both thieves. She might have found it in her to become his mortal enemy for that fact alone, but she had already learnt that life was unfair, there was no point bewailing the fact. So common sense, and a bond wrought somewhere beyond reason, decreed otherwise. Now they were both wealthy beyond counting, those days seemed so long ago, yet standing here by the open lattice of the window, the chill lent her body the memory of hunger.

She shivered fractionally as the memories invaded. She was sure there had been arms around her once, a mother, but she had no idea why she had been abandoned, or by whom exactly. She had vague recollections of constant travelling, sleeping in alleys, begging and stealing, and there remained a vivid memory of feeling alone in the world and distrusting anyone and everyone, even those who offered favours. Favours were never freely given – something would always be expected in return. And then Bran had come along; moved by her predicament, he instinctively did something about it – he bought her bread and made her eat it, after which he walked away. Because he had neither demanded nor expected anything in return, and because for the first time she had witnessed genuine compassion through a simple and straightforward act of kindness, she followed him.

He had known she was following, she sensed it, and when he turned she went to him, as timid as a whipped dog. And that moment, for both of them, had been the turning point in their lives, though they had not realised it then. Bran, she knew, had seen her not as a sex-gift but as an encumbrance he did not need or want. It had been her pleasure, as she ripened into the fullness of womanhood, to give him that gift of her own accord, not as some kind of reimbursement or thanks but because she wanted to. Because she loved him. Yet even as there was a part of him that she could not reach, a part forged by the alien harshness of an English public school, so was there a part of her that had been moulded by a different kind of exile. There was a penalty for lack of love in childhood, paid out week after week in chastisement and pain, but it never healed the inner wounds, and it never would. They both knew this and, over time, their dark bond became steadfast devotion. Olanthé turned from the open window of the past and left her room in a soft flutter of bright silk and oriental scent.

Christopher stood as she entered, a mixture of apprehension and eagerness in his gaze. He was not a tall man, his hair was greying and his body was padded with the excess of easy living. She gathered he felt silly in his robe, but it lent him a dignity that his normal, somewhat sloppy sense of dress did not impart. He had been a highly successful director for a long time and he was well used to dictating his terms, to cajoling women into submission with promises. He had agreed to be slave for a night and a day because it had been daring, because he had been challenged before others, and because he had been pulsing with need for her. Now he was here, she knew he was not entirely sure he wanted to go on with the charade.

Olanthé stood still and remained silent as she studied him, and she knew, as she listened to his breathing, that her sense of inner peace invaded his Western mind.

Eventually she said, 'I release you from your promise. Say the words, and I will leave.'

Her words were soft, but they were qualified by yet another unspoken challenge. Are you afraid? If so, speak out now. He licked his lips but remained silent, and she walked forward, a full turn around him, her voice a low taunt. 'Are you afraid of your body, your sexuality? Are you afraid of humiliation or pain? Are you afraid of me, a woman? You've used many women before, Christopher. I've heard the stories – are they true?'

He cleared his throat. 'I never ... In my position ...'

'Sss ... Don't lie to me. Yes, they throw themselves at you. They're desperate to succeed, to become stars, to earn big money, to earn the freedom that money buys them. I know how it works. How many women, Christopher?'

His eyes met hers, then sidled away. 'I don't see what that has to –'

She slapped his face, shocking him, silencing him. His eyes darkened and he stepped back, lifting his hand. She stood her ground, daring him wordlessly. He wilted fractionally and his hand slipped to his cheek, rubbing the faint sting.

'Hands behind your back! Answer me, slave.'

She saw it happen, saw the precise moment he decided to play the game. He did as he was bade and, as his hands clasped together, the arrogance slipped into disconcerted hesitation. He realised he had made a decision, but was not sure what.

'I don't know how many.'

'Hazard a guess. Five, ten, a hundred, a thousand?'

'A hundred,' he muttered.

Her lip curled, and she walked around him, one outstretched finger touching his gown lightly, as a child follows the line of a fence. His head followed. 'Eyes to the front! I did not tell you to move.'

He snapped into rigidity, like a soldier standing to attention on the parade ground, and she stopped behind him, slightly to one side, where his extreme peripheral vision would be aware only of movement, nothing else. Her hand almost touched the back of his head, and she felt the hair follicles rise to follow the movement. There was so much of the primitive animal within a person that was buried by day-to-day responsibilities. It took so little to bring it clawing at the veneer of sophistication, itching to be released from captivity.

'Hmm. Probably a low estimation. Let's see. You were a struggling actor for a few years, made two blockbuster movies, then used that income to make your own films. It was a risk, was it not? I heard you invested your whole personal fortune into something everyone else said would not work. That took guts. How old were you then?'

'Twenty-five.'

'Lucky for you, it worked.'

'Not luck – talent,' he muttered.

She shrugged, walked back around him, and draped herself in a wooden-armed chair. His eyes followed, though he kept his head facing front. 'Luck, too. People with talent and guts often fail. Then you became a god. Or as near as it gets. How old are you?'

'Fifty-five.'

'So, for thirty years you've been a god. Thirty years' worth of being the big shot, that's – let's see, hmm –' her eyes narrowed as her mind calculated '– nearly eleven thousand nights, and you've only fucked one hundred hopeful young women?' Her voice dropped, cajoled. 'Oh, no. I can't believe that. Come on, how many, really? Is it the thrill of the chase that does it for you? Does the pleasure wear off once you get into their pants, spurt into their tight young bodies? Or do you keep them on for a bit, persuade them to go further each time, do things to you they would rather not do? How does it work for you?'

She saw the flush work from his neck slowly up to his cheeks. His lips compressed.

'Ah, it's the latter, isn't it? You start off with the wining and dining, make them think they stand a chance. You even persuade them to believe it's love, don't you? You're despicable! Take off your robe.'

He blinked.

'Don't make me repeat myself, worm!'

He reached down, lifted the robe by the hem and slipped it over his shoulders. He was wondering why this simple act of becoming naked did not fill him with the same pleasure as it normally did; she could see it in his eyes.

He was right to be wary.

She felt a small flood of warmth between her legs, and interest in the task began to settle inside her. Men knew they were stronger than a woman. It was integral to their existence. For a woman to take that power away she had to be clever, she had to manipulate. Experience had taught her that control lay in the tone of voice, and in anticipation. Give too much, too quickly, and the anticipation would dissipate. Keep them guessing, keep them tense, frustrated, but not so much that they would leap on you, trying to take what they wanted. Not that she was worried about that. Ali and Timi were there, within earshot. But to need their interventions would indicate failure on her part. The game lay in taming the beast, persuading the man, the stronger being, to give you his power voluntarily. You pushed, then you offered the hint of promise, then you pushed a little more. Gradually they thought they knew what the game was, and they would go further and further, getting more and more sexually aroused, and more confident in their belief that your sole purpose was to give them the ultimate release they craved.

Then, suddenly it would be too late. A small purr of anticipation worked its way out of her throat, and from the glint in his eye she knew he thought he had caused it, pathetic creature that he was. 'Spread your legs. Lift your arms. Give me a star. I want to look at you.'

He obeyed, sheepishly drawing in his stomach, but he was not in such bad shape for a Western man who lived in the lap of luxury, she thought. 'Don't be shy,' she said, allowing her amusement to show. 'At least you're still able to view your love tackle without having to look in a mirror.'

She walked close, pressed her hands on his chest and inserted one leg between his. There was a faint stirring of activity. She circled her thumbs over his nipples, saw his eyes glaze, his fingers flex and relax. She nipped at his chest with her fingernails. He yelped, stepping back involuntarily, but kept his arms in the air. Well, he was trying, she thought.

'Naughty boy,' she murmured. 'I didn't tell you to move. Hmm. I know, you need a massage, you're far too tense.'

She clapped her hands.

A second later Ali softly entered the room. 'My Lady?'

'Look at this slave, Ali. He is tense, is he not?'

Ali looked. Christopher flushed bright red.

'Most certainly he is not at ease, my Lady,' Ali agreed, somewhat sarcastically.

She glared at him. He was hardly hiding his knowing grin, and that was not helpful. 'Fetch me the oils and the massage table. I would like to get him thoroughly relaxed.'

'Yes, indeed, Mistress.'

Christopher's arms ached. As far as he was aware, he had never in his life held them up in this manner, and was surprised at how much effort it took, but in spite of his obvious embarrassment, he was beginning to enjoy himself. Christ, it was worth it; she was one sexy bitch. Of all the women he'd screwed, and he'd certainly dipped his wick in some places that most people would probably like to forget, this was probably the sexiest one he had ever seen. She positively oozed sex. She was gagging for it. Christ, she had knelt in front of all of them, and taken that Greek guy's dick in her mouth. The thought warmed him.

He watched the dark man wheel in a portable table, knock the wheels out from under it, and leave, bowing as he did so. Stupid prick, Christopher thought derisively. He had seen massage tables before, but this one was subtly different. It had the expected padded circular hole for the face, but was a pretty substantial affair all in all, with two articulated joints that unfolded from the side of the trolley to support the arms a little away from the body, like an arrowhead. He struggled to keep his arms up above his head, vaguely amused with himself for playing her slave–master game instead of just jumping her and showing her what he was made of. He enjoyed watching her move around the trolley, adjusting things, sorting out bottles of oil. The butterfly-bright silk of her garment covered her from head to toe, but it shimmered around her body as she moved, leaving little to the imagination. He could even see the shape of her buttocks as she bent over, the smaller projection of her nipple nestling atop the plump mound of her breast.

He felt his heartbeat increase and his cock plump a little. It felt nice.

She was long-limbed, supple, and he imagined the pert bush of her hair in his face, her dark legs wrapped around his neck, his mouth moving up to her surprisingly pert breasts. She had the body of a young woman, ripe for plucking, and yet there were faint lines around her mouth and eyes that suggested she was older than she seemed at first glance. But that was OK. Age gave women like this – whores – experience in what a man liked, and that was something no teenager ever had, no matter what they thought. You fucked teenagers, that was good, gave a guy a kind of thrill to be the first in there, but they just lay back and took it unless you told them what to do, whereas older women fucked you right back. Yeah, she was right. A massage would put him in the mood.

As if sensing his thoughts, she glanced over. It was a sly, suggestive glance that made his balls buzz, and he knew he had been right to accept her challenge. Being a sex slave for a day was well worth what she was going to give him. He preened a little. And he wasn't paying a penny for the service.

'Come and lie down, Christopher, I'm ready for you.'

And she had a come-and-get-me little voice too. Oh, yeah. Let her get her pretty, dark little hands on his body. He jumped forward with alacrity and stopped just short of jumping on. The trolley was fitted with restraints at wrist, waist and ankle. His eyes caught hers.

'You're not going to use those?'

'Of course. That's what makes this fun. Let yourself go, Christopher. Let me do wonderful things to your body. Put civilisation aside; forget about being the boss. Just lie back and enjoy. You'll be surprised how sensitive I can make you feel. In all sorts of places.'

'I never agreed to this.'

'What, is the famous director afraid of being out of control? I'm not going to stick knives in you, I promise. I'm just going to use these. Honest.' She held her hands up, palms outward; they were small hands, long-boned and finely made. The seductive tone of her voice invited and taunted at the same time, then her hands turned over, and one finger crooked, invitingly.

Strangely, the excitement of being bound warred against his revulsion and fear. His people knew where he was, so how could anything bad really happen? It only really happened in the films he made. Laughing at himself he buried his reluctance and climbed on, face down as indicated, spreading his arms out along the cushioned pads but lifting his head to watch her as she walked around and buckled up the rather workmanlike padded restraints around his wrists and hands, like boxing gloves, leaving only the tips of his thumb and fingers free. They fitted snugly, comfortably, and as he tested them, a jolt of excitement shot through his belly.

Christ, that was strange. Strange, but delightful.

She walked down to his ankles and buckled the other restraints firmly. Again, they were not simply around his ankles but encompassed half of his foot also, leaving only the toes and the heel exposed. She smiled at him.

'Feel good?'

'Surprisingly, yes,' he admitted.

'Then relax, and enjoy.'

He plopped his head in the hole, closed his eyes and made himself comfortable, listening to her move around him. She must have tipped oil on to her hands and rubbed them together because, without warning, her hands slipped straight on to his shoulders and down the length of his back, smearing a generous portion of oil across his flesh. Her touch was soft but, even though he had been expecting it, he jolted, pulling involuntarily at the bonds. Then he pulled again, grinned to himself, and relaxed.

She began to work the oil into his back with sure, confident gliding movements. She circled heavily, just basting him all over. He knew how it worked; he had been here before. He stretched, moved a little and wriggled his bum in anticipation, wondering why the actuality of bonds around his wrists and ankles seemed to heighten his sensitivity, just as she had said it would.

She began to softly tease the muscles in his shoulders and upper torso, long sweeps with the full hand to bring the blood to the surface, then her fingers, stronger than they had appeared at first glance, began to dig confidently into his back, easing the tension, separating strands of muscle with considerable expertise. Oh, Christ, he groaned to himself as her hands gradually worked their way down to move his buttocks, separating, scrolling around, and pushing them back down. When she did that, everything stirred below, and he felt his balls tighten and his cock begin to push strongly against the padded bench. He had known she would be good. He hadn't realised she would be this good.

'Oh, yes,' he whispered. 'Touch me, baby. Do it.'

She stepped back at his words, and he heard the faint whirr of a motor. To his consternation the bench seemed to separate, gradually spreading legs and arms into a full Saint Andrew's cross, even though he was fighting against the movement, pulling against the restraints all the way. 'What are you doing?' he screeched. 'Let me up!'

But by the time the whirring movement stopped, he was almost immovably stretched and had difficulty lifting his head at all, let alone looking over his back to see what she was doing. It was then that she touched him all right. The resounding slap of a cane on his buttocks made him leap several inches off the deck. 'Christ, what are you doing?' he yelled.

'Pleasuring you,' she whispered. 'Do you want me to stop?'

'Of course I bloody want – ah!'

Her greased thumb slid into his anus, circled once, and exited, her fingers brushing along the exposed flesh beneath his balls. He drew breath as a long, drawn-out flame of desire ripped through him, tongue to toes. He had never experienced anything like it. A faint sheen of perspiration lined his face as he heard the double meaning behind her words.

'Do you want me to stop?'

'No,' he gasped, eventually.

The cane fell again, on his buttocks, and again, and again, and to his own shock he discovered pleasure in the pain. Not in the pain itself, but somehow because it seemed to heighten his senses, focus his awareness, his sense of anticipation. There was nothing now except his body, his driving need for sex, and the lines of fire caused by the cane, which seemed to reach right into the core of his being and join together at the one place he most wanted her to touch.

Sometimes a faint whimper fell from his lips as she worked but, as if anticipating it, each time he felt he could stand no more, she touched him gently between the legs, massaging his balls, his cock, or thrusting her fingers into him, and each time she asked the same question, forcing the answer out of him.

'Do you want me to stop?'

'No!'

She seemed to purr with satisfaction. He could have sworn she purred. But she didn't beat him this time – she lifted his head with a handful of thin hair. Not painfully, just demanding obedience. Before his eyes she dangled a padded leather mask. He stared at it for a second, his limbs pulling against the bonds in a kind of fearful expectancy. He should have known ... No way!

But then again, what man had not wondered?

'You've gone this far,' she said, her dark eyes swirling hypnotically before him as he panted, blood pumping hard. 'It will be good, I promise. Open wide.'

He groaned, closed his eyes and opened his mouth, wondering what the hell kind of a fool he was as the gag slipped in; it was only as she buckled the thing up, binding him into silence and darkness, that he realised just what a fool he was being. Now he could neither beg to be released nor see what she was going to do. A flood of terror drove through him. He yelled though the gag, whimpered, and fought against the restraints. He felt his head lifted by her hands, either side of his face. Her voice was clear; there was nothing wrong with his hearing.

'Calm down. Relax. Breathe slowly.'

He took long, dragging breaths through flared nostrils, and she kept talking in a low whisper until his breathing had regained a semblance of normality.

'Listen to me, carefully. I'm not going to damage you. I'm going to take you on a journey of discovery. You're going to learn things about yourself that you never knew, and when you leave this place you will never forget me, or what I've taught you. But you will not be harmed. Trust me. If you want me to stop, shake your head. It will finish instantly. You can leave here tonight; but the offer will never be made again. You will never know ...'

He heard the warning in her voice. If she stopped now, she stopped for good. She sounded different. Confident, in control, like a mother talking to a child, telling it everything was for its own good. He rationalised things. She had caned him, but already the stings were fading and the memory of that pain was, surprisingly, one of excitement and stimulation. Not pleasure exactly, but not terror. Not anywhere near terror.

For the first time in thirty years he was out of control, beyond the means of his not inconsiderable wealth, trapped in the silence and darkness of his own mind, bound to the whim of a beautiful and erotic woman. The darkness seemed to enhance the attraction he had felt for her earlier; it magnified it, making her more desirable, more exotic and exciting, and there was something about being naked, stretched wide, unable to anticipate where the next touch was going to come from, or what it would be: the stinging sensation of the cane or the soft touch of her fingers.

He had not felt so strangely exhilarated for a long time.

There was a space when he froze, analysing, confused by his own thoughts. Then she spoke again, softly, firmly.

'It is time to decide. It's your choice. If you want me to stop, shake your head. If you want me to carry on and take you places you've never been before, nod. Several times. I want to be sure. You must make it clear it's your choice. Once you make this choice, you honour your debt to me. You become my slave for this night and the next day – totally at my mercy, at my beck and call. Mine to do with as I see fit. If you stay, you'll enjoy the experience. You will take away something with you to cherish for the rest of your life. I promise you that.'

Slowly his head dropped. It could have been a mistake. Then he lifted it, and nodded three more times, more strongly at each action.

'Very well. It was your choice. Never forget that.'

He shuddered briefly as his head fell back to the bench. Instantly her voice lost the caring touch it had attained several seconds before, making him tense inexplicably. What was it with her damned voice that she could change it like that, second to second? If she had spoken to him in that tone of voice he would have shaken his head furiously. He groaned again, and tremors of excitement shuddered through him, making his skin ripple, his hair follicles dance.

What the hell had he agreed to?

An hour later, Olanthé stood back and looked at her handiwork. Christopher was moving faintly, writhing, making tiny whimpering noises. His back and buttocks were an inflamed mass criss-crossed with a purple mesh of lines, a small weight hung from his balls, and his bowels had been inflated to a point just this side of agony.

She left him to enjoy himself, with Timi quietly overseeing.

As Olanthé walked towards her own quarters she heard the soft sound of choral music. Her breath quickened and she stopped short, her eyes lighting with pleasure, before running forward eagerly. Bran clasped her to his breast for a moment, hand on the back of her head, holding her there as if they had been parted for years. It seemed like it.

She breathed deeply of his scent, then lifted her lips to his. The kiss was long and warm and deep, and Olanthé found herself melting inward to that place only Bran could take her. His pale eyes were heavy-lidded with need, and she knew he had missed her as much as she had missed him.

Finally he pushed her back, held her arms and just looked at her for a moment, then shook his head and smiled. 'I came here fully with the intention of killing Narcissus, only to discover you manhandling my tame director, you hussy.'

'Poor Narcissus,' she said, touching his cheek with a long finger. 'He would not deserve your vengeance. With him I share my body. With you I share my soul. With the director, so far I share only my expertise; but he hopes.'

Bran chuckled. 'And is he enjoying your expertise, my love?'

'Even he isn't sure about that. He probably never will be. But he most certainly won't forget it.'

Her glance caught his, and she frowned. 'What is it? Have I displeased you in some way, my Lord?'

She began to bend at the knee, but he caught her hand and held it to his face. 'No. I'm just afraid, with every new project that comes through your hands, my sweet pagan, that one of them will steal you away, that I'll come back here one day and find you gone.'

She cast him a mischievous smile. 'You always said I was no prisoner of yours; that I was free to go at any time.'

'It's true. But if you did, life would have no meaning.'

'Life always has meaning. I learned to believe that because of you.'

'If you ever stopped loving me, wanting me, my Olanthé, my life would have no meaning. I would walk the streets of Cairo barefoot rather than lose you.'

Behind them Beethoven's ninth crashed into its *grande finale*.

She reached up and ran her nail along the line of his lip, quivering with emotion. 'I could never stop loving you, my Lord. You know the others mean nothing to me.'

'Except Michael.'

'Even Michael. He was different, but I don't know why or how. I feel for him – oh, I don't know. I felt as though

I was losing a part of myself when he went, but not the same way. He was like the son I was never able to conceive. You mustn't be jealous. I will always carry love for him, but in here.' She pressed her hands to her eyelids. 'You, Bran, I carry in here.' She pressed her hands to her bosom.

Bran walked away from her, paced the room, and for a moment she was not sure if he had truly heard her. Then he turned and said dryly, 'Michael was indeed different. That's partly why I'm here.'

Her startled glance caught his.

'Oh, don't panic. Nothing has happened. I just thought you should know he's going to let us down. Of all of them, that surprised me most, I think.'

'Let us down? Michael? How?' She shook her head in bewilderment.

Bran took a silver monogrammed case out of his pocket, carefully plucked a cigarette from it and tapped it on the case a few times before slipping the case away and lighting the cigarette cupped between his two hands.

'It appears the dear boy has decided not to go into politics after all. He thought about it a lot, apparently, and decided he doesn't want to join a group of people who do not know the meaning of the word "integrity". Instead, he's joined International Voluntary Aid. And not only that, he contacted me and asked me to support him in this worthwhile venture. He somehow got the idea into his head that we have earned enough money for our selfish needs and that it's now time to start using it to do some good. He wants me to be his patron.'

There was a long silence, then Olanthé began to chuckle. 'He thinks we should now be altruistic? You and me?'

'Told the dear boy he was mistaken, of course. Told him we are not and never will be philanthropists, and that everything we do, we do for our own personal reasons. He said that while he could understand our need for security, he could not condone the sheer amounts of money we have amassed for our own personal greed.'

'He doesn't have to condone it. It's not his business – he can't do anything about it anyway.'

'I said that. So he threatened to tell the world about us, what we do, where this place is.'

'But he doesn't know.'

There was a certain amount of pride behind the glum words. 'Told you he wasn't stupid. He told me the exact map co-ordinates. Actually, come to think of it, that was rather stupid.'

'Bran?' Olanthé said after a long silence. 'You suddenly got very English. Exceedingly English, in fact.' He raised one eyebrow in a haughty query that did nothing to dispel her sense of foreboding. She put her hands on her hips and glared at him. 'Bran, what have you done? You tell me right now!'

'Put him where he can't do us any damage, of course,' he said guiltily.

Michael stood up in a rustle of chains as Olanthé entered the cell-like room, and gave her an enigmatic smile. 'We meet again, my fair torturer.'

Her hand went to her throat as she stared at him. Those dark eyes, the straight brows, the faintly sardonic curve of the lip. He wasn't built for beauty as Narcissus was; instead his body was strong, powerful, as was his mind.

His direct glance assessed her with equal intensity, before he added, 'I thought I would find my imagination had led me to recall you as more beautiful than you really are, but I was wrong. I hadn't recalled the half of it. God, you are truly lovely.'

'Oh, Michael. What have you done?'

She walked forward and he wrapped his arms around her, holding her, comforting her as though she were the one in chains. His chin rested on the top of her head, and she sensed his amusement. 'What have I done?' he wondered.

She pushed away from him in irritation, and he let her go. Though he could easily have held her, threatened her, it wasn't his way. He crossed his arms calmly and waited. She swivelled angrily. 'Why did you tell Bran you knew where this place was? Didn't you realise what would happen?'

He shrugged. 'I considered the possibility; but I wasn't going to break up his little scam without warning him first. It wouldn't have been fair.'

'You idiot!' Her hand slashed towards the manacles around his ankles. 'Is that fair?'

'It won't be for ever.'

'Of course it will be! What did you think, that you could threaten us and just walk away, free to destroy everything we've worked for?'

'I thought I could talk Bran into seeing things my way.'

'That was naive!' Her eyes flashed. 'Now what do we do with you? Tell me that. And what of your vow to remain silent about what happened here? Where's your integrity now?'

'That was before I knew just how much you two were worth.'

'You have no clue as to how much we're worth.'

'No, I couldn't find out the half of it, but I found out enough to be shocked.'

'So you thought you could blackmail us.'

'I said two Hail Marys, and God forgave me. Weighed up against the poverty in the world I decided it wasn't fair to keep my silence.'

'Not fair?' Her voice rose in disbelief. 'Won't you ever grow up?'

'If it means learning not to care about people, no. You and Lord Brandon forgot about caring for people a long time ago, but I'll never be like you.'

Her hand leapt out to slap him, but he caught it in mid-air, held it easily until the tension went from her. She'd forgotten how quick he was. She also didn't miss his wince of pain. 'What's wrong? Are you hurt?'

He shrugged again. 'Bruised. I'll mend. There were four of them, and I know I broke one nose and at least one arm before they got me trussed up,' he said with satisfaction. 'Mind you, that probably wasn't fair either. I suspect they were told not to harm me, or I would have ended up with more than bruises.'

Olanthé gave an involuntary chuckle and shook her head. 'When will you learn that life isn't fair, Michael? It never was, and never will be. You're a danger to yourself, you know that? People like you just shouldn't be let loose in society.'

He gave a wry grimace, sat back down on the narrow bed, which was the only piece of furniture in the room, crossed his arms and leaned tiredly against the wall. 'I'm learning. Looks like I'm pretty safe from now on then, doesn't it?'

14

Christopher felt as if he was in limbo. Soft hands had rubbed some kind of liniment into his back and eventually the stinging pain of the beating subsided to a residual soreness. He was left with the ache in his nether regions, only the twitching of his tired cock telling him that his body had actually appreciated Olanthé's efforts, but would like her to finish the job, please, and nicely. His limbs had gone numb and his jaw ached yet, in spite of that and the lack of sexual satisfaction, he felt light-headed, released from the burdens of society, of film-making, of any kind of pressure. As he could not speak, see or move, there was little point in worrying about any of it. How right she had been. Yet the more physical side of hunger and cramps eventually began to intrude on his solitude to the point of discomfort, and he made grunting noises of irritation that eventually brought attention.

He was released from the couch by a woman – not Olanthé, he was sure – and instructed to shower. By the time he had managed to remove the mask, he discovered himself alone in a locked room. The constriction about his balls remained, but as it appeared to be a metal collar locked by means of, perhaps, an Allen key – he couldn't bend close enough to see – he found himself walking around with a hand beneath his balls helping to take the weight.

Christ, what a woman.

He searched the apartment for food and discovered a minimal supper had been laid out for him but, though he craved a drink, there was no alcohol. Nothing to distance him from his inhibitions, to numb the strangeness. As he ate, savouring every mouthful, he realised it hadn't occurred to him that the whole slave thing would be like that. Sex without sex, so to speak. Did she get enjoyment out of that? He had rather supposed he would be following her around doing a bit of 'Yes Mistressing' like they did on the films before slipping her one. But perhaps it was the thought of a man at her mercy that turned Olanthé on. Or perhaps she'd thought that was what he wanted?

If so, he'd put her straight.

He looked at his watch and realised it was late evening. He had the rest of the night and the next day to go yet before he was released from his wager. But he knew he was kidding himself. She had already proved she would release him any time he asked. And with that thought he found he was actually anticipating her arrival, wondering what new kind of excitement it would bring.

Never before had Olanthé been in such a quandary regarding the men in her life. Bran had allowed himself to be secured to the phallic seat in her room and was waiting there in some discomfort for retribution to fall upon him. He said he deserved to be thoroughly chastised for kidnapping Michael, and knew she would not be merciful, but if she let Michael go free while he was incapacitated, her former project would ruin them both. Which brought her to Michael, who waited patiently, or perhaps not as patiently as it appeared, for a verdict on his future. She wanted to chastise him, to love him, but would not allow herself to do so because he was no longer a project. He was now a problem. In all honesty, she couldn't see what else Bran could have done.

Narcissus, her latest project, of course, was studying

the film script with avid attention to detail, not that he had any lines to learn. She knew she could safely leave him there for as long as it suited her, perhaps just give him a five-minute whipping before bed to keep his mind targeted. But Christopher had to be seen to, and removed from the citadel as fast as possible. He was an intrusion, a disruptive influence on the stability of the brethren, a thorn in the conceptual tranquillity of absolute sexual freedom. Although he was the one she least felt like abusing, he was, unfortunately, her priority.

She sighed; duty called.

The only satisfaction she allowed herself as she walked tiredly towards the chamber where, according to Timi, Christopher waited in some trepidation, was the knowledge that Bran was going to be bloody sore by the time she released him.

Christopher was wearing nothing but the weight when she went in, but it was interesting to note that he neither blushed nor turned from her. Already his experience had distanced him from his usual reality. He kept his hand beneath him supporting the weight, or playing with himself, she wasn't sure. But she was sure about the twitch of interest in his cock as she strode in.

She took a taper and lit incense sticks and candles and then turned out the main lights. There were times when electricity was best dispensed with, it was far too functional. The room turned instantly from a bedroom into a seductive boudoir, the thick candles and fine plumes of incense flickering on the soft breeze of innuendo.

A faint smile curved her lips as she wordlessly slipped her clothes from her shoulders in a single unexpected movement. Christopher's jaw dropped at the sight of her glistening dark body, and his cock plumped instantly to fullness, pulling the weight higher, closer into his body.

'I'm weary. Massage me.'

Her matter-of-fact voice jolted him into action. She casually threw a jar of oil towards him and strode to the couch, giving him the full benefit of her breasts and undulating hips. He grasped at the jar, missed, and had to scrabble under a table to find it in the semi-darkness.

It soon became obvious that Christopher had never massaged anyone in his life. He rubbed oil into her back, circled his hands around a few times with no consideration for the muscles beneath the skin and then, all too soon, began to target the globes of her buttocks. She felt his hands quiver, and his thumbs creep nearer to the small, puckered knot of her anus.

In a single fluid movement she rolled from the couch to her feet and glared at him, hands on hips. He jumped back, startled, his erection bulging and dribbling, his breath short and laboured. 'What do you think you were doing?'

He reddened fractionally. 'Massaging you. I thought that was what you wanted.'

'You were supposed to be pleasuring me, not you.'

'I thought I was.'

'You were not. For someone who's probably fucked a thousand starlets and bimbos you haven't a clue about pleasing a woman, you poor excuse for a slave. I expect they all had orgasms, didn't they? Were they good orgasms? Nice and loud? Did it make you feel good that you'd given all these women orgasms? Fool!'

His irritation flamed at her derisive comments, and he wet his mouth prior to defending himself, but she did not allow him that satisfaction.

'Silence! They were obviously acting for all they were worth, had you the sense to realise it, because you haven't the least clue about a woman's body, have you?'

'I –'

'No! Don't argue! Prove it. Bring me to orgasm, now.'

She flopped on to her back, put her hands behind her head and let her legs fall open invitingly. She was pleased to note his erection had diminished visibly.

'But I can't ... It doesn't work that way.'

'What doesn't work what way?' She was genuinely interested.

He searched miserably for the words, and found them difficult to say. 'I mean women need a man or a dildo inside before they get – ah – excited. It's the G-spot thing. I know about that.'

'Good God,' Olanthé said finally. 'You really mean that, don't you? Well, you pathetic bastard, you're about to have an education you should have had years ago. Western society really does have a lot to answer for, doesn't it? Come here. Put your hand here, like this, flat on my body. Yes, that's right.'

She positioned his right hand so that it lay on her belly with the forefinger just touching the skin above the hood of her clit, and his left on her breast. 'Now,' she whispered, 'just move, so softly you're hardly moving at all, smooth my body, touch every inch – gently, gently. No, don't push your fingers further down there. Not yet. And don't grab for the nipples, fool! Just lightly touch, everywhere, anywhere. Yes, that's better, but you can be even more gentle if you try. Pretend you're not touching me, just touching the air above my body. Stir the hairs with the air from your hands. For once in your life, be subtle.'

She closed her eyes and tried to make herself imagine she was enjoying the touch of his hands, but he was too self-interested, too keen to grab and touch and poke and prod. He just couldn't help clutching at handfuls of bosom, tweaking her nipples and flicking the small, sensitive sexual mound back and forth. Each time he strayed, she brought him back, but whenever she was beginning to relax, he got heavy-handed again, and she had to break the spell to correct him. Yet in spite of his lack of expertise her body began to blossom into interest under his intensive caresses. Her head stretched back and her back arched from the couch just fractionally. When she could stand his fumbling no more she took his forefinger in her hand, and used it to pleasure herself, and as the dangerously painful experience rose to climax, she pressed his finger close to her body to enable him to feel the tiny fluctuations of her orgasm. She held him still against herself for a moment until the euphoria diminished, then turned her head to face him.

He was flushed with excitement, and rampant.

'Hmm, you may yet learn,' she said dismissively, and stood up, stretching, totally ignoring his hopeful gaze. 'Now I've got some business to attend to. You'll await me here.'

'Yes – Mistress,' he said hesitantly.

'You may call me Lady,' she informed him. 'The word Mistress assumes I'm here for your pleasure. I'm not. You're here to serve me in my needs, whatever they might be.'

'Yes, Lady.'

'So.' She reached into a large chest and pulled out a stout leather belt with integral wrist restraints. 'Buckle this around you, then turn around. I would tell you not to pleasure yourself, but the majority of men haven't got that much self-discipline when it comes to their own sexual organs. In fact, there's only one I know who I could trust to give his word in that area, and keep it.'

'Lord Brandon?'

She cast him an irritated glance. 'No. Not even him. Breathe in and buckle it tighter. That's better. You could do with losing some of that flab.' She buckled his wrists behind his back and led him to the chest harness that hung from the ceiling on pulleys.

By the time she had finished, Christopher's ankles were parted with a stretcher, he was blindfolded and gagged, and a further weight had been added to his balls. He heard a door open and shut, and knew she had left him there while she attended to whatever other task it was she had to do. In his mind's eye he could still see her, slender, fragile and scented as an orchid, applying herself to the task of binding him. He wanted her so much he ached for her, and he could not get rid of the image of her sinking down before him, bending her dark head to his cock, and beginning to roll it on her tongue.

But he remained untouched and, in the enforced darkness, the strangeness of the aching, pulling sensation between his legs consumed him. He could think of nothing else. No manner of twisting and turning his body relieved the sensation – in fact, every minute movement enhanced it, bringing it more and more to the forefront of his mind. For a short while he likened the ache to pain and had visions of his balls being permanently damaged. He grunted his fears into the gag but, as the darkness and silence remained, he knew no one was there to hear, to rescue him from this untenable position.

His need for her turned to hatred.

For a while he struggled madly against his confinement, silently calling her all the names in his vast repertoire but, to his irritation, the excessive movement brought his previously unsatisfied sexual urge back, amplified, which had probably been her intention, the bitch, and with it the keenest wish to wank that he had ever known. He did not want Olanthé or any woman at that moment; he simply wanted to get his own hand on his own tool and wank it for himself. Eventually it drove all other thoughts from his brain; any fear, any pain he might have been experiencing were lost in the over-whelming need for ultimate physical satisfaction. His ineffective struggles eventually slowed, becoming gentle rotating movements of the hips accompanied by soft groans of need and desire, amplified by the sure knowledge that satisfaction of his own body was denied him, a concept totally alien to him, and surprisingly erotic.

Olanthé had not left, but remained in the room with him, not watching, but sensing him move from acceptance to anger to acceptance, and thence to a more primeval level of awareness. She drifted in and out of sleep, eventually to awaken fully with the sure knowledge that Christopher's state of awareness had attained a previously unknown level, similar to that attained by meditation. There was something now in the way he was almost still, yet the surface of his skin seemed to move with the odd rippling flush, that level of heightened anticipation that Europeans described with the unsavoury imagery of someone walking over your grave. Strange, she thought, that the so-called free Western world had long ago been granted a degree of promiscuity denied to the Eastern world; yet it had robbed the individual of that most exquisite of things, the true freedom of sexual enlighten-ment, which was so much more than the simple act of fucking.

She picked up the small silver-topped riding crop, which had never known a horse's hide, and walked towards Christopher. His erection had died but a fine dribble hung from the end of his cock, sharing with her the knowledge that his body was excited by the confine-ment. She made no sound, yet his heightened state allowed him to sense her presence – she saw it in the way his head tilted almost imperceptibly, his muscles tightened. She walked around him for a while, not touching, letting his senses follow her, allowing his imagination to run riot. He was no longer relaxed, but quivering like a greyhound waiting for the gate to drop.

His excitement transmitted itself to her. She raised her hand, and brought the crop down smartly across his buttocks. He gave a startled yell, wincing from the blow long after it landed. She waited a while, long enough for him to anticipate another blow a hundred times over, in a hundred different places. The original fine white line left by the first blow was rising to a dull red flush when the second blow caught him sharply, in virtually the same place. This time his feet left the floor.

He groaned and his hands clutched the air behind his back, then spread, as though to shield his buttocks from further punishment, but they were too high. Olanthé ran the tip of the slender crop along the fiery line, causing him to take breath sharply, then she ran it down the crack between his buttocks, pausing briefly, tantalisingly on his anus, before carrying on to touch his tender, aching balls.

He shot instantly into erection.

She laid her finger on his arm and walked around him once, twice, feeling his skin prickle under her touch, which was no more than a whisper against his risen hairs. Wherever she moved he tried to move towards her, to push himself on to her touch, but she retained control. For several moments she simply touched him, teased him with scarcely more than a promise. Then she leaned forward, took one nipple in her mouth and sucked hard.

He jolted and his hips began to thrust towards her. She avoided his touch, did not allow him to derive pleasure from it, heightening his need by still withholding satisfaction from him.

Then she backed off and began to labour again with the crop.

Three times more she teased him with pain followed by pleasure, until his frustration levels were an almost visible aura.

She reached up and removed the blindfold and gag.

Christopher blinked heavily for a moment until his eyes adjusted to the flickering candlelight, but even when sentience returned to his gaze, he still retained an aura of dazedness, like that of a man surfacing from sleep.

'So, do you like my little riding crop, Christopher?' she teased, running it down his chest and tapping his cock, which bounced once with eagerness.

'Please do it,' he gasped.

She pretended to misunderstand. 'You want more?'

'Please, I need –'

'Oh, no, my dear director. Most assuredly not yet. Tell me, what did you think of our Narcissus then? Will he look good on screen?'

'He's a sex stud,' Christopher said harshly, need written all over his face. 'And that's exactly what he'll look like. Please just –' He gasped into silence as she brought the crop down across his chest.

'Wrong answer,' Olanthé told him mildly.

'But he's only supposed to be pretty. He doesn't have to act. For goodness' sake, he's only going to be on screen for two minutes.'

'Five.' She lifted the weight with the crop, let it go.

'OK,' he gasped. 'Five, but still –'

'Five minutes, with credits.'

'You've got to be kidd– Ah!'

'Five minutes on screen, with credits.'

'But I – OK, OK, with credits, if you just – Ah!'

'Don't tell me what to do, you impudent little man.'

He was almost crying. 'Please, just do it. I'll do whatever you want. I'll give him lines.'

'I don't want him to have lines. I want him to be so beautiful, so charismatic that he will get more parts. I want you to be his sponsor.'

'Sponsor? You want me to nanny a stud?'

'Tell me what you want me to do to your body,' she bargained softly. 'Would you like me to climb up on to you, slip myself down on to you and slide up and down? Do you want me to kneel here, take you in my mouth? Do you want my finger to slip inside your anus and touch the magic gland while I do so? What would you like? What do you get your little starlets to do for you, my fine director? Whatever they did, I can do, and better, I promise.'

'Oh, God,' he groaned, staring at her with anticipation mixed with loathing. 'That's blackmail.'

'Tell me what you would like me to do to you. Be imaginative. Tell me everything you've been thinking these last three hours.'

'Three hours?' he said, aghast, looking around for the sight of a clock.

'Time flies when you're having fun. Tell me.'

'Just bring me off,' he howled. She smiled and stepped back. His expression of irritation turned to understanding. Olanthé laid the small crop with wickedly expert targeting, and Christopher babbled promises with every stroke. 'No, oh no. Ah! I promise. I'll do it. I'll make sure he gets more work. Better work. Ah! He'll be a star, I promise.'

'Thank you. Now it's time for bed.'

'About bloody time too,' he snapped, glancing over longingly at the silk-draped mattress as she began to release him from his bonds.

Olanthé poured a glass of wine and handed it to him.

He knocked it back and made his way to the bed with arrogant assumption. Then a look of surprise seemed to fill his eyes, and he fell over sideways.

She rang a small bell, and Timi entered softly.

'Tuck him in tightly,' she said, glancing down at the sleeping director. 'He's going to be pretty cross when he wakes, and he has a tiring day ahead of him tomorrow.'

15

Olanthé padded down the dark halls, sleep far from her mind. She stood in the doorway to the room where Michael slept, on his back, arms spread innocently as a child. Chains dripped away from his ankles to a hefty anchorage on the wall, but dark lashes covered the sensitive perception of his gaze as if he had not a care in the world. She grimaced. How could a man have reached such maturity, such clarity of understanding, without seeing the predicament he had now put himself in?

But, she realised, he did know. Yet his overdeveloped ethics had not let him do anything else.

He knew they could not let him leave. Their only option was to kill him, or keep him here in the citadel for the rest of his life, chained like an animal. Even here, if he were free to wander he would find a way to leave; he was too clever not to. So why? Why did he think that they, who had worked so hard for independence from a harsh world, would suddenly give back that which they had spent so long in taking? Nothing is for nothing, Michael, she thought bitterly. You knew that when you came here. You *knew* and you accepted the terms. Why could you not just honour the agreement?

And yet she knew in her heart that Michael's deeper agreement was with his own sense of integrity. And what did she care for that? Any integrity she might have once known had been lost in the streets of Cairo, many, many years ago. All that remained was to survive, and to love life itself. The projects, the sole purpose of which was to ensure that independence, were now distributed fairly around the globe, content to abide by the terms of their contracts.

All but one.

Michael stirred, rolled over and tucked one hand under his chin like a child.

Olanthé backed into the shadows, but he did not wake.

'Have you seen him?' Bran still sat on her stool, sweat drenching his pale forehead. His eyes followed Olanthé, but he made no mention of his discomfort.

'I've seen him. He's not afraid.'

'He's a fool not to be afraid.'

Her dark eyes met his. 'Please leave. Tonight I need to be alone.'

He rose slowly from the stool, wincing, his white skin reflecting the candlelit shadows. 'Don't shut me out. I had no choice.'

'You had a choice,' she said harshly, swinging on him. 'You could have had him killed –'

'And you would never have known. Had it been anyone else, or had he been doing it for personal gain, the choice would have been easier.' He shrugged. 'But Michael's . . . different. You know that.'

Her eyes softened. 'Oh, Bran, what will happen now?'

'We let him go, and close the citadel. We can find a new place, somewhere else.'

She shivered. 'The only place as inaccessible as this is the Arctic. Bran, you know I belong here. The desert is in my soul. I can't survive out there, in society. I'd rather die.'

His head snapped around. 'You wouldn't.'

'I'd die a slow death if I had to leave here. You know I would. The same death you would die if you were forced to live here and forgo the society *you* love so much.'

'Then we keep him here and carry on as before. Michael will learn to live with his new destiny. He chose it when he broke his word. He gave us the ultimatum, after all.'

'The brethren are here of their own free will. They won't tolerate Michael as an unwilling prisoner.'

'They can leave.'

She gave a brittle laugh. 'Stop being so arrogant, Bran! I can't survive here alone. I could bring in paid servants, but it wouldn't be the same. Besides, when individuals leave here of their own free will, as they all do, sooner or later, they say nothing. If they were to leave here with anger, bent on revenge, we might as well let Michael go now; it would have the same result. We've been sitting here in our desert stronghold, isolated for so long. Perhaps we got complacent. Yet all it took was one recalcitrant adventurer for our fortress to became fragile. If anyone learns about us, we will not survive; not here, not anywhere, and you know it. The world has grown too small, and I don't belong in it.'

Bran put his arms around Olanthé, his chin on her head, though it might have been for his own comfort rather than hers. 'I'm surprised we lasted this long, my love.'

'So am I, if truth be told.'

'So, I'll make a suggestion. Give us space to think. Let's finish this project, let the film be made, see Narcissus off to stardom, and leave the Michael problem until that is all finished.'

She gave a wet chuckle. 'He'll have to be patient.'

'Patience always was one of his most irritating habits.'

Bran watched Olanthé drift in the darkness of the pool. She was no more than a shadow, yet he felt like Peter Pan, lost in the world of grown-ups. If his shadow separated from him, his life would have no meaning. When, and why, had she become more important to him than anything else? He did not know.

Michael sensed eyes on him as soon as consciousness returned. He turned over to see Bran sitting on the stool staring at him, chin on hands. He realised he had never seen the English Lord look anything less than cool, but he was not cool now.

He lay still for a second, then slipped upright on his prison bed and crossed his arms, eyes narrowed. 'Is it good news, or bad?'

'We need time to decide what to do.'

'We?'

'Olanthé and myself.'

He shrugged. 'Time is meaningless to me at this moment.'

'Time is not infinite.'

Michael froze, then relaxed with a wry grimace. 'Ah. I see. I take it I should be worried.'

Bran leaned back, crossed his arms and smiled humourlessly. 'You should have been worried before now. Before this happened.'

'But I'm still here.'

'For how long?'

'If you're going to dispose of me, just do it. Don't hold it over my head like a threat. I took a calculated risk. It was my risk; I'll take the consequences.'

Bran stood suddenly and paced the small room. 'Dispose of? Christ, man, do I look that inhuman? Hell, don't answer that. Just because we're bred not to show emotion doesn't mean we don't have any. Damn it, why couldn't you leave well alone? Don't you realise what you've done?'

'Yes.'

'And you justified the risk?'

'Yes.'

He gave a bark of laughter. 'You're crazy. Do you know that? You're the first one I got wrong. The only one. Hell and damnation.' He glared at Michael with something akin to hatred. 'I'm going to ask you a favour. I need three months.'

'Children are dying of starvation while we dither about here.'

'I need three months for this damned film to be made, for Narcissus to be out of here and on his way. Then we deal with you.'

'I promise not to try to escape for three months, and you promise not to kill me in that time?'

'Something like that.'

'You pay IVA a suitable donation for the three months and I'll agree.'

'Christ.'

Michael grinned. 'Your money against my life? I think I'm the one with most to lose, don't you? And you know you can trust my word.'

Christopher was indeed cross when he awoke. He was more than cross, he was furious. He had been sexually excited beyond his expectations, drugged before he even got his end away, and had awakened alone, unable to satisfy himself. He pulled at the restraints on the bed when consciousness and realisation dawned, and he screamed at the girl who came to wash him. 'You get that bitch in here now or I'll fucking sue the lot of you!'

'Sue away, pal,' she said, shrugging, leaving him chained to the bed, hungry and dirty, thereby exacerbating his fury. After fighting his bonds for several moments he realised he was still hugely aroused and couldn't do anything about it, and that was the cause of his fury. He subsided, thinking about the previous night. Christ she was good, even if she was a tantalising bitch who didn't follow through.

He didn't ever recall anyone making him feel so horny, in fact.

Then she walked in. Christ, was she something. He yanked at the chains in irritation. 'You bitch, let me up. Now!'

She stood, turned around and stared at him with disdain.

'Why? So you can thump me? Or are you just trying to go back on what you promised last night?'

'I was made fucking promises, bitch!' he screamed, tearing at the restraints with disregard for his own skin.

Her voice was soft, seductive, calming. 'I said I would use you as my slave for a night and a day. I made no other promises. Anything else you might have wanted came from your imagination, not from my lips.'

He glared, hating her for being right. She stood there, slender and beautiful as ever, draped in shimmering fabrics that did nothing to hide those luscious curves from his avid gaze. This was like no other prospective conquest; he wanted her now with something that went beyond mere lust. He coveted that body. He wanted to use it because it had teased and tantalised him with unspoken joys, and had then been withheld. He knew that if he didn't have her, he would spend the rest of his life with that crazy need festering inside his brain.

She sat on the bed at his side and her scent drifted down to him. A soft smile curved her lips as she reached out and ran her nail from neck to navel, leaving a faint indentation. He was instantly aroused, as strongly as he had been the previous night. He groaned audibly.

'You tell me what you want me to do to you. What did you dream last night?'

He licked his lips, frustrated by his own thoughts, not sure of her intention. 'I dreamt you sucked me off.'

'Sponsor Narcissus and I will suck you off.'

'OK, I'll sponsor your Greek ponce.'

'Good. And I'll suck you when it's done. When I see Eugene's name in the first film credits, the tables will be turned: I'll be yours for a day and a night. I'll do whatever you want me to do. I'll be whatever you want me to be.'

The quality of her voice alone lent promise to her words, which sent a shiver from his scalp down to the soles of his feet. Then she stood up. 'But for now you're still my slave for a day. We have an agreement still to be honoured.'

'You expect me to –'

Her eyes bored into his. 'I don't expect anything from you. It's always your choice.'

'You think I'm going to wimp out, don't you?'

'If you did, I would be disappointed, of course. I assumed someone who had made it to where you are now would not have been scared off by a little adversity.'

'I'm not scared.'

She reached over and unbuckled the shackles from one wrist. 'Prove it. Shower, and eat, and be ready for me in one hour.'

'Where are my clothes?'

'Choose.'

She opened a cupboard door to where his suit was hanging, freshly washed and pressed. On another hanger was a scrap of vividly coloured silk. Her eyes dared him to choose which he would be wearing when she returned. He realised there could be no compromise.

Eugene was pretty fed up.

In this sybaritic society he gathered anyone could have any kind of sex with anyone they wished, as long as it was consensual – apart from him. He could do nothing at all for himself, and had not been able to from the moment he arrived in this damned place. His wrists were loosely manacled behind his back for no other reason, he realised, than to keep him from wanking. To keep him focused. He shrugged, trying to ease the ache in his shoulders. She had a real thing about him not pleasuring himself at all, and he had to admit it worked. Whatever else he did, there was a level at which his mind was always consumed by the need for self-gratification, simply because it was not his to control. What was it about her that made her want to exert this kind of control over him? In order to eat, read, or do anything at all, he needed the help of one of the house slaves – who provided for his needs happily and unquestioningly, save in that one area. That, it appeared, was Olanthé's domain alone. And on the times she did relieve him he had to admit it was more than gratification, it was more than simply a wank or a blow job or firing his load – it was a mystical experience that took him to another plane of consciousness.

He had heard the other slaves referring to him as a project. It had taken a while for the full import of those words to penetrate his brain, but once they had, other thoughts followed. He realised, therefore, he was not her first project, and in all probability would not be her last. He had already worked out that she was helping to train him to achieve his desire of becoming a film star, but why she wanted to do that defied explanation. It couldn't possibly be just for the money; she was already rich as buggery. And why she exerted total sexual control over him also beat logical rationalisation. I mean, what did the sex have to do with anything? Not that he minded having sex with her, of course, quite the contrary; though he thought it would be nice if she dispensed with the other more painful disciplines which, in her eyes, went hand in hand.

He looked at the film script without interest. He might not be able to quote it verbatim, but he knew it scene for scene, and had worked out in his own mind the best lighting, the techniques that would be best employed, the actors he could see playing the parts. In his mind's eye he had built the whole film from the ground up. He also realised that nine months ago he would not have been able to do that. In fact, he would not even have tried.

But presently his interest in the film had reached saturation point. He was frustrated. Ever since the film crew had arrived and had a good laugh at his expense, he'd been locked in a single room with nothing but his healing lash marks and the film script to keep him company – save for the one day he'd been paraded around like a tailor's dummy to stand in various poses under various lights so Christopher could plan the scenes. And where was Olanthé these last few days? For months now he'd been her toy, her ornament, her slave, and now and again her lucky partner in the most exquisite sexual adventures – then, suddenly, nothing.

Probably because that bloody English Lord was here. God only knew what her relationship with him was; with sex studs galore about the place, there was no way it was a sexual relationship. He couldn't imagine the cold-eyed git ever even having sex; there was not enough hot blood in his body to get a bloody erection.

And was this whole film thing going to turn out to be the biggest farce of his life? Was he really going to be in this film, get his face on screens all over the world? If Olanthé was right, he could be seen as the most exquisite male ever to grace the screen. Or he could be a laughing stock, a stud. He cringed at the thought of Christopher's power over his future. Even *she* didn't command people like Christopher Merrill, for God's sake.

Something stirred in his belly at the thought of having actually seen this icon of the film industry in the flesh, so to speak, and as he registered irritation, he knew it was also tinged with varying degrees of hope, excitement, and absolute devastation. To be so close, yet to be denied the chance to sell himself, and to be seen by such a man as nothing more than a sex stud, was a joke at his expense. Black humour filled him, but also a new level of determination.

Olanthé be damned. When he left here, he would live this down, whatever it took. He would have to do it the hard way, take the bit parts, take the crap jobs, lick some arses if he had to. But he would make it, one way or another, and on his own. As determination fired a more realistic approach to attaining his dreams, the door opened on the object of his indignation; but she looked different. He assessed her, blinking, trying to work out what had changed.

Her eyes were ringed with kohl, and her hair fell in a dark waterfall from a loose knot upon her head, emphasising the slender curve of her neck. She was dressed in a way he had never seen her before – sultry, yes, but *available*; more reminiscent of Western perception of a harem houri than the more powerful reality. Her belly was bare and a jewel glittered at her navel. A pair of flowing sateen trousers sat on her hips, drawn into cuffs over a pair of curl-toed sandals, her arms were wreathed in a tangle of snakelike bangles, and a tiny cropped top laced at the seams covered all but the hint of a cleavage. What was also different was that she trailed an older male slave on a lead affixed to a collar about his neck.

The only other thing the slave wore, save jewellery, was a brightly coloured silk hood. Eugene's eyes narrowed. From the fish-pale colour of the man's skin, he had not been here long.

'Jealous, my Narcissus?'

'Should I be, my Lady?'

'Oh, no,' she purred. 'The film crew have gone, and I had a splendid idea.'

A sense of foreboding filled Eugene's breast. That bright, excited gleam in her eye usually meant she was going to enjoy herself and he was not, and he was still healing from her last efforts. Except, he conceded, she somehow managed to make him discover enjoyment in just about anything she did to him.

Even as he was bracing himself for whatever was to come, there was the clanking sound of steel-shod feet marching through the hallways, and Olanthé stepped back in surprise as four burly men in the flowing robes of ancient Saracens stepped into the room. Their white turbans were topped with glittering spikes and at their sides hung huge, curved scimitars, the hilts of which were studded with precious stones. It was instantly obvious that they were soldiers of some kind, and he also gathered, from the hard set of their faces and the narrow slits of almost black eyes, that they meant business. One of the men bowed low to Olanthé.

'I beg your pardon, Lady. The Lord has said this slave must be taken to the dungeons.'

'But he's mine! I won't –'

She tried to move, but the man blocked her way deferentially with the size of his body alone, hands stretched placatingly, while two of the soldiers grasped Eugene firmly around his upper arms with rather more authority. Even without his present manacles he was no match for one of these men, let alone four, but he would have given a lot to have his hands free at that moment. 'Olanthé, what's going on? Let me go, damn it!'

She didn't glance his way, but he recognised the glitter of anger in her eyes as she tried to outstare the guard. 'How dare you touch me! Get away from me!'

'My Lady, I'm sorry. The Lord won't brook your defiance in this matter. He said he has been tolerant but things with this slave have gone far enough – too far.'

She frowned. 'Too far? What does my Lord intend?'

'Be calm, Lady. He is not to be killed. My Lord knows you desire to keep this slave, so for your own protection he is to be emasculated so that you may keep him in your chambers.'

Her anger, never far from the surface, erupted. 'What? No! He can't do that!'

Eugene, in the process of being dragged from the room, dug his heels into the floor in panic, but he was no match for the muscles sported by the terrifyingly large Saracens. 'Olanthé!' he yelled in consternation as he slid past, but her response gave him no satisfaction.

'Don't worry, Narcissus. I'll sort it out before it goes too far.'

'My Lady, my Lord left with the sunrise.'

'The coward!' she snapped.

The image of Olanthé's face, slack with disbelief, lingered in Eugene's mind as he found himself manhandled down a narrow set of stone steps into long, dark corridors he had never seen before. 'Tell me this is just another one of her tricks,' he panted, struggling, but his frantic optimism was answered by utter silence.

Shit, was that bastard Englishman really going to have his balls cut off? The thought of the cold Englishman seeped in jealousy was a new image, one that made the acid taste of bile rise in his throat, because it was all too believable. An iron door was opened with a vast key, and clanged shut with a dull thud behind him. The corridor he was now dragged through had never been brought into the new century. Its darkness was broken by flickering torches of what looked like oiled or waxed fabric, and the walls were made from vast stones that had been chiselled and laid so precisely that mortar had not been necessary. The corridor opened into a wide chamber filled with an assortment of weird metal contraptions sporting restraints, spikes and wheels. There were also metal cages hanging from the ceiling by pulleys, and manacles dripping from virtually every wall. To one side a row of ancient wooden doors with tiny grilled windows marched along, stoutly bolted and barred from the outside, and the wall opposite was nearly filled by a huge, spoked wooden wheel. Everything was draped in flickering light and shadow from the torches, making it far more terrifying.

The whole vivid nightmare culminated in the black-masked man who stood silently at the far side. Eugene realised he had never seen such a large man in all his life, but that was not the most terrifying part about it. The scariest part was the black-toothed smile of anticipation that slowly dawned below the leather mask and the way he snapped a pair of large iron shears up to Eugene's face to give him a good view of the lethal cutting edges.

'Oh, Christ. Tell me this is a charade,' he begged, feeling his legs turn to jelly.

'Where do you want him, Aaron?' one of his captors asked.

The man considered for a moment. 'Put him on the wheel. Make sure you spread him nice and wide. Is it just the balls, or the whole works?'

'All, I think. I'd better check before you do it, I suppose.'

'And mind you don't bleed him to death like you did one of the others,' one of the soldiers said. 'You have to admit he's pretty enough to serve my Lady's needs for a few years.'

'Just as long as he doesn't have the tools to pleasure my Lady, eh?'

They all laughed heartily.

Eugene was dragged, cursing and nearly crying, to the large wheel. In spite of his desperate struggles his hands were freed from the dainty shackles he was already wearing and he was hoisted up and clamped tightly against the spokes of the wheel by larger, more substantial shackles that hung on chains from the wheel's rim. A thick belt of leather was tightened around his middle, then his legs were spread wide, as the giant had ordered, and tightened until he was fixed immovably, his limbs echoing the shape of the spokes.

They stepped back and surveyed their handiwork, then Aaron stepped forward and spun the wheel a half turn. Eugene gave a startled, panicked cry as he spun upside down. Fingers prodded his well and truly exposed balls.

'No! You can't do this,' he gasped, instantly light-headed. 'She promised I wouldn't be damaged. She promised. This isn't happening. It's all part of her games. I know it is. It's got to be.'

'S'pose I'd better tie them off to stop the blood,' Aaron commented thoughtfully. He took a piece of soft shoelace leather out of a bucket of water and, ignoring Eugene's increasingly feeble exclamations of horror, wrapped it around the soft flesh and tied it off. He then rotated his captive into an upright position and tapped his arm playfully.

Black spots danced behind Eugene's eyes for a moment, then his vision cleared.

'The leather shrinks as it dries,' Aaron the torturer said informatively. 'Once the blood stops, the balls turn black, but it's not as painful as it looks, and it's much safer this way. Better find out if he wants that removed too.' He flicked Eugene's cock and turned away, incongruously glancing at a watch on his wrist. 'Hey, it's time for lunch. Wonder what we've got today.'

They began to chatter in another language as they walked away, then the large man turned back and winked once. 'Don't go away. We can have some fun while we're waiting for the leather to shrink. Pain doesn't always have to leave marks on the body, you know.'

Left on his own, Eugene lapsed into stunned silence. He glanced up at the stout iron chains and thick leather shackles that buckled his wrists and began to pull and twist, knowing that these shackles had been designed to hold a man whatever was being done to him, and they were not going to break just because he willed it.

He whimpered slightly and thought about the leather binding around his balls. The more he tried not to, the more he thought about it. All he could feel was a dull ache, but he knew the leather was drying, slowly and inexorably tightening, cutting off the blood supply.

Then, in the half-light before him, a shadow seemed to move.

A man stepped forward, but how he came to be there, Eugene had no idea. There was no door nor alcove that Eugene recalled, and the man had most certainly not been there a moment ago. It was as if he had appeared by magic. He was strangely dressed, almost in a male version of what Olanthé had been wearing, save that his chest was bare. Rings of gold hung from his nipples, gold dripped from his hands and neck, and his head was wrapped in a turban similar to that of the Saracen soldiers. His skin seemed to have a faintly golden sheen, yet there was something about the cold eyes that was familiar . . .

'Lord Brandon!' he gasped.

He gave a chilling smile. 'I am also known by that name. Tell me, did you enjoy my Lady's favours?'

Eugene groaned and closed his eyes briefly. Jealousy personified. He was to be emasculated because of jealousy? This was not real. 'I haven't had any choice in anything I've done since I came to this accursed place. You know that. I curse the day I ever saw that wretched advert. She told me nothing was for nothing. I should have believed her.'

Bran stepped forward; he had to look up to meet his captive's eyes. 'You're just a pawn in her games, I know. It's not your fault.'

'So why –'

'It's a matter of honour. An Eastern man would realise, but you'll probably never understand. A debt has to be paid; a crime has been committed against me, and some-one has to pay the penalty.'

'But it wasn't my fault!' he howled.

'I can't harm my Lady. You must see that.'

Eugene yanked angrily against his bonds. 'I don't see that at all! I promised to do whatever Olanthé told me to do for one year, and I was doing that. Why do you blame me?'

'But I don't blame you,' Bran said. 'Not at all. I'm just punishing you for what's passed between you.'

'That's not fair!'

'It doesn't have to be fair – it just makes me feel better.'

'It makes you feel better? What about me?'

Eugene's voice rose to the point of shrieking, but the other man seemed to shrink back into the wall and disappear. His angry yell petered into a whimper. 'Where the fuck have you gone? What's going on? Don't leave me here like this, you bastard. Not like this. Who the hell are you anyway?'

Eugene was left on his own in the semi-darkness long enough for his stretched muscles to complain, and for his arms to go numb, but the anticipated constriction of his balls didn't happen. In the flickering darkness, understanding dawned very, very gradually.

'Olanthé, you bitch,' he whispered to himself. 'You *are* playing games. You said you wouldn't harm me. I'm not harmed. You've scared me, but I'm not harmed. I'm not.'

He waited in the flickering darkness until she appeared. He knew she would.

'Ariaz,' he said softly.

'Ah, my slave,' she purred. 'Are you enjoying your role? I tried hard to make it authentic for you.'

'Yes, Lady,' he lied.

His attention sharpened to the small pair of scissors that were advancing on his balls. He tensed his muscles, but she slid them beneath the leather and snipped, saying softly, 'And Ariaz took the Greek soldier from her Lord's dungeon, and into her chambers to be her slave of love. And there he remained, chained to the goddess's whim, unable to flee, for the moment he left the safety of her chambers his true age would descend upon him.'

She slipped him from his bonds and he sank to the floor, stifling a groan of pain as the strain went from his arms. It was there he noticed the slave that Olanthé still had in tow. His hands were tied behind his back, probably to stop him from playing with the erection that was straining madly in the flickering light of the dungeon. Hmm, Eugene thought, new slave, not used to seeing people being bound, whipped, tortured. He'd get used to it. Probably.

If one ever got used to it.

'Come,' Olanthé said in a stage whisper. 'We must go before my Lord discovers us here.'

He forced himself to his knees, then to his feet, again stifling a groan. Why was he the only one to end up bloody hurting in this charade? And why were they doing it? Or didn't Olanthé – bless her – trust him to bloody act the part?

Olanthé smiled, knowing her slave was hovering between relief and anger, but she did not regret what she had done. He had become complacent, and somewhat less than grateful for her attentions, when she had been working so hard on his behalf. It served him right for doubting her.

There was a one-way mirror in the dungeon, behind the barred window of one of the doors, disguised by the flickering lights, and it was from here she had watched her brethren bind Narcissus to the wheel and leave him as they had been ordered. She had pleasured herself on his fear, his knowledge of what was to come, and had watched with amusement as Christopher grew the most enormous hard-on he had probably ever had. People needed excitement, she mused. Why did they deny themselves these little pleasures?

She had rubbed herself to orgasm while Christopher stood beside her, unable to accord himself the same relief, his interest flickering between the terrified man bound on the wheel in the torture chamber and the extraordinary sight of a woman touching herself in front of him without the least hint of embarrassment, in absolute dedication to her own needs. It was a sight that would stay with him for a long time. There had been no excessive writhing or groaning, just a stiffening of the spine, a shortening of the breath into small gasps, and that inexplicable way her eyes seemed at one point to be looking into her own soul. Why he thought that, he did not know, but it had been so. It had been at that moment he knew she had been right. All of the orgasms of all the different women he had ever been with had been faked.

He loathed her for giving him that knowledge. He now trotted along beside her on his lead, following the tight, naked butt of the slave Narcissus with his meshwork of fading lash marks, and wondered whether the guy had really thought he was going to have his balls cut off or whether he was simply a really good actor. One thing was sure – Christopher had believed he believed it, and the excitement had triggered an erection which, even now, refused to diminish.

They entered a room as large as a hall, and Olanthé looked around, pleased. It was lined with mirrors, shot with subtle lighting, and curtained throughout with gossamer fabrics, which draped and curved, giving the room a greater sense of mystery and depth. The centrepiece was a single tall, carved pillar from which strands of coloured fabrics were strung like exotic bunting. Behind the shimmering organdie jewels glittered, and everywhere the floor was piled with cushions. She spread her arms and spun around with the simplicity of a child, laughing. Everywhere she turned there were replications upon replications of herself and her two slaves in diminishing clarity.

Then several of her male brethren entered, led by Ali, bringing steaming bowls of scented water strewn with petals.

'Wash them,' she said, indicating both her slaves.

She draped herself on a pile of cushions and watched the process. The two men were both naked, but scarcely comparable. Christopher spread his legs as ordered and allowed himself to be washed, but she could see a dull stain of embarrassment flush down his neck at the experience, and his erection seemed to shrivel up inside his body. She had chosen to use men for this ritual cleansing out of a perverse sense of humour, knowing he would be uncomfortable with the process.

She turned her gaze to Narcissus. He stood, arms outstretched, and his eyes never left hers while he was being washed. In society Christopher might reign supreme, but here Ariaz's unknown Greek soldier was godlike in his perfection; the personification of erotic beauty. His broad shoulders and narrow waist were even more trimmed and honed than when he arrived. His dark golden hair softly curled to his shoulders, but there was nothing effeminate about him at all. His glorious, sultry mouth and perfectly shaped cheekbones were carved into a look of almost supercilious disdain for the process, and the proof of his last whipping still ornamenting his body made a real man out of him. She drew in a long shuddering breath, thinking he would surely even have roused a hot-blooded heterosexual man's desire.

When they had been cleaned and dried with scented powders, her brethren left silently. She crooked her finger at the Greek. 'Come, slave, and pleasure me.'

'My Lady's pleasure is my greatest desire.'

He knelt gracefully, subserviently beside her, then waited, eyes lowered. She was pleased by the sensual tone of his voice, the absolute wish to serve, yet a slightly petulant expression entered her voice because she realised he was now truly acting. 'I'm tired and hot. I wish to sleep. Remove my clothes. Smooth my skin with oils while I rest.'

He reached up and took the pins from her hair, allowing its luxurious length to pile around her coffee-coloured skin, then spread it neatly like a halo around her. She lay, watching him from beneath heavy lids, not moving, but the sensation of his hands on her hair reached deep into the core of her. She caught the faintest drift of a smile on his lips; he knew what he was doing, damn him. Then his hands slid to her bodice and gently pulled at the strings that held it together. He parted the fabric from her bosom, slid it aside, lifting her body slightly with one hand in the small of her back to enable him to remove it totally. He was so strong, her Narcissus, yet with such sensitive hands.

A shudder of desire rippled across her bared skin and her nipples tightened and lifted visibly. He reached behind him, damped his hands in the oil, rubbed them together, lifted her own long brown hand in his light golden one, and began to smooth her, gently, as one would a child. His fingers separated hers, touching every single millimetre of her hand before working his way slowly and surely towards the elbow, the shoulder. She sighed, revelling in the light touch, knowing he was repaying her with the knowledge she had given him. Subtlety, and the long drawn-out breath of anticipation.

Her eyes closed.

When he had completed one arm he rose, carefully, so as not to disturb the cushions she rested on, not to break her mood, and began to circle her other arm. She drifted into a higher state, somewhere this side of sleep, and delighted in the sensuous touch, so soft it seemed to reach inside her, touching her very soul within. His hands glided along her cheekbones and his thumbs rasped along the carved line of her lips, causing her to gasp at the electric touch. Then they slid down the long length of her neck, getting stronger as he reached the larger muscles of her shoulders and torso, easing the tension he found there. Yet still he was gentle.

Time seemed to stand still.

Once again he moved, sideways this time, and removed her golden slippers, one by one, almost reverently bending down to kiss her feet. She felt the touch of his lips upon her, sensed the heat in them, and knew he was rampantly aroused by his own actions. He reached up, slipped the cord of her sateen trousers and gently, oh so gently, slipped them over her hips, down the length of her legs, over her feet, hardly disturbing her. She writhed softly as the action stoked her desire and she felt an overwhelming pull to have him ride inside her body. She imagined the feel of him thrusting slowly, surely, into the space between her legs, overpowering her with his strength, his maleness, holding her there for his pleasure.

Yet still he simply smoothed her skin, from the sensitive soles of her feet, easing every tight muscle, working his way up her legs so slowly it was torture to her raw needs. And still he had not even laid hands upon her torso. Her breasts cried out for his touch and dampness seeped between her legs. Almost of their own volition her legs parted invitingly, yet though he moved between them, holding her thighs apart with his own, he reached up and began to smooth her belly, his large hands pressing along the flat middle, gently sliding over the swell of her hips, her buttocks, and back again.

Olanthé was now fired with need. In the silence of her mind she was willing him to touch her breasts, to touch the core of her sex. Her eyes opened the merest slit, but he noticed, and the sultry glance washed over her in a wave of expectancy. Her hands grasped and opened on the air around her. She bit her lip to stop herself from commanding, begging. He saw her need, and it was echoed in his own eyes.

It was now he put his hands on the cushions either side of her, and bent his face down to hers, so slowly that she held her breath. He tasted her lips softly, and ran his tongue over the shape of them, finding the line of her teeth; but he did not force himself into her even though she was ready, waiting, wanting. Instead he nibbled at her neck, under her chin, and worked his way down until he found one dark nipple and brought it into his mouth. And still he was gentle. She moaned, caught herself, and was silent again. He began to suck harder.

Now she could not contain the need; she could no longer pretend the coolness she was trying to maintain. She lifted her hips towards his, inviting, thrusting. His eyes seemed to smile at her as he ignored her demands, moved over to her other nipple, and began to savour that in the same way.

She slashed a hand at him, grazing his face.

'Now, damn you,' she whispered. 'Fuck me now.'

He caught her hand too late, but forestalled further damage by containing her wrists in his own hands, while continuing to take his time, feeding upon her body. Olanthé gasped at the flood of warmth that filled her at the instant he took control away from her.

Now she could feel the strength of his body holding her still for his pleasure, and she savoured it. It was her strength, her pleasure. He lowered himself slightly; she could feel the warmth of him teasing strongly at the entrance to her body. He rubbed the ball of his piercing along her clit, over the mound and back, until she whimpered and growled, drowning in the need for fulfilment but not able to reach it. She thrust herself at him, but he backed off, retaining control until her struggles ceased. Now she simply lay and stared at him.

It was now, and only now, that he lowered himself slowly, surely, into the clutching cavity of her body. She drew breath and sucked him in, every glorious milimetre, as tight as he would go. Then he began to move, his cock abrading her aching cunt with every stroke. At first he moved slowly, to pleasure himself or her, she was not sure, but there came a time when a new look stole the humanity from his face, when his own gaze became introspective, and when he began to pump into her with great heaving thrusts until she felt the heat of his come bursting inside her body. But, though Olanthé had shared the culmination of his enjoyment, he was aware she had not come herself. He eased himself from her and began to suck her breast and rub the swollen nub between her legs until her body arched backward, and she stilled his hand with her own, pressing it down upon her clit. She was so horny it was almost painful, and it took her only moments to achieve the ultimate satisfaction of a cunt-pulsing climax.

She sighed, pushed Narcissus aside with a purr of contentment, then looked over to where Christopher still stood where he had been left. He was tense and vicariously excited by what he had just witnessed; an impressive hard-on had exploded at his groin and was throbbing redly between his legs. His hips were moving slightly, and she guessed his hands were probably working too, and she knew he wanted nothing more than to kneel down and sink himself into her already lubricated pussy.

She rolled over, stood up, sublimely uncaring of her nakedness, and clapped her hands once, summoning service, not stopping even as her brethren filed in: 'And so the plot progresses. To the Greek soldier whom I freed from my Lord's dungeon I gave the gift of everlasting life, yet now he tires of that life with me. And so now I, Ariaz, curse him. I curse this slave for wanting to leave me. I curse him for his beauty. I curse him in that if he should speak another word for the rest of his whole life he shall become his proper age, and die. And so, in my anger, will I chastise him to force him to speak his last words, to beg me to stop, to beg for forgiveness. Ali, place Narcissus on the rack. I'll come to him when I'm ready.'

And, taking Christopher by his lead, she led him out.

She had made him watch her have sex with Narcissus, not because it gave her any particular personal satisfaction but because it pleased her to violate his predetermined concepts of acceptability. He might have watched porno films, and he had certainly fucked a good number of desperately hopeful young women, but she was prepared to bet he had never stood and watched a real scene of exquisite arousal followed by rampant sex in his whole life. She had seen his face. He had been shocked and excited by his enforced voyeurism. Maybe in the process he had incidentally learnt something of the art of pleasing a woman; for Narcissus had most certainly pleased her. Not least because he had subjected her to the animal lusts of his fine body, and satisfied the animal needs of her own, but also because that had been the culmination of the experience, rather than the whole of it.

'Well, my dear director, time to go home.'

His eyes shot to hers. 'But – the dungeon scene?'

'That, my would-be voyeur, is best left to your imagination. But tell me, does not my Narcissus have a certain – presence?'

Christopher shuddered. 'Christ, yes. He didn't give a toss that I was watching, and by God, I wish I had that scene on film. If he can be that dedicated, he'll probably make it on to the big screen on his own. What's he doing here anyway?'

'Learning. That, Christopher my love, is what I do. I take people who have not yet realised their potential and strip them down to their bare skin, their basest instincts, their animal ancestry, even their bare souls. Then I build them again from the bare bones upward. Believe me, my pupils leave here with more than they came with.'

'I believe you,' he said fervently.

She brought him to the door of his chamber, where Timi waited.

'Shower and dress. The helicopter will be here in an hour. I will see you back here to film the seduction scene with Narcissus in one month. It will be a beautiful scene, filled with emotion, with scarcely a sexual body part in sight.'

He hesitated at her unspoken threat, then wet his lips as Ali released his wrists.

She gave him her most seductive smile and her voice dropped to a suggestive whisper. 'If you dream it, Christopher, I will do it. I promise. When Eugene's name is at the head of the credits of your next blockbuster I will come to you. For one day and one night I will be your dream-woman, your whore, and service your basest animal needs.'

He grimaced at himself, probably for wanting her so badly, for feeling so frustrated. 'What makes you think you're a prize worthy of such risk?'

'I dare you to find out.'

Michael had been divested of his clothes and was wearing the body-hugging chains of a murderer in transit: his wrists were attached to a chain around his middle, and from that another went down to ankle cuffs separated by no more than six inches.

'Those things will kill you,' he commented.

Bran was by the pool when they brought Michael to him. He was sitting in a small patch of shade, eyes narrowed against the sun, and was inhaling pleasurably from one of his favourite brands of cigarettes. He glanced sideways through the slit of his narrowed lids. 'You told me yourself that we take educated risks. That's mine. The only sure thing in life is that one day we die.' He tapped the ash carefully into an ashtray. 'I've put three million pounds at the disposal of IVA under your name. I trust that meets with your present criteria?'

'A million a month? I suppose that's reasonable payment for my present co-operation. Very well. It will suffice. Can I now dispense with these?' He indicated his chains.

'Insurance. You'll find it more difficult to leave this place with those on. You've already proved your word is worthless.'

Michael flushed. 'A man's word is his bond, eh?'

'Something like that. Besides, that word was extracted under duress. People like to save their own skins from torture, save their own lives, that I can understand. But your previous word – your bond not to talk about this place – was not extracted under any kind of duress. You knew the terms. You agreed to them when you came here.'

'So a decision can't be altered to save other lives, only your own?'

'Not at my expense, damn you.'

'You can afford it.'

Michael seated himself by the pool and dangled his legs in the warm water. Bran found himself irritated by the youth's confidence, his overwhelming belief that this would all end up happily ever after; that he wouldn't end up in a shallow grave out in the desert somewhere, providing a feast for the vigilant scavengers. What was it about the young that they thought bad things only happened to others? Had he been like that? He did not think so. Bad things had been his birthright, and he had chosen to leave them behind.

'That's not the point. You wanted to become a politician. We gave you the chance, and you've thrown it back in our faces.'

'It's very much the point. I wanted to be a politician because I thought I could change something that way. When I came here, that was my goal. Then, when I saw what was going on around me, I realised that I could make even more difference. My goal hasn't changed, just the way I wish to achieve it. That's all.'

'That's all.' Bran gave a snort. 'Don't you realise that where money is concerned that is never all? Money commands life, but it can also command death. How could you put yourself in this stupid position?'

'Because I trust you to do the right thing. I believe you're a good person.'

'Your naivety stuns me.' The sound of a helicopter hovered on the hot air. He stubbed out his cigarette, gave a wry grimace and stood up. 'Guards!'

Michael was instantly surrounded by a small phalanx of Bran's personal security team who had been waiting nearby.

'Put him in the far dungeon. I don't want him talking to anyone.'

'For three months? Bran, no –'

'And gag him. Now. I want him unable to communicate with anyone other than me,' he said, his cold eyes meeting Michael's bitter glance without flinching. The guards obeyed, lacing Michael into a leather mask despite his angry protests, but Bran knew Olanthé was right. The brethren knew Michael was not here of his own free will and would not tolerate the situation for long. That wasn't what this citadel, this oasis from civilisation, was all about. It needed to be resolved, and soon, not in three months' time. Michael had achieved more than he knew. He had single-handedly turned this co-operative utopia into a dictatorship.

16

Eugene felt the euphoria of sex drain away from his body as he lay stretched in place on the rack in the semi-darkness of the dungeon. The torturer, Aaron, had turned out to be no more than one of the brethren, after all, and no longer had the ability to instil terror, but he had taken his responsibility seriously, testing and tightening every bond thoroughly before leaving the prisoner alone to Olanthé's tender ministrations.

This was obviously Aaron's domain.

As he waited, he rested his face against the cool stone, knowing that she was going to beat from him any pleasure he had unexpectedly discovered in having what amounted to almost normal sex with her. Almost normal, because someone had been standing there watching, which seemed odd in hindsight. Someone who had been given a raging hard-on by watching. He had never exactly forgotten about his audience, but had been so engrossed in what he was doing, the fact had diminished in importance. Yet now, in the cold aftermath, he wondered why. Everything that had happened to him to date had been either alone with Olanthé or before the whole gathering of her brethren.

Yet this man had been different – an outsider, a voyeur. He couldn't quite pinpoint it, but he sensed that the *Curse of Ariaz* scenes had been played out for the man in the hood – or were still being played, for he realised the worst was yet to come, from his point of view, of course. He even thought he knew who might be inside that hood, but he told himself not to be such a fool; it was neither possible nor was it, in fact, desirable. God only knew, he did not want anyone as well known as Christopher to have watched him having sex; but then, he reasoned, in the unlikely event that it was Christopher Merrill under that hood, the man was most certainly not going to admit to it any more than Eugene was going to admit to where he had been and what he had been doing for this last year – should anyone ask he would most certainly lie.

The door behind him clanged open and he tensed, thinking, here we go again.

He raised his head, but to his surprise a young man was hustled past, resisting all the way, virtually being carried by the same four men who had earlier been dressed as Saracens. They were now dressed in something that looked more like conventional desert army battle-dress with berets.

One of them glanced at Eugene and his eyes widened. 'What the hell's he doing down here? Brandon didn't mention him.'

'Shit, that'll put the cat among the pigeons.'

Eugene's eyes narrowed. He assumed they were more truly security guards than anything else, even though they had been roped in to play Olanthé's charade earlier, and from the muffled angry sounds that continued to come from the cell after they retreated, he was convinced that the prisoner was truly that. Quite why he thought that, he was not sure.

He tried to persuade himself he was wrong – his own panic earlier today would have led anyone else to suppose he was about to be tortured and killed – yet he could not convince himself. There was something disquieting about the silent desperation of the man's struggles.

* * *

Olanthé was in as near a state of panic as she had ever been. Her desert boat had been well and truly rocked, and she was not sure yet whether it was actually going to sink. And of all of them, it had to be Michael who had caused it. At that moment she hated him. She stood on the topmost corner of her citadel and gazed out over the turbulent storm-tossed waves of the desert, uncrossable to most, but a haven for those who had discovered it. Never, until now, a prison. From here the citadel appeared only as a wide swathe of flat roofs, all coloured like the sand. From far above, with the shimmering waves of heat, it was virtually invisible, and anyone in an aeroplane who thought they might have seen something far below would normally shake their heads and smile at their own foolishness, and know it for a mirage.

It was silent and still, the waves of sand gleaming and rippling innocently into the far distance on all points of the compass. Not so when the wind blew, whipping the sand into lethal projectiles, filling the air so thick with sand that unprotected mouths and noses would be filled and unprotected skin flailed from the bones. A harsh landscape, yet she loved it. She was a person out of time. She did not belong in civilisation as Bran did; ironically, for her, all civilisation afforded was the money to shield her from it.

Michael knew how much she valued the privacy, the secrecy of her desert stronghold; he must also have guessed that Bran would kill to keep it alive for her. So why would he risk his freedom, his life, for people he did not even know? It was bizarre.

Although he was silent, she sensed Bran behind her; he had his own particular smell of aftershave and cigarette smoke. She turned.

'We have to tell them,' he said.

She gave a wry smile. 'Mutiny in the ranks?'

'Not yet, but it will happen. Michael won't have to escape; the brethren will free him.'

'Bran, how rich are we?'

He reached for his cigarette case, tapped it a few times with a single finger, then placed it back in his pocket unopened. 'I don't know. Once it started it just escalated somehow. Even I don't know the full extent of our wealth.'

'If you don't know, who does?'

'No one. I dislike accountants and I've got no intention of paying anyone any tax.' He gave her a brief childlike grin. 'But I've got a room full of bits of paper if you want to start counting.'

'Then would it be so bad to let him have some of it?'

'Probably not, but it's blackmail. Once it starts, where does it end?'

'I think the ending started the day Michael arrived here. We just didn't recognise it.'

Michael was cursing himself for his stupidity. He squinted sideways through the bars of the cell and could just make out the man lying strapped to the rack. He had a fine body, Michael realised; he had taken that much in as he was dragged past. He had seen startled comprehension dawn in the green eyes, followed by a consternation that hardened the chiselled perfection of his model face.

Her latest project was not as stupid as he had at first assumed.

What was he destined to become out in the real world? How much money would he generate to fill Lord Brandon's bottomless coffers? One thing was for sure, you couldn't pre-guess from seeing people in here.

He did not see her arrive, but knew she was there. She had her own particular presence that filled the senses. He knew, only too well, how a man could drown in her, lose his identity, his sense of self. Once he had left the citadel his course of action had seemed so obvious: she was just a woman, as Bran was just a man. They were greedy, selfish, and deserved to have the financial rug pulled from beneath their feet.

But Bran was right – he had been naive. Why had it not occurred to him that Bran had not become rich by caring about an individual's freedom or life? He was no one's fool, and he was not about to be blackmailed. Comprehension came to him too late, bound hand and foot in the back of the helicopter, but it wasn't until he stood in the darkness of the cell that the dire straits of his situation truly dawned on him.

He realised he was going to die.

He only had to see Olanthé to recall she wasn't human. How could he have been so mistaken? She was like something out of legend; the epitome of a man's most secret dream, a siren, a whore, the original temptress. He tried to reach his hands up to the mask to remove it, to spit out the infernal gag, talk to her: to ask her to consider his motives, or just to beg her for his life, maybe? He did not really know.

He doubted that Olanthé and Lord Brandon would listen to him. He sank on to the small pallet, knowing he was truly at their mercy. They would talk about him, choose whether he lived or died; and he had the grim feeling he knew the answer. He would disappear from the world having helped no one at all.

Then he heard the first heavy stroke slap on to bare flesh, followed by a harsh indrawn breath. He was human enough to go once again to the grill to watch. Not to be a voyeur but because the sound brought memories flooding from his own psyche, bringing their own brand of frustration. He recalled the strangely erotic confusion of pain and pleasure that she had awakened in him, and amusement lightened his dark mood. He was, after all, still alive enough to recall those pleasures.

But as Olanthé struck the bound man again, Michael realised her mood was bleak. He also realised in some indefinable way that he was the cause, and that the man lying unable to defend himself was simply the object on which she was venting her spleen. And by God, she had plenty of spleen to vent, he recalled. She also had a heavy hand. She lashed out three more times before the man cried out, and in the flickering darkness he caught the glint of tears in her eyes. Don't do it, he willed her. Keep control. You always kept control. But as she kept lashing out in fury at the bound man, Michael could think of no other way to get her attention than to throw himself at the unbreakable door, again and again.

Olanthé was lying on her bed when the security guards brought Michael in to her. He looked as though he had been given a truly bad beating; his body was adorned with slowly ripening bruises, the sight of which made her wince. He stared at her through the holes in the leather mask, and she felt as though his gaze stripped her, laid her innermost feelings bare to him.

She did not like that.

'He's going to be a film star,' she said, then added angrily, 'you don't need to look at me that way. It's your fault. If you hadn't made me cross, I wouldn't have hurt him. I hadn't meant to do that. And you wouldn't be hurt either. Why did you do that to save someone else's skin? Someone you don't know. I don't understand you.'

He gave an expansive shrug, as if to say what he was like did not matter; they were going to kill him anyway. She stood up and paced; his eyes followed her. Finally she stopped before him.

'We're going to send you home.'

Michael closed his eyes briefly. She could see relief flood his body. He had really believed they were capable of disposing of him. She dismissed the guards, and when they glanced at each other, she sighed. 'It's Lord Brandon's decision.'

When they were gone, Michael growled and yanked angrily at his chains. She reached up and unbuckled the mask. He stretched his mouth about, trying to relieve the dryness. She picked up a glass of water and fed it to him. His eyes never left hers.

'We're not monsters, Bran and myself. We're just different. Your first instinct was right. We don't want the world to intrude on us, but we don't want to have to kill people to keep it out. So it's up to you now. You hold our lives in your hands because we won't succumb to blackmail. If you tell people where this place is I'll send everyone home, raze it to the ground and walk out into the desert.'

'You'd risk that?'

She shrugged. 'I'd have nowhere to go. I'm fully aware that I'm an anachronism in the modern world. And if you tell anyone how much money we have accumulated, Bran will destroy all of it. He will turn it into paper and burn it.'

'That's blackmail too.'

'Yes. You see, with blackmail no one wins.'

'So I see.' He grimaced. 'I've told Bran I wouldn't try to escape for three months. Will you take the chains off now?'

'No. It pleases me to see you naked, and in chains.'

'I'm not your slave now.'

She shrugged. 'Quite what you are, apart from a pain in the arse, I don't know. But I promised Bran I wouldn't take them off, and his word is my law.'

One brow lifted. 'Bran also said I wasn't to talk to anyone.'

She glared at him. 'I'd be happy to put the mask back. No? Very well. If you speak to anyone about your intentions, in the citadel or outside, we're finished. So it's up to you now.'

'So when do I leave?'

'In three months. When this project is completed. If it is to be the last one, I would at least like to see a level of success before you pull the plug. Narcissus has been a slave to his own driving need for success for many years now – as you were. It would be a shame if it had been in vain.'

'It doesn't have to be that way.'

'Yes, Michael, it does. Now, lie down.'

'Why, so you can beat me?'

She gave a slow smile. 'It would be no more than you deserve. I want to put something on those bruises of yours. Just do as you're told without arguing, please?'

His brow rose. 'Please?'

She scowled, and he added, 'OK, OK, I won't tell anyone you said that. I promise.'

Olanthé released the chain around his middle, allowing him to stretch out on the bed with his hands under his thighs, and very, very gently began to dab an ancient remedy on to cotton wool pads and smooth it over the purpling skin. He winced a couple of times where the skin was broken but otherwise said nothing. Olanthé found the gentle action soothing and continued to smooth his skin long after every bruise had been well and truly balmed.

'Turn over.'

Michael would not look at her. She realised he had had no intention of allowing himself to make love to her, but she gave him no choice. She straddled his thighs. Her fingers moved subtly along every inch of his skin, along the closing piercings of his nipples, from which he had removed the rings, down his sides and buttocks. She knew him so well. She closed her eyes, revelled in the familiar contours, allowed the anger and hurt to flow away from her.

Gradually his abused body became pliable, softened beneath her fingers, and hardened again with a different kind of tension. His balls rose and tightened, his cock swelled and he began to move underneath her – slow writhing movements he could no longer control. She slithered up his thighs and felt the heat of his prick touch her bare skin. His eyes snapped open, shadowed with lust.

He tried to lift his arms, to pull her closer, but the web of chains snapped tight against his ankles. He cursed and then rolled them both off the bed, on to their knees, to take her from behind. She loved the way he took control, chains or no chains. His control was as gentle and insistent as Bran's was domineering and harsh. He lifted her skirts and thrust himself into her, hands on her buttocks, then he stilled, gasping with the electric pleasure of entry, before beginning to move in long, slow, pleasurable glides.

Olanthé shuddered and put her hand between her legs, massaging herself in time with his leisurely movements. Every so often Michael forgot about the cuffs, and tried to stretch his arms around her, snapping the chains tight between them as his movement was halted. Olanthé delighted in his semi-captive state. She knew he wanted to touch her breasts, pull her up against him, but even with the cuff about his waist released, the deceptively fine silver links held his chained wrists and ankles together, restricting total freedom.

He cursed, pressed his hands back on to her buttocks and leaned down to nuzzle her back with his mouth before jolting upright again and thrusting himself into rapid movements which culminated in his coming. As his hot seed pumped into her, Olanthé allowed her own orgasm to blossom, and for a long moment they were joined by absolute sexual fulfilment.

'Oh, God,' Michael murmured breathlessly, leaning his weight down on to her. 'I didn't think I was ever going to do that again.'

Olanthé nudged at him. He released her and slid away to sit against the bed, knees drawn up to his chest, his cuffed wrists around them. She stood, stretching happily, and said, somewhat smugly, 'You couldn't help yourself.'

'No,' Michael corrected wryly. 'I meant I didn't think I was *ever* going to do that again. With any woman.'

The present situation flooded back in, breaking the spell. She clapped her hands, and the slave Yasmin entered, staring curiously at Michael.

'Take him to be washed and fed,' Olanthé snapped at the open-mouthed girl. 'And put him back in his cell. He's mine alone to control. Make sure Aaron knows that.'

'But I thought . . . I was told –'

Michael stood up, and turned obediently to allow Olanthé to re-fasten the chain around his middle. 'That I was dragged in here kicking and screaming? That's true, but I'm here because I want to be. Aren't we all?'

He winked at Olanthé, fuelling her irritation as he left, having successfully diffused the slave crisis with a couple of well-chosen sentences.

Olanthé eased herself into the warm pool, drifting in the sun-dappled light that glittered between the broad palm leaves. She wasn't so much washing Michael's scent from her body as allowing the water to caress her, embedding the memories of his touch deep into the storehouse of her mind. There had been so many men, each of them different; some she recalled in full clarity, some were just names, some were totally forgotten, but what would be her purpose in life if this all came to an end? She did not regret Michael for one moment, but she knew also that he would not be able to contain his anger about the money; he was too damned nice for his own good. The issue would rise again once his relief at still being alive had mellowed into complacency.

A shadow fell over her. She looked up, and pleasure lit the back of her dark eyes.

She watched Bran slowly take his clothes off and slip into the water beside her. He had a sunburned V at his neck, but other than that he was as pale as the cold fish she had heard him likened to. But whoever had said that, and she could not recall, did not know him at all. One thing she had learnt from her occasional forays into the outside world was that people rarely saw beyond the persona they were presented with. Employers did not know their employees, husbands did not know their wives, mothers did not know their children; and all were far, far too wrapped up in day-to-day living to even realise they did not know. To her, Bran was not cold. His outward persona was his protection, his armour against a cold world, but she had learnt long ago how to prise the cracks of his armour apart and creep within.

He would say she had been his salvation.

She knew he was hers.

He sat on the shallow ledge and pulled her backward. She lay against him, spreading herself on the water, her dark body in stark contrast to his. The brethren, seeing them there, crept away to leave them in privacy, not understanding at all the dependency between her hot red Eastern temperament and his cold blue English blood. But they did not have to understand. All they had to do was keep her small world running smoothly, and make love whenever they wanted. For that they could share her citadel, eat her food.

She closed her eyes, felt Bran's breath upon her head, and sighed.

'You've been with Michael,' Bran commented without rancour. 'My security guards told me. I hope he was suitably appreciative.'

'Mmm,' she murmured. 'He was.' Then she rolled over and lay on top of Bran in the water, her forearms on his chest, her eyes troubled. 'Should we have killed him?'

Bran grimaced. 'We may yet wish we had.'

Olanthé smiled down at him and smoothed his damp hair back from his forehead. 'No,' she said. 'No, we won't. Michael will work something out. You'll see.'

'That's what I'm afraid of. How's the Greek?'

'Bruised. Sore. Not as sore as he would have been if Michael hadn't interfered. I was cross.'

'So I understand, my sweet Olanthé.'

'You're laughing at me!'

'Would I dare, I wonder?'

Her eyes met the pale reflection of a smile in his. 'When do you leave?'

'Tomorrow. When I return I'll be bringing the film crew. I'll let you know. Keep Michael out of harm's way when we arrive. I don't know if he'll cause trouble, but I'd rather not find out. And don't trust him. His motives are far too altruistic for my liking.'

The sound of an aeroplane hovered on the air, and Olanthé rolled over, narrowing her eyes to watch the faint white line of its disturbance cut the empty sky in two. Bran cradled her breasts in his cupped hands. 'Do you have another project in mind?'

'Possibly,' he said evasively. 'It rather hinges on what happens here.'

'So it comes to this. Our whole future depends not on

our ability to amass a fortune, as we once thought, but on one person's knowledge of that fortune.'

'But he has got a point about the money. I was rather wondering what we should do with it.'

'I thought you wanted to buy your old family estate back?'

'I did that years ago.'

'You didn't tell me.'

'It didn't seem important. Somehow once I owned it, I couldn't see why I wanted to. Just having the money to be able to afford it was what I really wanted, I guess. This place is my ancestral home now. It holds my greatest treasure.'

She laughed, delighted by the compliment. 'Then what should we buy? You said we needed a new helicopter. Can we afford one?'

'We could afford a fleet. Two fleets.'

Olanthé pondered on that revelation. She knew just how many millions a helicopter cost. 'I don't think there's anything I want, Bran. Not really. Do you remember when you found me?'

'How can I forget? It was your eyes I noticed most. Beautiful, mysterious, even though you were like a little stick insect.'

'I was starving. I've been here so long I've forgotten what it was like to be hungry. I had even forgotten there were hungry people out there. Perhaps I should feel guilty, but I don't.'

'Nor I.'

'Then perhaps Michael was sent to be our conscience.'

'Maybe he was sent to be a thorn in my side.'

'Don't make a decision while you're still angry.'

'No. I need to unwind. The past is intruding.'

'Let me help.'

He sighed, stood up, walked out of the water and sat

cross-legged in the shade, his eyes narrowed as the warmth dried him almost instantly. 'Be ready for me in a couple of hours. I have some business calls to make now, while the Western world is still awake.'

Olanthé took her time getting ready for Bran. She relaxed in her room to the sound of Eastern reed instruments and had Ali rub oil all over her body to ease her limbs, then she dressed in the laced black leather dress Bran had brought from the Western world. She put dark kohl around her eyes and shaped them upward at the outer edge, painted the edges of her mobile lips with a dark maroon line, and stepped into some obscenely high-heeled shoes with a strap around the ankle. She looked and felt like a high-class call-girl, exotic and sure of her power over the men in her life.

This was a game they played. It excited Bran like no other, and she knew he carried a photograph of her in his wallet dressed in a similar vein. Did he show it to his colleagues, she wondered, when they got out the pictures of their loved ones? There were times she doubted it; his standing in the outside community was among the elite – that of inherited wealth, impeccable taste and a titled lineage that could be traced back to the Normans. But there was another side to his character, the one that liked to see how far he could go to shock his peers and still have them fawn and agree with everything he said.

Behind his cool exterior she had discovered a wicked sense of humour.

She finally slipped her arms into a pair of long black gloves, placed a long cigarette holder between the fingers of her right hand and minced in small, tight steps into the office where Bran was working.

'Daahling,' she drawled, 'I'm ready to go out.'

His glance left his papers and travelled the length of her body, from the pointed tip of her shoe to the tight, shining knot of hair which crowned her head. 'You slut,' he enunciated coldly in a most upper-class English accent. 'You dare to come to me like that, knowing we're going to my family home?'

'Why not?' she responded, flicking a lighter into life and casually drawing a long puff of the cigarette. 'It would do those cold bastards good to see how a real woman looks. Get a little blood into their lifeless lily-white peckers.'

'Whore!'

She rubbed her finger and thumb together and gave a sly smile. 'If they wanted, I might oblige. For a price, of course.'

He stood up suddenly from behind his desk, knocking papers flying, and she could see the bulge had already formed in the front of his trousers. 'Mmm,' she drawled, rubbing a suggestive hand down one tightly sheathed thigh. 'I can see you like my dress, my sweet.'

'You have no idea how much I like it,' he said. 'But it's not for my family to see. Haven't you learnt anything about what's acceptable and what's not?'

She put on an ingenuous expression. 'How to be a pretentious society wife? Oh, welcome to my home, my dear sister-in-law. That sack you're wearing is absolutely adorable. And that corset! It must take your husband three weeks to get into it, not that he would bother, when you've got a moustache a camel would be proud to own.'

'Bitch!'

'I thought one was supposed to tell the truth to one's relatives? Or one's husband's. And your sister is a fat cow.'

'My sister is a lady.' Bran came around the desk,

snatched the cigarette from her hands and ground it into his ashtray. 'And you, my wife, are about to learn a lesson you won't forget in a hurry.'

'What do you think you can teach me?' she sneered, and turned away.

He snatched her wrist and hauled her back into the room, dragging her unwillingly towards a door to one side of his office. Olanthé felt her blood begin to pulse. Ah, she loved the dominating feel of a man's strength against hers. It sent shivers right through her spine.

'What are you doing?' she gasped, trying hard not betray the lust that sprang damply to her lips.

'You're acting like a mare in heat, so by God, I'm going to treat you like one!'

The room they entered was lined with rough wood, hung with saddles, bridles and various other equestrian tackle. 'The stable? Brandon, daahling, stop it, you're scaring me!'

'I haven't started scaring you yet, my sweet. Get your foot on that rail.'

'I will NOT!'

'I suggest you hold on to the rail.' She squeaked realistically as he pulled her right foot a couple of inches from the floor, hooked her spiked heel over a bar and strapped her ankle with a leather thong to an upright part of the sturdy fencing. She grabbed the bar hastily.

When he grabbed her left ankle and stretched it wide along the bar the leather skirt split up one seam with a loud tearing noise. Her legs were spread wide enough to be almost painful, and excitement was too great now to allow her to carry on with the facile comments. She clung tightly to the top rail as ordered while he strapped her left ankle to another upright. She felt a trickle of liquid slip into her lacy tanga briefs.

He then came around the other side of the railings,

grasped one of her wrists and, pulling her over the rail to hang with her rear pointing skyward, pinioned her wrists to her ankles. There was a long moment when Bran stood there, panting loudly in the silence, then he walked back behind her and very gently began to lift her torn skirt, and rub his hands on the tightly stretched globes of her buttocks.

Able to do nothing to stop him from touching any part of her body he wanted, Olanthé gasped as her helplessness shot an electric jolt of lust between her legs.

'Oh, yes,' he whispered, quivering against her. 'You like that, don't you, my sexy beauty?'

She knew better than to scream in the affirmative, and whimpered, 'No, no, don't hurt me, my Lord. I promise I'll be good. I'll try to be a proper English lady in future, truly I will.'

'Too late for promises,' he said, grinding himself up into the stretched V of her legs. 'Far, far too late.'

She felt the heat of his erection press against her as he ran his hands hard against the outsides of both legs, up the silky length of her stockings, and back down again. His hands shook slightly, then stilled. Bent over the rail as she was, she could see nothing but his legs between her own, but she knew he was bringing to bear all the training of his horrific childhood, controlling his emotions behind an engineered ice-cold façade while living out his most poignant hurt within private, lustful dreams.

What had that wife of his been like that she had left such scars in his mind?

The curious part of her wanted to know what this woman looked like who had beguiled the English Lord with promises while wanting only his money and his title. Was she blonde or dark? Tall or short? All she knew was that Bran's ex-wife had been beautiful and scornful, and had further scarred his already damaged soul.

She gasped with shock as Bran gave her buttock an almost playful, resonant slap.

Then he grasped the remnants of her skirt in both hands and ripped. The fabric parted up to the waistline, and he grunted with effort as his muscles bunched once more until the fine leather tore right through. His breath whistled between his teeth as he slipped the ravaged fabric from beneath her, then accorded her bodice the same treatment. The cheeks of her arse were uppermost, framed by the fine lace of her suspenders, separated by a brief sliver of fabric, while her full breasts bounced strongly from confinement to hang temptingly between her spread legs. Now her flesh rose in goosebumps, not with the cold but with the shivering excitement of anticipation.

God, she loved it when he played rough.

Bran knelt to taste first one breast and then the other. He was still fully clothed but the thrill of his arousal was betrayed by the narrowing of his eyes and the shortness of his breath. As he fondled her breasts, the cool touch of his fingers and the heat of his tongue sent shivers of desire to Olanthé's every extremity. Her fingers curled within the restraints, and the lubricating juices began to flow.

'Ah, you whore,' Bran whispered between nibbles, hearing her faint moan of pleasure. 'You really like being exposed and fucked, don't you? You want me to ram myself inside you. Well, patience, my dear. First of all you're going to regret betraying me with all those other men. I'm going to beat you once, just once, for every single time you have ever taken another man's cock into your faithless body.'

'No, please don't,' she managed to gasp, while in the darkness of her mind the words 'beat me, please beat me!' echoed wildly.

He stepped over to the wall, his eyes scanning the available accoutrements. She tensed, strained, knowing already what he would choose. She felt a stir of air brush over her exposed rump only seconds before the familiar fire of the antique riding crop flamed across her buttocks. She jumped and bit her tongue to stop herself from crying out – not from fear or pain but from the excruciating excitement of arousal, and her own inability to assist towards her own fulfilment.

Bran struck her again and again, until ridges of weals flowered, criss-crossed along her buttocks. He had a steady hand and a sure aim. She felt the precision with which he kept his strokes within the lacy guidelines of her underwear, causing weals to flame on top of weals. Gradually she began to drift into that strangely removed state caused by surface pain mingled with erotic desire, scarcely realising she was making small keening noises as her abraded flesh tried to crawl away from the stinging lines of fire.

Then he stopped.

After a while her breath began to slow and her eyes slipped open, searching for him. He had divested himself of his clothes and was slouching in a cushioned seat, sipping at a glass of whisky while avidly drinking in the sight of her bound over the rail, her stretched legs exposing the tiny strip of fabric that scarcely hid her sex lips, topped by the pulsing redness of the raised cheeks of her backside surrounded by delicate lacy briefs and suspenders. His erection remained impressively untouched, his ability to control his needs almost superhuman at times.

He deliberately put the glass down and stood.

She tensed in anticipation.

Very gently he bent and kissed the flaming lacerations, causing her to gasp, as each touch of his lips was like fire against her desecrated flesh. Then his fingers slipped under the lace of her briefs. She felt a faint pressure as he sliced them through and flung the panties aside, exposing her for his delectation. She saw in her mind's eye the small puckered entrance to her anus above the large, swollen, ready lips of her pussy. She was his to plunder, wherever he would; she could neither move to assist nor deny, and therein lay the most exquisite of anticipations.

He stroked his finger down the length of her crack, brushing carelessly against her most private of places and jolting against the inflamed lump of her clit. She shuddered with the delicious pause of anticipation, willing him to slip inside her, not gently, but selfishly, using her as she was ready to be used, with passion, lust and selfish male satisfaction.

But he was gentle. She wanted to curse out loud as he slowly, slowly entered and pushed as deep as he could into the tight warm dampness of her cunt. She held her breath as he eased back out. She heard the shortness of his breath and knew his eyes were half closed with self-gratification afforded by those deliberately slow movements. Again and again he rode her, gently, too gently, until she wanted to scream at him to just fuck her. Then his thumb slipped into her backside, and her body trembled at the added invasion, the pain from the unlubricated abrading of his thumb indistinguishable from pleasure.

He suddenly began to ram harder, again and again, then he pressed tight and held himself there for a moment; not for him, but for her. The roughness of his tight balls rubbed her most sensitive nub of flesh, causing the coil of flame inside her to instantly burst. She cried out as she exploded with release, felt him slip from her as the dying fluctuations of her orgasm were still pulsing. Then he pushed his heated erection, lubricated with her own juices, against the tightness of her anus.

Slowly her body opened for him, and he slid in.

Now he used her for his sole and selfish needs, the tightness causing him to make small grunts of pleasure as he thrust. His hands were on her hips, using her as a lever to thrust himself into the satisfyingly constricting circular band of muscle. As the pleasure of her own orgasm diminished, so the pain from her lash marks began to impinge on her consciousness. Unable to close her legs, she began to clench involuntarily against the onslaught of his loving, further tightening around his swollen cock, increasing his pleasure. Finally he came with a groan, and stood there for a moment, buried inside her, the dying pulses of his orgasm shuddering against her wet sex.

Then he relaxed.

He rubbed his hands along the length of her back, leaned over to fully circle her breasts, then stood again, rubbing his fingers possessively along the warm, swollen stripes that were now beginning to sting unmercifully. 'I love you like this, my sweet,' he whispered.

She heard gentle amusement in his voice and was happy, knowing that his ghosts had been purged once more, and that his love for her was as strong as it had ever been. She smiled to herself. Bran's ex-wife, who had married him for his status and his inheritance, had divorced him when she discovered his wealth was a sham. Olanthé hoped she now lived with the knowledge that her once-bankrupt husband was a multi-millionaire.

She knew it was a little vindictive, but the thought pleased her.

'Will you untie me now, Bran?'

He knelt down between her legs, kissed her lips through the bars, then reached for the buckles. 'Tempting though it is to simply leave you there, ready for when I come back, I suppose I'd better.'

'Do you have to go?'

She stood up and wavered a moment, disorientated. Bran held her back against his chest while she regained her equilibrium, his chin resting in that familiar way against the top of her head.

'I must.'

'And Michael?'

'I'll deal with him when I come back. Use him if you wish, but don't trust him an inch.'

'I won't.'

17

'Narcissus?'

'The name's Eugene.'

'I do hope it's not as bad as it looks.'

'I've been informed not.'

'I'm sorry. It was rather my fault.'

Strapped face-down to the pallet, Eugene winced as he twisted painfully to look over his shoulder, and realised the man who had quietly addressed him was none other than the man who had previously been wearing a leather mask, and was now wearing a colourful array of bruises.

'I thought you were the one who stopped it.'

'That too.'

'You acquired some impressive bruises in the process, so I guess we're about even.'

Eugene's eyes narrowed as he surveyed the heavily manacled man who stood in the doorway. He wasn't quite sure why Olanthé had laid into him with such skin-splitting venom, but had been relieved when the muffled screams and thumps from the cell at the end of the dungeons had penetrated her fury, causing her to glance down at him with a brief expression of shocked comprehension. Although he was aware it had been a pivotal moment in his year's contracted slavery to see an almost normal expression of contrition on her face, in hindsight he would rather have been denied the experience.

'Can I come in?'

'I can't exactly stop you.'

'Then I'll go away.'

'No. No, don't. I'm so bored I'd speak with the devil himself.'

The manacled man gave a wry grimace and shuffled in to sit on the stool at Eugene's side. 'Judas, maybe, but not the devil.'

'I don't understand.'

'That makes two of us; but some interpretations of the scriptures suggest Judas was doing what Jesus bade him do.'

'What did you do to make her so angry?'

'I didn't do what I said I was going to do with the money.'

Eugene's interest pricked up. 'You were a slave, like me?'

He nodded. 'Enigma was my slave name. I wanted the money to give me leverage into the political arena.'

'And what did you do? Fritter it?'

'Sort of. I gave it to charity.' A distant smile flitted across the man's face. 'Which, as you found out, made her furious. Lord Brandon has an unerring eye for a money-spinner, and they don't like it when their little scams don't go according to plan.'

'It wasn't Bran who picked me.'

'Of course it was.' Michael flashed him a charming smile to take the sting out of the words. 'He'd singled you out as a target long before the interview. I didn't realise till afterwards either. He put the advertisement your way and made sure you applied for it, not that you'd have guessed. That's why they're so mad at me because I was all set to be a ground-breaking politician, fighting for the rights of man.'

'So did you change your mind?'

'My ideals haven't changed, just my methodology. I want to be out there doing it, not talking about it.'

'Good God. A do-gooder. I see their point. You're not religious, are you?'

'No. What I feel about people has nothing to do with religion.'

'So why are you here? Don't tell me, they brought you back to brainwash you into going along with the original plan?'

'Something like that.'

'So what's this, some kind of warning? Do as you're told or end up back here in chains?'

'No, I just thought you might like someone to talk to. I heard you're going to be a film star.'

Eugene grimaced. 'I wish.'

'It'll happen, make no bones about that. Bran might do the choosing, but it's Olanthé who wields the power. She'll give you all the help you need to get started. Can you imagine any man refusing to do what she wants in return for a little of what she has to offer? She'll have a few directors drooling into their pants for her, then once you're on your way she'll cast them aside. She enjoys the power of her sexuality, but only has eyes for one man in the end, and it's not you or me.'

Eugene's brow rose. 'Bran? You've got to be kidding. He's an iceberg.'

'He's a very private person.'

Eugene grunted, tried to ease himself into a more comfortable position, then slumped back down with a grimace. 'Say, I don't suppose you'd undo these cuffs for a bit, would you? Didn't think so. Well, I'll tell you one thing. I wouldn't want to get on the wrong side of him. If you did, you're a braver man than me.'

'Not brave. Stupid, perhaps, or impulsive. That's always been my weak point. I ought to be going. I don't think she'd be happy if she realised I was in here fostering insubordination.'

'You aren't fostering anything. I've nearly served my time, and if you think I'm going to lose it all now because of anything you say, you're crazy.'

'No, but you'll remember me, won't you? When I come begging for handouts when you're rich and famous.'

Eugene echoed his cheeky grin. 'If you make me remember any of this, I won't thank you!'

Over the following weeks, Olanthé rubbed the essential oils gently into Narcissus's back herself until the lacerations healed, then snapped at him to keep still and stop whingeing as she teased his tight muscles apart with strong fingers. She was relieved when Timi had told her that, although the lacerations had torn the surface skin quite badly, the muscles had not been damaged. He also might be lucky enough to have escaped without scarring, though the starkly white marks which presently decorated his dark skin would probably add a level of reality to his slave scene. She would talk Christopher into leaving them exposed.

Her latest slave had not come through the experience unscathed though; she noticed he now wore a deeper level of grim determination about his mouth and a new awareness in his eyes. She had seen it before, many times. Where he had at first been simply resigned to his fate, he was now impatient to complete his term.

Her fledgling was ready to fly the nest.

Without fail there came a time when the subtle realisation dawned on her slaves that their initial perceptions of this adventure – one year of bondage for a massive remuneration – had been simplistic, not to mention erroneous; that in reality they had been given an education second to none. The term had been both a prison sentence and a unique sexual adventure, but also had deeper, more lasting implications. While their bodies had been restrained, their minds had been freed of the chains imposed by culture and upbringing. They entered with inflexible mental barriers and exited with those barriers exposed for what they were, and dissolved by the knowledge. The diploma of this school was not simply a large amount of money, but a level of maturity it took most men half a lifetime to achieve, and the bonus of an open door towards realising their aspirations.

If, she thought grimly, digging her fingers firmly into his thick shoulder muscles at the thought of Michael's betrayal, they chose to walk through it.

'Ouch!' Narcissus grunted.

She slapped his backside. 'Be quiet. I'm hardly touching you. Did you learn the lessons I set you yesterday?'

'Yes,' he said grumpily. 'I wasn't in a position to do much else.'

'Good. In a minute I'm going to test you.'

He muttered under his breath about not needing another load of scars, and she realised she was going to have to do some heavy remedial work to bring him back into line. If he thought she felt guilty or sorry that she had hurt him, he was much mistaken. She was irritated at herself for losing control; that was all.

As her nimble fingers began to ply their trade around his buttocks and along his muscular thighs, she saw the first signs of his sexual organs beginning to tighten. She realised he had not had sex for several days, which was probably why he was miserable and bad tempered. She had discovered long ago that men were predictable creatures whose temperamental barometers were totally ruled by their animal need to spurt their seed. She felt her own interest blossom as the familiar sense of possession filled her. She would miss this slave. He was so easy to manipulate, and a real pleasure to use.

When she saw his hips begin to move gently in time

with her hands, she stepped back and unhooked a cord from the pillar, which ran to the ceiling on a pulley.

'Stand up.' In spite of his dawning state of insurrection, she was pleased to see he knew better than to ask why.

'Hands behind you.'

He obediently presented his wrists and she tethered them behind him, that simple act alone sending his erection sky-high. His eyes were bright with wariness, yet his body quivered with anticipation. He didn't know whether he was to be loved or beaten, but was excited anyway. She felt a small purr begin in the back of her throat. He was just a man. Predictably, she could excite him by doing practically anything. That his excitement fuelled hers was the end game at this moment.

She put her hand to his cheeks, stood on tiptoe and kissed his lips with featherlight touches. Her eyes caught his and locked; dark chocolate reflecting Mediterranean promise. He stood rigid while she teased, working her way down his body. She nuzzled his ears, licked her way down the fine fuzz of his chest and kissed his nipples, tugging the rings gently with her teeth. His mouth parted fractionally and he made small panting breaths as she worked her way downward, slipping to her knees before him. He thrust at her hopefully, but she nipped his foreskin playfully with her teeth, making him gasp and take a step backward, to be pulled up short by the cord which hung from the ceiling to his joined wrists. She pulled a stretcher towards her and strapped his ankles widely to either end. His breath began to shorten as his helplessness increased, and sexual introspection turned his eyes inward.

One slender hand began to fondle his hard-on, long gliding movements that lent slickness to his dark, throbbing organ. The other she slipped between her own legs, only to find that she came almost instantly. She realised with irritation she had been thinking far too much about Michael, the enigma, and had not pleasured herself for several days.

She snatched a film from the pile and thrust it into the video player.

Eugene felt full of fury as he realised she had moved away from him. He was frustrated to the nth degree and just wanted fucking. Plain and simple, no-nonsense, good old-fashioned fucking. And there she was, damn her, already settling herself back on the divan to take her siesta, her mind far into that other place she disappeared into when she was not feeling in the mood for sex. With aggrieved frustration he watched her put a film into the video and walk away.

He scowled. *Scent of a Woman*. He hadn't liked that film before, damn it; he wasn't likely to have changed his mind. He shuffled and wished his erection and the need to have sex would simply go away, but he knew they would not, they never did.

Eugene glared at her coldly.

She still had the power to move him sexually; there was something about her that a man could not resist. She was different, and would always be different, but he was no longer in thrall to her beauty. Perhaps it was what that other guy, Enigma, had said. That she was not his, she belonged to another. Or perhaps it was like the slow rift of a broken marriage, he wondered, clinically staring at her rich swathe of dark hair, her luscious figure and sensuous movements as she stretched on the divan. He had spent several boring days waiting for his lacerations to scab, and for the scabs to heal, and he was ready – more than ready – to be used. He would fuck her because she was there, because she was as exquisite as ever and he needed sex, but the excitement and the magic had disappeared, and he dreamed of moving on to pastures new.

He was ready to scream his frustration. He saw the soft rise and fall of her chest slowly deepen. Bitch! Olanthé was evil incarnate to leave him this way.

His eyes flicked from her to the screen. Scabs or no scabs, she would make him pay if he did not give the film his full attention. If he thought he was frustrated now, the bitch had ways of making him worse. She could do things with cords and marbles and crocodile clips and weights just the thought of which made his balls shrivel.

And he wasn't in the mood.

He choked back a groan. He'd had enough and wanted to leave. His wrists were presently pinioned by a cord from the ceiling of an Eastern woman's boudoir, and he was rampant with desire for her. Yet he did not belong here. This was not his world. Besides which, he wanted to be free to masturbate whenever he chose. At breakfast, dinner and tea.

For a week now she had rubbed oils on his back, perhaps in penance for wounding him in the first place. Her proximity had filled his senses and his body had risen each time to her ministrations, yet she had contented herself with leaving him to cool off on his own each time. To prevent the scabs from opening, she had informed him maliciously. So in spite of really, really wanting to get his hands on his tool he had been able to do nothing but read scripts and wait to be fed and watered, never mind the other personal things that he could *never* get used to others assisting him to achieve. And with the end of his year of slavery marching ever closer, his mind had subconsciously reasserted his individuality, bringing Western values into his consciousness. The thought sent his eyes sliding to the screen.

In this strangely unreal life, the one constant remained

the film he watched each day; sometimes old, sometimes new, but always with a specific objective in mind. How had the director arranged the lighting? How had tension been achieved? Why had the actor won academy awards for that performance? Whether he would or not, his knowledge of the film industry now encompassed the complete caboodle, the job spec of the director, the producer, the cameraman, the rush cutter, the gaffer and the make-up artist's tea boy. While he was in one way quite pleased with himself for his present somewhat unexpected depth of understanding, he had also been made aware of the sheer naivety of his previous goals.

His superficial wish to be a film star was now firmly backed by the knowledge of the odds he was playing; and there was a small part of his mind that still wished he did not know. But you could not give knowledge back. Once you had it, it was there forever. And he had to admit to himself there was enjoyment to be gleaned from knowledge, from the way you saw the films with more depth, analysed them, enjoyed them at a deeper level.

He grimaced at the film's irritatingly childish opening. At this moment all he wanted to do was masturbate, not watch rich college brats made dickheads of themselves. And there was the blind Al Pacino himself, dreaming of the scent of a woman in the darkness of his mind while planning to top himself. In spite of himself Eugene became engrossed. It wasn't a good film, largely sentimental and supremely unbelievable, but it was powerful acting. The film wound its way to the end. He watched the credits and the inevitable snowstorm, and as the machine clunked into reverse his mind went into overdrive.

Suddenly, with blinding comprehension, Eugene understood. Christ, how had he missed the whole fucking point before? Still standing in the middle of Olanthé's room, he shuffled around and looked towards the latticed opening which was cut with shards of sunlight, but he wasn't truly seeing it. As his sun-blinded vision adjusted he knew that being a film icon wasn't enough.

Two lusts warred within his body, and became subtly entwined.

With equal intensity he wanted to have sex and to be an actor.

Olanthé had not been sleeping. There was a state of mind akin to hypnosis, or meditation, and she was able to achieve it at will. She heard the sound of the film on one level, felt the security of her desert domain around her at another level, and at the same time sensed something subtle shift within her slave, Narcissus. What it was, or how she recognised it, she would never be able to tell anyone; but she knew it had happened.

Her eyes opened.

He was facing partially away from her, staring intently towards the light, his back a mass of healing whiplashes. She drank in the sight of the thick yellow mane of hair, the pinioned arms pulling back the broad shoulders, expanding the exquisite definition of his chest. The legs, parted by the stretcher, were tensed magnificently at the thigh and buttock, and the fine golden hairs of his body glistened in the rays of sun. His head tipped back slightly, as if hearing something outside her senses. He was a tethered beast, unwillingly chained, straining towards freedom beyond the confines of his cage.

God, he was magnificent. He had been beautiful before, beautiful and shallow, vain as a popinjay. He was now beautiful like a dolphin in water, sleek, at one with his element.

He must have heard her stir; his attention moved to

her. As he turned she saw his tight erection tremble with eagerness, yet there was something in the depths of his eyes that had not been there before. He was the lion awakened.

He had discovered himself.

She rose from the couch and touched a button to rid herself of the Western world; the silenced video and screen slid silently out of sight. Narcissus watched her every move. She felt clumsy before him. Almost hesitantly she knelt before him and kissed his cock.

He drew breath sharply, then said, 'No. Let me make love to you.'

Before, he would have been only too pleased to have received a blow-job – it was the stuff men's dreams were made of – yet now he wanted to share something with her. She was touched.

She released him slowly and silently and stood trembling like a virgin with her first man.

Oh, yes, the lion had awakened.

He took her by the hand and led her to the couch. Then, taking her face in his, he began to kiss her. He kissed her eyes, her nose, the edges of her lips; soft, feather-light touches of electric contact.

Olanthé shivered with expectation. Although she wanted to grasp Narcissus by the shoulders and press her mouth to his, she resolutely kept her hands at her sides. Waiting was an exquisite torture.

She felt a tiny growl of pleasure rumble from his chest and knew that it was costing him equally, to not simply rip her clothes off and dive inside the heat of her body. His eyes snared hers for a moment, then slowly the thick lashes lowered, leaving the merest glint of green. As he bent, showering his kisses down her neck and shoulders, his hands slowly, sensuously, pushed the silks aside from her shoulders. The fabric hung for a moment, suspended on the warm air, then softly shimmered into a puddle at her feet.

She felt him shiver with delight as he knelt before her, his hands sliding down her back to rest on her middle. Holding her about the waist, he began to kiss one nipple. Warmth welled between her legs as he suckled, his tongue chafing the underside of the breast then slowly pulling half of it into his mouth in his eagerness. Her feet spread for support, her head lolled back; eyes half closed, she revelled in his lover-like touch which seemed to join every sexual part of her body. She felt herself fluctuate with need, and gasped with the pleasure-pain of thwarted desire.

She put her hands on the back of his head, pulling him in towards her, hinting that she was ready, more than ready. He lifted his head and those sleepy golden-flecked green eyes glowed with a mixture of lust and amusement, then he lowered his head and suckled on the other nipple while the first rose into a hard knot where the warm breeze chilled against her damp skin.

His hands moved down in unison to encompass her buttocks, and the weight of his hands on her flesh prickled the already-fired nerve endings into exquisite agitation. Then one hand moved firmly into the small of her back while the other sought the damp secret place between her legs.

She hung on to his shoulders for support as his fingers worked their way inside her, but it was his thumb that focussed her mind. Gently, so gently it was hardly moving, it pressed against the hood of flesh above her clit. Now her eyes closed and she simply wallowed in the pleasure he was inflicting on her willing body.

Beyond that, time stopped.

She was vaguely aware of being lifted, pushed back

gently against the bed, to lie spread widely in abandonment. She felt the thick thighs push hers apart, lifting her knees to accommodate him. She felt the warmth of his prick enter her, and keep entering as though impaling. Heat spread. He began to ride her gently, his body movements teasing her lustful appetite; slow and strong and even. Without volition, her body began to dance to his tune.

Her hips rose upward, pressed against him, demanding, claiming more than he was giving.

He lifted her legs, one at a time, and trapped them with his shoulders, pressing her almost in half, lifting and spreading her sex lips the better to accommodate his body. He pressed closer, seeming to expand to fill her. His movements subtly changed, becoming harsher, more demanding, and now, with every long, slow stroke, he was abrading the sensitised core of her sex. She gasped with desire for fulfilment, her hands clawing at his buttocks, his back, trying to pull him in closer, to enticep him to push harder, faster, the better to bring her to culmination.

For a short while he held her there, teasing himself in and out, pleasuring himself, not giving in to her unspoken demands, but his lips were parted, he was panting, and his eyes were half lost in lust. She growled and dug her fingernails in, and within seconds he began to ride her hard, with no thought for anything except his own pleasure.

For Olanthé the experience was both pleasure and pain, and somewhere between the time of his increased thrusting and his shout of culmination, she knew she had come herself, but the moment had been flooded by the whole experience and lost, making his coming her ultimate pleasure.

Why did that happen to women?

Within seconds of his orgasm, she felt her individuality reassert itself, yet waited for his breathing to slow, to ease, before shoving at him, letting him know she wanted to move. Yet he held her there, her wrists in his hands, his lust-sated eyes smiling down at her as she lay trapped, folded beneath him in that most submissive of positions. She frowned and arched against him, but scarcely shifted him a jot, and she was irritated at his smug look.

'What?'

'This is how I want to remember you,' he said finally. 'Not with the whip, or the robes, or your damned glass marbles, but as my whore, with your body spread open for my pleasure.'

She growled.

He bent his head and kissed her, his tongue lapping at her teeth. She opened her eyes wide, daring him; but he did dare. His tongue invaded her, slid over and between the dangerous white teeth, while she pulled ineffectually at the hands that trapped her wrists.

Finally he lifted his head, released her hands and knelt up, allowing her legs to unfold around him.

'Get off,' she snapped.

'Yes, my Lady,' he said instantly, but there was a new tone in his voice. It lacked respect.

He stood, backed away calmly and waited while she snatched up her robe and stalked to her bathroom, angrily ringing the bell in passing. She stood and looked at herself in the mirror. She was truly older than she looked – time was being kind to her. Age was showing in the tiny crows' feet around her eyes, in the way her breasts were not as firm as they had been; yet no one but her would notice. Age was that indefinable thing that registered in a person's eyes, along with their very soul. Ali entered and, without being asked, began to wash her body in the scented water. She stood enjoying the luxury of his asexual touch on her sensitised skin.

'It's nearly time, Ali.'

'Yes, Lady,' he agreed. 'Will you go with him to the Western world?'

'No, not this time. There's still the problem of Michael.'

'And the new one?'

'Not yet ripe for the plucking. That will be all.'

He nodded and bowed himself out.

Narcissus was standing, waiting between the pillars with his arms folded. She had never seen him like that before. Even before she told him to re-buckle the stretcher between his legs and to present his wrists behind his back, his expression told her he knew his arrogance was to be punished.

She pulled hard on the rope and he folded in the middle, arms high behind his back.

She hung a weight from his depleted, sensitive sac and fed him with marbles until he could accept no more, yet he gave not a single indication of discomfort. In irritation she grabbed the riding crop and began to land slow and even strokes over the whole of his exposed buttocks and thighs. Not hard enough to break the skin, but enough to have him drawing breath sharply and closing his eyes at each stroke.

They both knew it was now a waiting game; there was nothing more she could teach him.

Eventually she sat back on the divan, and he lifted pain-filled eyes to hers. 'I'll be a good actor, Olanthé. You'll see.'

'I know. I always knew.'

'If I hadn't come here, it wouldn't have happened.'

'You might have still made it, somehow.'

'No. I might have become an icon. I would never have become an actor. I think . . .'

She shrugged, then frowned. 'What is it? What are you trying to say?'

'I'm trying to say thank you.'

Olanthé felt something warm blossom inside her. It was born somewhere deep inside and gradually manifested itself as a wide, pleasurable smile.

No one had ever thanked her before.

Not even Michael.

Epilogue

In solitude, Michael imagined the helicopter lifting Eugene out into the sun and on towards his new destiny. He had seen a small portion of the film rushes, as had all the brethren, and like them he had been stunned by the sheer sexual magnetism the godlike Greek stud had exuded on screen. He knew that Narcissus the slave would indeed become an actor second to none.

A shiver of disquiet filled him regarding his own future. He wondered whether he had one.

He couldn't find it in himself to hate Eugene for his single-minded determination to be adored. Instead he felt slightly jealous of this simplistic need; there was a kind of innocence in being so absolutely intractable that transcended mere selfishness. The world needed such people now and again. Maybe when Eugene had satisfied that need in himself he might find it in him to think of those for whom the dream was simply to eat, to survive.

But maybe not.

He lifted his head, trying to see something, anything, but the darkness was complete. He lay gagged and bound on the cold stone floor of a cell he had never seen before. Its whitewashed walls were less overtly bleak than Olanthé's toy dungeon with its whips and chains and instruments of torture, but in the circumstances this was far more frightening, for it had not been the brethren who had surrounded him and secreted him away but Lord Brandon's personal guards.

He had been easy to take: finally freed of the irritating

restraints, dressed to leave, or so he had been told, he had been relaxed, off-guard. They had been quick and discreet, taking him by surprise, and he doubted anyone realised it had happened. He struggled unsuccessfully once more to free himself but did not cry out, knowing it was pointless. This room was far below the level of the desert floor and along an ancient, winding tunnel. He reasoned that a few million tons of sand lay between him and the citadel, and that the brethren remained innocently unaware of this particular place.

He reflected bitterly that it was his own fault for being too honest. He had kept his word. He had not tried to escape for those long months while the film crew came and went, while Eugene's education was completed and the wheels set in motion for his future, but it seemed Olanthé and Lord Brandon were not going to accord him the same treatment. If they had, it would have made sense for him to leave on that helicopter with Eugene, as he had been expecting, instead of being incarcerated in a secret prison.

Shivering, he rested his cheek on the chilled stone floor.

Eventually the sound of footsteps echoed in the tunnel. He tensed. There was the harsh jangling of keys and he blinked in the sudden brilliance of an electric light. As his sight returned, what he saw didn't inspire confidence. Lord Brandon stood there, looking coldly down upon him in the manner in which one would look at a cockroach before crushing it underfoot. One of the guards leapt forward at some unseen signal, grabbed him by his shirt front and propped him up in a sitting position in the corner, ripping away the tape from his mouth.

Bran surveyed him coldly. 'As you've no doubt guessed, we've been re-thinking what to do about you.'

'Olanthé said you'd decided to let me go.'

'You might be interested to learn you did go. Just now, on the helicopter. Everyone saw you climb on board.'

'Bastard!' Michael swore, muscles bunching ineffectually.

'I'm pleased to inform you that I can disprove that particular accusation.'

Michael subsided into grim silence and leaned his head back against the wall, staring at Lord Brandon bleakly. So, this was it. The end of the line. The tentacles of the English Lord's strange financial dealings reached all over the world, so why had one solitary orphan dared to think he could actually make a difference just because he cared?

'You see, my dear boy, I thought about what was said before, and though I think you truly believed you could walk away from us, I realised later you would never leave us alone. You might for a bit, then you'd be yapping at my door again, asking for donations for this, money for that.' One brow rose. 'Do you think that's a fair summation?'

He shrugged, not denying it. 'So I just get exited quietly out of the picture.'

'You have to admit it's the surest way to preserve our privacy. But think on it this way: even if this is the end, you did first scrounge another three million out of me for a good cause.'

'So if you're going to do it, get on with it already!' Michael snapped.

'That's what I like about you, dear boy. No nonsense, straight to the point. You really should learn to be a bit devious, Michael. Try lying now and again. Very useful talent.'

'I'll try to remember that in future.'

Lord Brandon chuckled. 'There's not an ounce of artifice in your body, is there? You couldn't be devious if you tried.'

'I don't consider that a defect.'

'No, but it's naive. Tell me, how much money would it take to satisfy you? Four million, six?'

'It's a fairly pointless question in the circumstances.'

'Humour me.'

'I don't know. I suppose I'd be content with a percentage of your income.'

'Ha! So I was right! Fifty per cent? Eighty? Ninety?'

'Damn it, I don't know what you're worth.'

'Nor do I. But it's in the billions. Just think of the good you could do with all that money.'

'Christ, rub it in.'

'And even if you had it, it wouldn't be enough to make a difference, you know.'

'It would make a difference to some people.'

'What, feed a few people for a few years, then let them starve when the money runs out?'

'No! I want to help put in the infrastructure to help them to help themselves.'

'Well, that's a fairly sound premise. How about we settle on seventy percent?'

'I'd settle for seventy.'

'Very well. Seventy it is.'

Michael's eyes narrowed. Was there just cause for the sudden surge of hope that leapt into his breast? Bran took out a cigarette, tapped it on the metal box, then lit it carefully. For the first time, Michael realised this was a ruse to cover a moment of insecurity or hesitation. Then those pale eyes lifted, caught his, and he shivered fractionally, not quite knowing why. 'Do you believe me capable of having you killed in cold blood, boy?'

'Yes.'

'Then you won't doubt that if ever you discover the seventy per cent is not enough, and ask for more, this will truly happen.' His hand swept around the bare room, Michael's situation.

'I don't understand.'

'I think you do.'

Michael found himself swallowing hard, trying to contain all the panic that had previously seemed pointless, but strangely rose to mind in the light of optimism. 'But if you're serious, why –'

'Why the charade, or why the seventy per cent?'

'Well, both I guess.'

'The charade was to put the fear of God into you.'

Michael gave a mirthless laugh. 'You achieved that. I thought you were going to kill me. In fact, I'm still not sure you're not. But why the money?'

'Neither Olanthé nor I have need for it – well, not all of it – and it's serving no useful function sitting in various banks around the world. Yet we couldn't think what to spend it all on, and we haven't got the inclination to do good works with it. So, instead, we decided that you shall be our conscience. If you want the job, of course.'

'Christ! Yes!'

'In the light of the alternative, I rather thought you might. Free him.'

The guard sliced through the bonds around his ankles and leaned him forward to reach his wrists. From the almost inhuman expression on his face, Michael thought he would as easily have sliced through his neck. He struggled to his feet, fighting pins and needles of returning blood-flow.

'We have just one thing to ask in return, my somewhat naive philanthropist.'

'My silence?'

'That I take for granted. No, you'll come back here for two weeks each year, and you'll come back alone for two reasons. Firstly to present me with your accounts. In doing so, incidentally, you'll be putting yourself totally at my mercy should I not approve of your usage of my money.'

'And secondly?'

He gave a dry smile. 'Olanthé wishes it so. And now, dear boy, she intends to wish you godspeed in her own inimitable style. You might just wish I had finished the job here, today.'

Olanthé stood on the roof of her desert stronghold watching the helicopter return. Eugene had gone on to his new life out there in the other world. She would not miss him; she had already been tiring of him. She glanced down at the photograph Bran had given her. This young man was African with almost jet-black skin, and he had a beautiful, sensitive face, his doe eyes so heavily lashed they almost appeared rimmed with kohl. In the picture his smile was hesitant, but genuine. Even while struggling to survive as a student architect in grim circumstances, he had visions for innovative buildings which exceeded those of his more educated peers. Bran suggested he could become an architect of the first water, if he became confident of himself and his status in society. He needed to lose the mixture of diffidence and shyness that would forever hinder his career. She rubbed a finger possessively over the shining surface of the photograph, her mind already tackling this new problem. Joseph Magubwe did not have a clue that powers outside his control were conspiring to teach him that confidence. 'He-llo, my pretty artisan,' she crooned gently. 'You *so* badly need a sabbatical year to raise a little bit of money. Don't you worry. Your guardian angel is looking down on you.'

'Lady, Michael's ready for you now.'

'Thank you, Ali.'

A year ago her feelings for Michael had been such that she had felt torn asunder by his departure, yet his recent interference in their plans had angered her. She turned in a soft swirl of seductive silk, secure with the knowledge that life as she knew it was going to carry on, for the time being anyway. Her optimism was not boundless, but reflected the practical realities of the situation. It was not in Michael's interest to betray them if he had the use of so much of their money; quite the opposite. The more people who came through her hands, the more money he would have for his damned charity.

Contrary to what Michael himself believed, she had been party to his latest trauma, had helped to instigate it. She'd seen enough barely noticed deaths during childhood to know how little they meant in the grand scheme of things, and in the same way, different slaves came and went from her small world. Once they were gone, it didn't really matter to her whether they were alive or dead. Even Michael would not have been allowed to shatter the fragile harmony of her world. She would have killed him herself first.

She still might.

He had always been an enigma – her naming of him had been prophetic. She would probably have been sad for a while had Michael had to be terminated, but she would have buried her sadness and carried on, for beyond her life here, nothing mattered. Now, before they sent him on his way once more, she wanted to punish him for rocking the stability of her sand-locked citadel, even if just for a while.

He now awaited her in the grand hall, spread wide for her delectation. He must be very wary, certain she was going to make him pay in the only way she knew how.

She smiled faintly. He would be right. Before they released him to begin his new altruistic life, she was going to give him a taste of what he was going to get every year from this point forward. Two weeks of her absolute, personal attention. This was the beginning of a new yearly ritual, and the brethren were all going to watch. The year Michael stopped coming would be the year the money stopped flowing, or the year he died, and he knew it.

The thought sent a tingle of excitement through to her curl-toed shoes.

His reluctant compliance would stretch the boundaries of even her imagination.

LOOK OUT FOR THE ALL-NEW BLACK LACE BOOKS – AVAILABLE NOW!

All books priced £6.99 in the UK. Please note publication dates apply to the UK only. For other territories, please contact your retailer.

FULL EXPOSURE
Robyn Russell
ISBN 0 352 33688 9

Attractive but stern Boston academic, Donatella di'Bianchi, is in Arezzo, Italy, to investigate the affairs of the *Collegio Toscana*, a school of visual arts. Donatella's probe is hampered by one man, the director, Stewart Temple-Clarke. She is also sexually attracted by an English artist on the faculty, the alluring but mysterious Ian Ramsey. In the course of her inquiry Donatella is attacked, but receives help from two new friends – Kiki Lee and Francesca Antinori. As the trio investigates the menacing mysteries surrounding the college, these two young women open Donatella's eyes to a world of sexual adventure with artists, students and even the local *carabinieri*. **A stylishly sensual erotic thriller set in the languid heat of an Italian summer.**

STRIPPED TO THE BONE
Jasmine Stone
ISBN 0 352 33463 0

Annie has always been a rebel. While her sister settled down in Middle America, Annie blazed a trail of fast living on the West Coast, constantly seeking thrills. She is motivated by a hungry sexuality and a mission to keep changing her life. Her capacity for experimental sex games means she's never short of partners, and she keeps her lovers in a spin of erotic confusion. Every man she encounters is determined to discover what makes her tick, yet no one can get a hold of Annie long enough to find out. Maybe the Russian Ilmar can unlock the secret. However, by succumbing to his charms, is Annie stepping into territory too dangerous even for her? **By popular demand, this is a special reprint of a free-wheeling story of lust and trouble in a fast world.**

Coming in June

WICKED WORDS 6
A Black Lace short story collection
ISBN 0 352 33590 0

Deliciously daring and hugely popular, the *Wicked Words* collections are the freshest and most entertaining volumes of women's erotica to be found anywhere in the world. The diversity of themes and styles reflects the multi-faceted nature of the female sexual imagination. Combining humour, warmth and attitude with fun, filthy, imaginative writing, these stories sizzle with horny action. Only the most arousing fiction makes it into a *Wicked Words* volume. **This is the best in fun, cutting-edge erotica from the UK and USA.**

MANHATTAN PASSION
Antoinette Powell
ISBN 0 352 36691 9

Julia is an art conservator at a prestigious museum in New York. She lives a life of designer luxury with her Wall Street millionaire husband until, that is, she discovers the dark and criminal side to his twilight activities – and storms out, leaving her high-fashion wardrobe behind her. Staying with her best friends Zoë and Jack, Julia is initiated into a hedonist circle of New York's most beautiful and sexually interesting people. Meanwhile, David, her husband, has disappeared with all their wealth. What transpires is a high-octane manhunt – from loft apartments to sleazy drinking holes; from the trendiest nightclubs to the criminal underworld. **A stunning debut from an author who knows how to entertain her audience.**

HARD CORPS
Claire Thompson
ISBN 0 352 33491 6

This is the story of Remy Harris, a bright young woman starting out as an army cadet at military college in the US. Enduring all the usual trials of boot-camp discipline and rigorous exercise, she's ready for any challenge – that is until she meets Jacob, who recognises her true sexuality. Initiated into the Hard Corps – a secret society within the barracks – Remy soon becomes absorbed by this clandestine world of ritual punishment. It's only when Jacob takes things too far that she rebels, and begins to plot her revenge. **Strict sergeants and rebellious cadets come together in this unusual and highly entertaining story of military discipline with a twist.**

Coming in July

CABIN FEVER
Emma Donaldson
ISBN 0 352 33692 7

Young beautician Laura works in the exclusive Shangri-La beauty salon aboard the cruise ship *Jannina*. Although she has a super-sensual time with her boyfriend, Steve – who works the ship's bar – there are plenty of nice young men in uniform who want a piece of her action. Laura's cabin mate is the shy, eighteen-year-old Fiona, whose sexuality is a mystery, especially as there are rumours that the stern Elinor Brookes, the matriarch of the beauty salon, has been seen doing some very curious things with the young Fiona. **Saucy story of clandestine goings-on aboard a luxury liner.**

WOLF AT THE DOOR
Savannah Smythe
ISBN O 352 33693 5

30-year-old Pagan Warner is marrying Greg – a debonair and seemingly dull Englishman – in an effort to erase her turbulent past. All she wants is a peaceful life in rural New Jersey but her past catches up with her in the form of bad boy 'Wolf' Mancini, the man who seduced her as a teenager. Tempted into rekindling their intensely sexual affair while making her wedding preparations, she intends to break off the illicit liaison once she is married. However, Pagan has underestimated the Wolf's obsessions. Mancini has spotted Greg's own weaknesses and intends to exploit them to the full, undermining him in his professional life. When he sends the slinky, raven-haired Renate in to do his dirty work, the course is set for a descent into depravity. **Fabulous nasty characters, dirty double dealing and forbidden lusts abound!**

THE CAPTIVE FLESH
Cleo Cordell
ISBN O 352 32872 X

18th-century French covent girls Marietta and Claudine learn that their stay at the opulent Algerian home of their handsome and powerful host, Kasim, requires something in return: their complete surrender to the ecstasy of pleasure in pain. Kasim's decadent orgies also require the services of Gabriel, whose exquisite longing for Marietta's awakened lust cannot be contained – not even by the shackles that bind his tortured flesh. **This is a reprint of one the first Black Lace books ever published. A classic piece of blockbusting historical erotica.**

Black Lace Booklist

Information is correct at time of printing. To avoid disappointment check availability before ordering. Go to www.blacklace-books.co.uk. All books are priced £6.99 unless another price is given.

BLACK LACE BOOKS WITH A CONTEMPORARY SETTING

☐ THE TOP OF HER GAME Emma Holly	ISBN 0 352 33337 5	£5.99
☐ IN THE FLESH Emma Holly	ISBN 0 352 33498 3	£5.99
☐ A PRIVATE VIEW Crystalle Valentino	ISBN 0 352 33308 1	£5.99
☐ SHAMELESS Stella Black	ISBN 0 352 33485 1	£5.99
☐ INTENSE BLUE Lyn Wood	ISBN 0 352 33496 7	£5.99
☐ THE NAKED TRUTH Natasha Rostova	ISBN 0 352 33497 5	£5.99
☐ ANIMAL PASSIONS Martine Marquand	ISBN 0 352 33499 1	£5.99
☐ A SPORTING CHANCE Susie Raymond	ISBN 0 352 33501 7	£5.99
☐ TAKING LIBERTIES Susie Raymond	ISBN 0 352 33357 X	£5.99
☐ A SCANDALOUS AFFAIR Holly Graham	ISBN 0 352 33523 8	£5.99
☐ THE NAKED FLAME Crystalle Valentino	ISBN 0 352 33528 9	£5.99
☐ CRASH COURSE Juliet Hastings	ISBN 0 352 33018 X	£5.99
☐ ON THE EDGE Laura Hamilton	ISBN 0 352 33334 3	£5.99
☐ LURED BY LUST Tania Picarda	ISBN 0 352 33533 5	£5.99
☐ THE HOTTEST PLACE Tabitha Flyte	ISBN 0 352 33536 X	£5.99
☐ THE NINETY DAYS OF GENEVIEVE Lucinda Carrington	ISBN 0 352 33070 8	£5.99
☐ EARTHY DELIGHTS Tesni Morgan	ISBN 0 352 33548 3	£5.99
☐ MAN HUNT Cathleen Ross	ISBN 0 352 33583 1	
☐ MÉNAGE Emma Holly	ISBN 0 352 33231 X	
☐ DREAMING SPIRES Juliet Hastings	ISBN 0 352 33584 X	
☐ THE TRANSFORMATION Natasha Rostova	ISBN 0 352 33311 1	
☐ STELLA DOES HOLLYWOOD Stella Black	ISBN 0 352 33588 2	
☐ SIN.NET Helena Ravenscroft	ISBN 0 352 33598 X	
☐ HOTBED Portia Da Costa	ISBN 0 352 33614 5	
☐ TWO WEEKS IN TANGIER Annabel Lee	ISBN 0 352 33599 8	
☐ HIGHLAND FLING Jane Justine	ISBN 0 352 33616 1	

❏ THE CAPTIVATION Natasha Rostova	ISBN 0 352 33234 4
❏ CIRCO EROTICA Mercedes Kelley	ISBN 0 352 33257 3
❏ MINX Megan Blythe	ISBN 0 352 33638 2
❏ PLEASURE'S DAUGHTER Sedalia Johnson	ISBN 0 352 33237 9
❏ JULIET RISING Cleo Cordell	ISBN 0 352 32938 6
❏ DEMON'S DARE Melissa MacNeal	ISBN 0 352 33683 8
❏ ELENA'S CONQUEST Lisette Allen	ISBN 0 352 32950 5

BLACK LACE ANTHOLOGIES

❏ CRUEL ENCHANTMENT Erotic Fairy Stories Janine Ashbless	ISBN 0 352 33483 5	£5.99
❏ MORE WICKED WORDS Various	ISBN 0 352 33487 8	£5.99
❏ WICKED WORDS 4 Various	ISBN 0 352 33603 X	
❏ WICKED WORDS 5 Various	ISBN 0 352 33642 0	

BLACK LACE NON-FICTION

| ❏ THE BLACK LACE BOOK OF WOMEN'S SEXUAL
FANTASIES Ed. Kerri Sharp | ISBN 0 352 33346 4 | £5.99 |

To find out the latest information about Black Lace titles, check out the
website: www.blacklace-books.co.uk or send for a booklist with
complete synopses by writing to:

> Black Lace Booklist, Virgin Books Ltd
> Thames Wharf Studios
> Rainville Road
> London W6 9HA

Please include an SAE of decent size. Please note only British stamps
are valid.

Our privacy policy
We will not disclose information you supply us to any other parties.
We will not disclose any information which identifies you personally to
any person without your express consent.

From time to time we may send out information about Black Lace
books and special offers. Please tick here if you do <u>not</u> wish to
receive Black Lace information.   ❏

Please send me the books I have ticked above.

Name ....

Address ....

....

....

....

Post Code ....

Send to: Cash Sales, Black Lace Books, Thames Wharf Studios, Rainville Road, London W6 9HA.

US customers: for prices and details of how to order books for delivery by mail, call 1-800-343-4499.

Please enclose a cheque or postal order, made payable to Virgin Books Ltd, to the value of the books you have ordered plus postage and packing costs as follows:

UK and BFPO – £1.00 for the first book, 50p for each subsequent book.

Overseas (including Republic of Ireland) – £2.00 for the first book, £1.00 for each subsequent book.

If you would prefer to pay by VISA, ACCESS/MASTERCARD, DINERS CLUB, AMEX or SWITCH, please write your card number and expiry date here:

....

Signature ....

Please allow up to 28 days for delivery.